SWEET SHOCK

Gillian sat still, shocked to her toes. Thorne's lips were cool and touched hers lightly at first, but when she didn't move, they pressed harder, growing warmer and softer, and hers responded. She would have sworn she hadn't meant them to. But as that thought crossed her mind, he was pressing harder, and his hand moved to her waist. Her body arched forward to meet his. A low moan began in her throat when she felt his other hand on her shoulder, but when it moved down her arm, perilously close to one aching breast, she jumped, pulling away.

Thorne let her go at once. He smiled. "You are the first woman I've ever kissed who purred like a kitten," he said.

Clearly it was time for Gillian to show her claws— before it was too late!

AMANDA SCOTT, winner of the Romance Writers of America's Golden Medallion *(Lord Abberley's Nemesis)* and the Romantic Times' Awards for Best Regency Author and Best Sensual Regency *(Ravenwood's Lady)*, is a fourth-generation Californian with a degree in history from Mills College in Oakland. She lives with her husband and teenage son in Folsom, California.

suggestion. Swiftly she unfastened his lead and tucked him inside her cloak. Then, by tying the lead around her waist, she was able to hold both the dog and her hitched-up skirts in place with it, making it possible, though not easy, to climb. Deciding she must think only of reaching the point where the grass grew, she began her careful ascent. The sharp edges of the rock tore her clothes and scraped her hands, but she managed to reach a ledge a quarter of the way up where she could sit down for a moment.

The waves mounted steadily higher, and Gillian, always a realist, knew her life depended on reaching a point nearer the top of the rock where she would be safe. About two-thirds of the way, when her head was no more than a foot or two below the tuft of grass, which she saw now was still a good way from the top, she was forced to stop. She could grasp the great slanting slab ahead of her and balance her weight on one foot, but the rock was wet from the drizzle and too slick to climb. If she slipped, even if she survived the fall, she would never manage a second ascent. The position she was in provided no shelter from rain or wind, but it was at least a position she could hold for a while.

The wind dropped a little, but when Gillian looked down, she saw to her horror that the water was rising more swiftly than ever. There were no boats to be seen, no other wanderers, and not so much as an inch of the shingle where she had walked so unheedingly before. Marcus stuck his head out through the opening in her cloak and licked her chin, then struggled to free himself. Clinging to the rock with her right hand, Gillian managed to lodge him in a crevice near her left shoulder.

A huge wave broke violently over her from behind, soaking her, smashing her into the rock, where she clung frantically with both hands, straining her left arm and shoulder to protect Marcus from being swept away, until at the very moment she thought she would be ripped from her perch, the water dropped away. Seeing that she still was not safe, though the water eddied well below her feet now, she pulled the dog from the niche and put him back inside her cloak. Then, with a superhuman effort, she got her left foot into the crevice where he had been and heaved herself upward. She could find no good place to put her right foot, but she wrapped her arms around a craggy knob near the top, and knew she was as safe as she could be from the waves. The next few broke below her, and she dared to hope the tide was on the turn.

She had no idea how long her climb had taken her, but it was darker now, and she wondered if anyone at the castle had noted her absence. Even if they searched, they were unlikely to find her, for she had come too far, but she reminded herself that if she could hold on until the tide went out, she could simply climb down again and walk home.

The thought no sooner crossed her mind than she knew she was underrating her danger. She could hear her own breathing now, and she became aware, as she had not been in her fear, that her arms ached, her hands burned one minute and felt numb with cold the next, and her body was wet and shaking. She would never be able to hold on until the tide went out. One way or another, she had to find a safer position.

Marcus, too, was wet and cold. She could feel the dog's body quivering against her own. In what light remained, she could see the cliff top, several feet above and beyond her but enticingly near. In her misery it seemed to lean out toward her, to beckon, to suggest that if she stood atop her rock, she could jump to safety. The thought—or more precisely, the absurdity of it—nearly made her smile. The cliff top might as well have been a hundred miles away, for she knew that even if she could pull herself to the top of her rock, she could not stand upright there. With the wind howling around her again, and the increasing darkness making it impossible to see what she was doing, even to attempt such a feat would be the act of a lunatic.

Uncomfortable as she was, clinging to her rock and trying to soothe the dog, at least she was out of immediate danger. She made her position less contorted by finding at last a niche for her right foot, and a spot where she could occasionally lean one of her elbows. The lightning had stopped, but the rain was falling more heavily.

Suddenly Marcus stiffened against her, then struggled to free himself from her cloak. Believing the dog could no longer bear confinement, she helped him emerge, steadying him as well as she could against the rock face. His ears were pricked, his head turned toward the cliff, and for a moment she hoped he had heard voices, though she could hear nothing herself but the wind and the waves. When he relaxed and the wind dropped again briefly, she strained her ears, easing her hold on him as she did.

Marcus shook free, and before she realized what he was about, he had scrambled to the pinnacle, taken a mighty leap, and, to her horror, hurled himself at the cliff top. Her throat went dry, and her heart pounded in her chest when she saw his rear legs flailing wildly over the edge. He wriggled, seemed for a heart-stopping moment to hover between death and safety, and then his back feet found purchase at last and he was gone.

Though she sighed with relief, and uttered a swift prayer that he would find his way safely home again, Gillian felt bereft by his departure. She was sure now that the water was receding, but it would be hours before she could attempt to climb down, and she was certain she would not make the descent unscathed. The most she could hope for was to make it without killing herself in the process, and that only if she could manage to cling to her present perch until it was safe to begin the attempt. If she fell before then, she would most likely be swept out to sea, and no one would ever know what had become of her.

She wondered who would miss her. Her father perhaps, though he was not one to express his feelings. Estrid would not, nor would Dorinda, Estrid's elder daughter. Perhaps Clementina, the younger one, would shed a tear or two. At twelve, she still did not know much about the world and had little ambition to make her mark in it. When Dorinda had boasted of the success she expected to enjoy in the spring when she would make her come-out, Clementina had remarked only that she thought London would be amusing, then wondered why Gillian—at the ripe age of one and twenty—had not yet enjoyed a proper Season if such a thing was as important as Estrid and Dorinda so clearly believed it was.

Gillian could have explained the matter to Clementina had she chosen to do so, but she had not. The subject was not one she wished to discuss with anyone. The truth was that having anticipated sharing the delights of her first Season with her mother, she had not wanted to go without her the year following her death. Talking about her mother was still painful, indeed impossible. She had never talked about the late countess's death with anyone, not even with her favorite uncle, the Honorable Marmaduke Vellacott. She had therefore informed her father when the time came that she was not interested in being displayed as one of the offerings on the Marriage Mart.

The earl, more interested in his hunting, fishing, and gaming than in doing the fancy in London, was content to let her have her way. It had never occurred to him that she might not be entirely contented as the acknowledged belle of Devonshire society. Moreover, as Gillian knew perfectly well, he preferred her to be at home to deal with such day-to-day decisions as his steward might not wish to make alone. That the earl was a wealthy man at a time when many fortunes were at risk was due not to his own efforts but to those of his father before him and to his daughter and his remarkably honest steward at present.

Sudden barking, apparently quite nearby, startled Gillian so much that she almost lost her grip. Clutching the rock, she shifted her gaze to the cliff top, searching hopefully for the shadowy little figure she expected to see; however, the massive dark shadow that loomed at the cliff's edge belonged to no dog.

"Good God!" The wind dropped again just then, enabling her to hear the words clearly, spoken in a deep masculine voice. "Hold tight! Don't let go!" The shadow vanished.

For a moment Gillian thought the figure must have been an illusion, a product of her own wishful thinking. She stared at the place where it had appeared and saw that Marcus was there now. She could hear him panting, and she could see his tail wagging. The little dog was vastly pleased with himself.

Time proceeded slowly, but she knew that only a few minutes passed before the shadowy figure loomed again at the edge of the cliff. "Good," he said placidly, "you're still there."

"Where the devil else would I be?" she demanded.

"Pretty language, child, but since I have not got the least notion how you got where you are now, I can scarcely be expected to know where you might have gone next," he replied. He was doing something with his hands while he talked, and she realized she could see a little better than before. Glancing out to sea, she perceived through the lingering drizzle that the storm had nearly blown itself out. There was even a faint glow of moonlight in the clouds overhead.

"Can you reach me?" she asked, having no desire either to attempt to convince him that she was no child or to try to make explanations until she was safe, if then.

"I do not know." His tone was still calm, maddeningly so. "Can you tell me if this cliff top appears, from your perspective, to be thick enough to bear my weight with yours added to it? I should not like to be plunged to my death, you know, through simply trying to play the Good Samaritan."

"Well, that is pretty talk, I must say! Did it occur to you that my life is the one presently in jeopardy?"

"Certainly, but it also occurs to me that the better part of valor might simply be to see that you do not fall from there before the tide goes out, when you will be able to climb down and walk to safety. To risk both our lives because you were foolish enough to climb out there seems a trifle foolhardy to me."

"Gracious, do you think I merely stepped out here for a better view? You must think me half monkey to have accomplished such a feat!"

"A most injudicious monkey."

"I did no such thing! I climbed up here. There was nowhere else to go once the cove was cut off by the tide, and the water just kept coming!" She heard her voice rise sharply on the last words, recognized the betraying note of panic, and fell silent.

"It was foolish of you to wait so long to leave the shore."

"Oh!" Gillian ground her teeth together, welcoming the surge of anger for the strength it seemed to give her, but trying to remember at the same time that she was a lady and that it was no part of her intent to make him walk away and leave her.

While he talked, he had continued doing whatever he had been doing, and now he said matter-of-factly, "I am going to throw this line to you. You must slip your hand through the loop I've made and grasp it firmly before you attempt to do anything else." He made a swinging motion, and she felt the brush of something across her back, but she made no attempt to grab it. "Do not simply lie there, girl. Take the line. Here!"

She felt the thing touch her back and fall away again. She could not see it, however, and reaching for something she could not see seemed ill advised under the circumstances. But to her annoyance, her voice sounded small when she said, "I cannot do it. If I reach out as you want me to do, I will fall."

He said in a reasonable but measured tone that showed he still thought her a fractious child, "It is raining, and I am getting very wet. If you believe I can be of no use to you, say so, and I will get back in my carriage and drive away again."

"No, don't! You have a carriage?" A vision loomed large in her mind of shelter from the rain and the penetrating cold.

"There is a road near here, you know. Your dog dashed out practically under the hooves of my team. When I stopped, he did not run away again but stood barking at me. I began to get down to chase him out of the way, but he dashed off toward the cliff, and when I took up the reins again, he ran back under the horses. Tempted though I was to throttle him, I followed to see where he would lead me instead. But now that my curiosity has been satisfied, even he cannot object if you do not want me to stay."

"Don't go. Please don't!" Her voice caught on a sob.

"I won't," he said, "but you must take this line. Once you have it, you will be a great deal safer than you are at present." When she did not reply, he said, "Come now. You have already shown you have some spirit. Don't let it desert you when you need it most. I will attempt to direct the line so that it falls right across you, but it is not heavy, and the wind is unsteady, so it is difficult to predict exactly where it will go."

This time when the touch came, it was across her shoulders, and the line did not instantly slither away again. Gritting her teeth, Gillian turned her head and trapped it beneath her chin. Then, moving slowly, realizing that she was stiff from the cold and that her danger was therefore increasing by the moment, she managed to hold herself in place with one hand while with the other she grasped the line, which proved to be flat leather.

"This is part of your harness."

"One of the reins," he replied. "I have the others here. Do you have that one firmly in hand?"

"I think so."

"Let it slide through your fist as I pull, until you feel the loop I mentioned. It is arranged in such a way that you can open it to slip it over your head and shoulders. Then if you fall, maybe I will be able to hold you."

"Maybe?"

She heard him chuckle, a singularly heartless sound at the moment. He said, "Though you are obviously older than I first thought you, I cannot tell from this vantage point how large you are. If you should prove to be six feet tall and weigh twelve or fourteen stone, I shall be hard pressed to hold you. In fact, I daresay the rein would snap."

"I am three inches above five feet," she said, "but I do weigh seven stone and six. The rein may still snap."

"If it does," he said grimly, "my stable master will shortly require a new post. Have you got the end?"

She had it. There were a few more terrifying minutes to be endured before she managed to wriggle the noose over her head and shoulders, but at last the thing was snug beneath her armpits and she could feel his firm grip at the other end. For the first time in hours she felt safe. She knew the feeling was illusory, but that knowledge changed nothing. She did feel compelled to inform him that while she was grateful for his assistance, she had long since given up hope that she would be able to climb down the rock when the tide finally receded.

"I know you cannot," he said. "I feared so earlier, but I knew it when you could not move to grasp the rein. I am going to throw you another now. Do just as you did before."

His attitude was so calm, so matter-of-fact, that it no longer occurred to her to doubt that she could do as he asked, and soon she had all four reins tied around her. She realized that the drizzle had stopped, and wondered when it had done so. The rock was still wet, however, and she was sodden. Trying to shift her position, to find a more comfortable one, she slipped, but his firm hand on the lines steadied her and she did not fall.

"I think," he said grimly, "that we had better not wait any longer. You never answered my question about this cliff. Some are fragile at the edge. Can you see how this one is formed?"

"It looks solid," she replied. "What do you want me to do?"

"I want you to try to stand on the top of your rock."

"You must be jesting!"

"No, I will help you all I can, but I do not want to have to try hauling you up over the edge of the cliff if you are swinging free beneath it. I am cold, too, and I do not know if I have the strength to hold you as a dead weight. It will be easier if you can climb nearer so that I can control you better."

"I don't think I can do it."

"Don't be a little fool," he said harshly. "Of course you can. Try for some resolution and cease your whining."

Her anger stirred again, and she found the feat easier than she had expected. With the lines and his steady strength to aid her, she was soon poised atop the pinnacle, reaching toward him. For one breathless moment she swung wildly in space before she shot upward to be snatched into his arms. They folded around her, and she leaned against him gratefully, shivering, hearing his heart thud in his chest, its rapid beat telling her that in those last moments he had been as frightened as she.

"Can you stand alone?" he asked.

"I think so." The minute he held her away from him to untie the traces, the wind touched her wet clothes and her shivering increased. He had stripped off his heavy cloak to help her, and he leaned down now to pick it up. He wrapped it around her.

" 'Tis wet, I know," he said as he gathered the reins into a coil around one bent arm, "but it will protect you from the wind. There are furs in the carriage. Where do you live?"

"The castle," she said, her teeth chattering. "I am Gillian Carnaby." She waited for him to tell her his name, but he was silent as he helped her over the rocky ground to the road and a light sporting chaise that was drawn up there. He opened the door and lifted her to the seat, pulling coverings from beneath it to tuck around her. Putting Marcus on a rug at her feet, he went to readjust his harness. Then, jumping up beside Gillian, he fastened the protective leather apron across their legs, picked up the reins, and gave his horses the office to start.

When he still had not spoken by the time Gillian's teeth stopped chattering, she said, "You have not told me your name, sir. I should like to know to whom I am beholden for my safety."

"It is of no consequence." She could not see his face, but his tone was curt. Then, as if he realized his response was less than courteous, he added, "I am only glad I was passing and could help. I was sailing this morning when the gale came up, and took shelter at Ilfracombe, so I spent the afternoon visiting a friend at Braunton Burrows. I was on my way back."

"I have never sailed in the Bristol Channel," she said encouragingly. " 'Tis a pity the weather is so dreary."

"So long as the wind blows from the right quarter, Lady Gillian, the sailing is generally fine."

"You know who I am?" She had not mentioned her title.

"You said you were from the castle," he reminded her, "so Marrick must be your father. Neither the name nor your demeanor suggest the serving class. Won't they be searching for you?"

"Perhaps." But she knew her doubt was clear. Glancing at him, she said, "I am no longer my father's only child, sir. I have become of small importance now that he has a proper heir."

"I see," he said. "I knew he had married again. In fact, I believe I have heard something about your stepmother."

"Well, you may believe whatever you have heard of her," she said with some asperity. Then, biting her tongue, she said, "My besetting sin is that I nearly always say the first thing that pops into my head, but I ought not to have said that."

"Why not? Is it true that his horse unseated him on her doorstep in Leicestershire?"

"Very nearly."

"Then I suppose that most of what I have heard is true. I disbelieved only that part."

Gillian chuckled. "Pray, who are you, sir, that you hear such tales as you must have heard of him? You must tell me."

"My name is Josiah. My friends call me Josh."

"I may not do so, however. I have been taught better manners than that. Pray, sir, what is your family name?"

"Haw—That is, Hopwood."

"I, too, recognize quality, sir. It is not plain Mr. Hopwood. Of that I am certain. I would wager my best gown that I ought to be saying 'your lordship' when I speak to you, but I do not recognize Hopwood. Still, it is Lord Hopwood, is it not?"

"If you must. I prefer Josh." His tone was easier now. "It's an insignificant barony, nothing more. There is the castle yonder. You will soon be quite warm again."

"My father will want to thank you, sir," Gillian said. "You must come inside with me to pay your respects."

"I think not. If we should encounter Marrick, he is

welcome to thank me, but I will not risk encountering your stepmama in all my dirt, I assure you.''

"You sound like my uncle. He hasn't yet risked encountering Estrid at all. He slips in and out at Carnaby like a ghost.''

"It is not the same. Only look at me.''

She did so, and in the glow from the torches lighting the open passageway through the curtain wall to the courtyard, she could see that he was no sight for a lady's drawing room. He was as sodden as herself, and the front of him, where he had lain upon the ground, was muddy. His hair was plastered to his brow, and so wet she could not guess its natural color, but she thought his countenance a handsome one, and was conscious of a desire to know him better. That he meant to set her down and drive away she found distressing. "You are dreadfully wet,'' she said. "You must come in to warm yourself. You need not stand upon ceremony, and you must have dry clothing. You are larger than Papa or Uncle Marmaduke, but I daresay there will be a cloak to fit you and perchance some other things as well.''

"No,'' he said. "I thank you, but I have not far to go, you know, and I would as lief not be seen like this.''

She pressed him, but his attitude chilled alarmingly and she fell silent. He seemed suddenly aloof, more distant than he had seemed even when he had scolded her from the cliff. Still, she could not think him other than kind, and when he set her down on the flagstones in the courtyard with Marcus, she thanked him again. But he brushed her thanks aside, telling her to go inside before she caught her death of cold. She did as he commanded, but was sorry she had not insisted upon his accompanying her when she discovered not only that her family had not yet missed her but that only Clementina believed her tale of danger and rescue.

She was forced to endure a scolding from her stepmother because she had missed supper and ruined her dress, and there were weeks of teasing to be endured from her stepsister Dorinda, who took it upon herself when they returned to South Devon to inform everyone they knew about Gillian's Baron Hopwood. No one seemed to have heard of him, which increased Gillian's mortification, but she thought of him often, wondering if perchance she *had* dreamed the whole, as Dorinda had accused her of doing.

1

London, March 1800

> Certain persons will be fascinated to learn that an announcement of the forthcoming marriage of one of the ornaments of the *beau monde* will appear tomorrow, albeit rather cryptically, in the South Devon *Gazette*. We take the liberty to print the notice as it will appear, to wit: "The Earl of Marrick announces the betrothal of his daughter, Lady Gillian Carnaby, to Josiah, Baron Hopwood, of London." Can it be that the earl does not know Baron Hopwood to be but an honorary styling for the notorious M—— of Th——?

PORTLY, FAIR-HAIRED Peregrine, Lord Dawlish, along with two other dinner companions at Brooks's Club, had been watching the rapidly changing expression on the Marquess of Thorne's face as he silently read the notice, which Dawlish had obligingly pointed out to him only after they all had finished their meal. Dawlish said, "Well, coz, what about it? We knew you were up to something with these secret little jaunts of yours, but marriage? And to Marrick's daughter? Bad blood there, Josh. You don't want anything to do with that lot. Does he, Andy?"

The exquisitely attired gentleman thus addressed was twisted about in his chair, his handsome features screwed up in a frown as he peered anxiously about the eating room at Brooks's. "Where are the damned waiters? Never about when you want them. Here, waiter," he shouted, "can you not see that our glasses are empty? Stir your stumps, man, and bring a fresh bottle! And take away these damned platters while you're about it. That poultry is as old and tough as your grandmother. Moreover, the pastry was made with rank Irish butter, and that cheese, which you claim is cheddar, is nothing but a pale imitation, damme if it ain't!"

Dawlish, balked of support from that quarter, turned to the fourth gentleman at their table, a slim, lanky gentleman with the muscular shoulders and thighs of a sportsman and the demeanor of a man about town. "You tell him, Crawler. The duke won't like this. You can take my word for it. A Tartar, that's what he is. You don't know him as well as I do. Stands to reason, since you mostly went home on holiday, while I went as often as not with Josh to Langshire, but my uncle's said he won't stand any more of Josh's nonsense. Means it too. Never says what he don't mean."

Lord Crawley glanced at the marquess, then back at Dawlish before he said, "His grace is not noted for tolerance, I know, but Josh is his only son, after all. He won't eat him, Mongrel."

"Don't be too sure of that," Dawlish replied, paying no heed whatever to the odd nickname, for the simple reason that he had lived with it since his days at Eton, where his name had undergone transformation, thanks to his chums, from Pedigree Dawlish—thanks to his relationship to the marquess—to Pedigree Dogless, to the present, much simpler appellation, about which he had long since ceased to complain. He went on, "After that bit of fluff in Brighton last summer—saying she wanted to be set up in a castle of her own—and then the opera dancer, followed by that little incident at Badminton when we went for the shooting—stands to reason, he ain't going to look kindly upon a betrothal to the daughter of a man who marries any woman who picks him up when he falls off his horse. Shouldn't have done that, Josh."

"I didn't," Thorne said brusquely, sitting back in his

chair and absently thrusting a lock of his dark hair out of his eyes.

"Says you did, right there in the London *Gazette.* Be in the *Times,* I daresay, by morning. Your father don't necessarily read the *Gazette,* of course. Stands to reason. Mine don't. Don't read any of the popular press. But he's bound to read the *Times.* And when he does, my lad, he'll want your liver for carving."

"Here's that damned waiter," the exquisite interjected, adding, "That bottle had best be a sight better than the last, my man. When a club's wine cellar extends clear under St. James's Street, a man expects better than a mere infusion of malt with his meal. The port was musty, and the sherry we had was sour. I don't know what Brooks's is coming to, but I can tell you that both our dinner and dessert were not fit for the consumption of gentlemen. If you cannot do better, we shall soon find ourselves under the necessity to change our subscription to White's. And how will that suit you, my man? Answer me that!"

"Ignore him," Thorne said to the waiter, "and put the dinner to my account." When the waiter, clearly relieved, had taken himself off, the marquess added gently, "You mustn't run your rigs here, Andy. They may do for a coffeehouse or tavern, but you mustn't play them off in Brooks's. First thing you know, you will have the secretary demanding your resignation."

The exquisite blinked at him, then grinned ruefully and drawled, "Habit, I expect. One does so dislike being made to waste the ready on mere foodstuffs when one might keep it for the tables through the use of a simple ruse or two. It's too much like giving money to one's tailor, that is. So frequently, when one complains that the fish is not warm through, or the port has turned to vinegar, mine host begs one not to pay. Damned decent of you, Josh, to stand the nonsense for us today."

The marquess shrugged, turning his attention back to the *Gazette.* He read the notice again, his lips tightening as he did so, and when he looked up again, it was to glare at the others. "If this is someone's notion of a jest,

I hope I may discover his identity without further loss of time so that I can make plain to him its lack of humor.''

Crawley held out his hand. "May I? Mongrel told me what it said, but I have not actually read the thing myself.''

Thorne handed him the paper, casting a speculative glance at Dawlish as he did so.

That young man hastened to reassure him: "I had nothing to do with it, I swear to you, Josh. I only told Crawler and Andy. Not that it matters, though," he added. "Nearly everyone in town will have read it by now, except—one hopes—my uncle.''

Another of the club servants approached the table with grave dignity, bearing a silver salver in his outstretched hand.

Thorne said grimly, "I think perhaps your faith in my esteemed parent's choice of reading matter is about to be proved faulty, Peregrine." When the servant held out the salver to him, Thorne took the folded missive and grimaced when he saw the ducal seal. Breaking it, he scanned the message briefly, folded it again with exaggerated care, and tucked it into one pocket of his heavily embroidered waistcoat. Only then did he seem to become aware of the avid curiosity on his companions' faces. "I am bidden instantly to Langshire House. Perhaps, Peregrine, you will be kind enough to arrange for my obsequies. Nothing too gaudy, I beg. You must allow Andy to advise you.''

Corbin smiled amiably at him. "Damme, but I think I might just exert m'self to do it, too, Josh, for you. Daresay you're having a game with us, though, for if you cannot string the old gentleman 'round your thumb again, you ain't the man we all know.''

Dawlish, not taking his eyes from his cousin's face, said abruptly, "It ain't funny, Andy. This is dashed well just the sort of nonsense my uncle meant. You ain't going to try to tell him you knew nothing about it, are you, Josh? I'll lay you any odds you like that he knows the whole, even if we do not.''

"Then he knows a deal more than I do," Thorne said, "and I shall beg him to enlighten me.''

"But you must know the girl at least," Dawlish exclaimed. "Ten to one she misunderstood your intentions or some such thing. Well, it stands to reason, don't it, but one simply don't announce a marquess's betrothal without his permission, no matter what sort of a misunderstanding there might have been."

"There was no misunderstanding," Thorne said.

"There must have been," Corbin insisted. "Surely you can't marry the chit. She don't even have your name right."

"That was certainly an error in judgment," Thorne agreed.

"Yours or hers?" Crawley demanded, his dark eyes narrowed.

"Mine, I'm afraid."

"Good Lord, coz," Dawlish said, "surely you must know better than to play fast and loose with a girl of our own station, let alone to pretend to be someone else when you do so."

Thorne looked at him and said softly, "You have mistaken the facts, Peregrine. I believe, if you will take a moment to think for once, you will realize that you are very much mistaken."

Dawlish flushed, glanced at the other two, both of whom remained silent and unhelpful, then looked back at his cousin. "To be sure," he said hastily. "I am anything you like."

"So long as you are silenced," Thorne said. "I should not like to hear that you have discussed this business with anyone. Not with anyone at all." He flicked a glance at Crawley, another at Corbin. "Nor you two. I should be rather put out, you see."

Corbin said, "Owe you that much for a fine dinner, Josh. We shall be as close as oysters, the lot of us. You do know the chit, though. Can't be mistaken about that."

"No, you are not mistaken. I have met her. Once."

"Unfortunate," Crawley said. "Is it possible you did say something she misconstrued, or is she simply a lass who—like my humble self—keeps an ear cocked for opportunity's knock?"

"I thought she had cause to be grateful to me," Thorne

said, getting to his feet. "You must forgive me, gentlemen. I have been commanded not to tarry, and I've a stop to make on the way."

Crawley said wryly, "South Devon is some distance out of your way to Langshire House, Josh."

"The offices of the London *Gazette* are not, however."

He left them, making his way past other tables to the doorway without pausing to talk with anyone else, but unable to ignore completely the curious glances of several others who had obviously seen the notice in the paper. His temper was rising, but he had had a great deal of practice concealing the signs, and there was nothing in his demeanor or casual stride to indicate that he was anything but mildly amused by his own thoughts. At the top of the stairway, he paused to exchange a word with Mr. Fox, who was on the point of entering the card room. Then, nodding to another acquaintance, he descended the stairs, claimed his hat and cane from the porter, nodded to the club secretary, and stepped outside into fading sunlight and the clatter of traffic in St. James's Street.

He had a house of his own in Brook Street, and he paused briefly to weigh the merits of repairing there first to change his attire to something less likely than the pantaloons and florid waistcoat he presently wore to inflame his sire's temper even more, but he dismissed the notion. The duke was a greater stickler for promptness than for sartorial perfection, and Thorne did not want to face him before he knew more about the matter at hand than he presently did. Therefore, he went back inside the club long enough to scrawl a message and request that the porter have it delivered at once to his house. Then, since he had walked to Brooks's with the others, he also asked for someone to hail him a hackney coach.

Giving his order to the jarvey, he climbed inside and settled back against the shabby leather to do what he could to calm his temper. Finding that the offices of the *Gazette* were still open soothed him a little; however, he was kept waiting for some time only to learn that the sole person who might prove helpful to him was not on the premises.

That combination of events set a muscle high in his cheek to twitching.

The young clerk who had given him the unwelcome information said, "I am very sorry, my lord, that Mr. Thistlethwaite was so unexpectedly called away, but if you would care to have him wait upon you at a future time, I will certainly inform him of the fact." The man's eyes were wary. He had clearly heard of the Marquess of Thorne, and what he had heard stirred him to speak with extreme courtesy.

"You can tell me nothing of how this notice came to the paper?" Thorne's voice was gentle, even mild.

The young man colored up more furiously than ever. "Only that it was Mr. Thistlethwaite who made the decision to print it, my lord. He does, now I think of it, have a cousin or a brother in Honiton, who is on the paper there. Perhaps that is how word came to him. If you like, I—"

"You may tell Mr. Thistlethwaite that I look forward to making his acquaintance," Thorne said in the same mild tone. "He must do me the honor to call upon me at his earliest convenience. You will remember to tell him that, will you not?"

"Oh, yes, my lord. Certainly, my lord."

"See that you do."

The young man, pale now, agreed fervently that he would, and Thorne left him. His own carriage appeared some moments later, as he had commanded in the message sent to Brook Street, and he permitted himself a small sigh of relief at the sight. He did not mind hacks, and the distance from Fleet Street to Langshire House was not so great that comfort was a factor, but since he was certain he would need every ounce of his dignity to face what lay ahead of him, he was glad to see not only the elegant crested carriage but the liveried driver and footman who accompanied it.

He considered what little he could tell his father. The duke would not be interested in the business that had taken him to Braunton Burrows, for he had already made it clear that he wanted no part of Thorne's interference in anything having to do with the Langshire estates, giving it as his opinion that Thorne should practice patience and wait until the estates were his own before he meddled with their management. And since Thorne had not the least notion what might have been in Lady Gillian's mind to have done what she had, he was at something of a loss.

He smelled the Thames before he saw, through the dusky twilight, the tall, blue, gilt-trimmed iron gates of the house. Langshire House, nearly two hundred years old, was tall, massive, imposing, and was surrounded by extensive, well-tended grounds that overlooked the busy river. When the carriage rolled briskly through the gates into the walled, torchlit forecourt and drew up at the entrance, the footman jumped down from his perch and moved swiftly to open his master's door and let down the step.

Thorne emerged, twitched a cuff into place, brushed a bit of lint from the lapel of his coat, and firmly suppressed the recurring wish that he had chosen a less flamboyant waistcoat. Taking a deep breath, he turned toward the wide, shallow stone steps leading to the arched entrance. Both doors opened as he approached, but hearing his carriage roll away toward the stables at the rear of the house, he felt strangely forsaken. Reminding himself sharply that he was nine and twenty and not a ruddy schoolboy, he nodded casually to his father's porter, handed his hat and cane to a starched and heavily powdered footman, and said casually, "His grace is in the library, I expect."

"No, my lord," the porter replied. "His grace requested that you attend him in his dressing room."

These words conjured up childhood memories that, under the circumstances, were most unwelcome, but when the footman moved to a side table to set down his things, Thorne turned in his wake to cross the huge hall. Behind him the porter cleared his throat.

Thorne looked back to see the man grimace sympathetically and roll his eyes toward the cross-vaulted ceiling. A moment later the expression was gone, and the wooden countenance of the perfect servant had fallen into place again, but this time when Thorne turned away, his step was lighter.

He did not have far to go, for his parents' private rooms were on the ground floor. He had only to cross the great hall and pass through the formal dining room to reach the nearest door to his father's dressing room. Short though the journey was, however, his lighter spirits did not survive it, and his expression was grim again when, with the lightest of scratches to announce himself, he pushed open the door and entered the room.

The curtains had long since been drawn, but the room was lit by a multitude of wax tapers in wall sconces and in candelabra set upon nearly every piece of furniture that would bear them. A fire roared in the marble fireplace, reflected in a red glow on the fender and in flickering highlights on the marble hearth.

His grace sat in a caned armchair beside a dressing table of exquisite floral marquetry, his right hand held out to a servant who knelt to pare his nails. The duke still wore his wig, but he had removed his coat and replaced it with an elegant dressing gown of sapphire-colored silk that matched his still brilliant eyes. He was a man of regal bearing, who had been handsome in his youth and had retained his youthful figure. He looked up when Thorne entered, and his demeanor was stern, but he did not speak for several moments. The servant continued with his task as though there had been no interruption.

Thorne reminded himself that he was at least two inches taller than his father now and nearly a stone heavier. The mental reminder had much the same fleeting effect upon him that the porter's grimace had had, but the longer the silence continued, the more conscious he became that he was standing like the schoolboy of whom he had been reminded earlier. His palms were damp enough to make him want to wipe them on his pantaloons, but he was damned if he would do so. He was sorely tempted to offer his father a casual greeting and stride as casually across the room to take a seat in one of several other caned armchairs. Well aware, however, that to do so would be a grievous tactical error, he remained standing where he was and held his peace.

At last the duke said to his servant, "That is all. You may go." The man disappeared through a jib door that led to the servants' passage, and when the door had been closed again, Langshire said coldly, "I must suppose from your attire that my message found you in a gaming hall, though in my day, we dressed properly even to honor with our presence such low places as that." Imperiously he held out his right hand.

Thorne stepped swiftly forward and knelt to kiss it. There was no welcoming squeeze of the hand for his own, however, and when he looked up, there was no softening in the eyes that gazed sternly into his. He stood up, deciding that it would be unwise at this stage to request permission to sit. He stepped back toward the hearth but stood straight, making no move to rest his arm upon the mantelpiece.

The duke said, "Have you nothing to say for yourself?"

"Since I have no doubt that you are already several steps ahead of me, sir," Thorne said evenly, "I should be most unwise to speak until I know at least as much as you do."

The gleam in Langshire's eyes told him instantly that he had hit the mark, and it was with increased confidence that he added quietly, "I must assume that you have made the acquaintance of one Mr. Thistlethwaite of the London *Gazette*."

"Ah, yes, a most enterprising old fellow. May I ask how you knew that I had had that honor?"

"My knowledge of your methods, sir, and the information recently given me that Mr. Thistlethwaite had been called away from his office. Since I appear to be a step behind you, may I ask what information that gentleman was able to provide?"

"Certainly you may ask. It seems he has a cousin who prides himself upon having memorized the genealogy of every duke, marquess, and earl in the country. When the young lady gave the notice to the South Devon paper—one must suppose with her father's knowledge and consent—Thistlethwaite's cousin, recognizing the title, took it upon himself to apprise his relative here in London of his conclusions. One does wonder, however, just what action of yours prompted the young woman to believe herself betrothed to Baron Hopwood. Perhaps you will be good enough to explain that part of the business to me, Josiah.''

The chill that entered the duke's voice with the last sentence was sufficient to stir a prickling sensation along Thorne's spine, but he replied with commendable calm. ''I cannot explain, sir, since I have never indicated an intention to link myself by that name or any other to any young woman.''

''You are very casual, sir,'' Langshire said grimly. ''So casual, in fact, that I believe you do not comprehend the serious consequences of this latest folly. No, don't attempt to deny the term. I do not doubt that you have concocted a glib explanation, but glibness will do you no good. This is Marrick's daughter, Josiah, the daughter of a belted earl, not some scrub from the stews or member of an opera chorus. She is a lady, and whatever one's opinion might be of her father, her maternal uncle is Vellacott of Deane, scion of a wealthy and distinguished family even older than our own. Indeed, Josiah, if you had made this connection in the proper manner, I should be pleased, for Lady Gillian must be a considerable heiress. But you did not do the thing properly. You have niggled in the wrong pond this time, sir, and this time you will pay the consequences.''

Thorne's teeth grated together, but with an effort he held his temper. After a short silence he said, ''Am I to understand that you desire me to marry the young woman, sir? I must warn you that she told me her father now has a male heir.''

''Damme, sir, I know that, but if you have led her down the garden path, of course you must marry her! What manner of man are you, that you think you can dally with ladies of quality as though they were but common trulls?''

Thorne flushed. ''If that is what you think of me, sir, there is nothing left to say. I will bid you good night.''

The door opposite the one through which Thorne had entered crashed back upon its hinges, and a round little pink-cheeked lady in a lavender silk dress and a lace-trimmed mobcap stumbled into the room. "Oh, my goodness," she exclaimed, recovering herself and bestowing a blinding smile upon first Thorne and then the duke, "that door does stick so! We must have someone see to it, my love. But why did you not send to tell me that dearest Josiah was here?" She turned back to the marquess, holding out her hands and hurrying toward him, still talking away. "How are you keeping yourself, my darling? 'Tis an age since you visited, and I have missed you prodigiously. Whatever is the use of our both having houses in town if you do not come to see me?"

Thorne found himself hugging a generous armful of lilac-scented lady, and grinned in spite of himself, not believing for an instant that his mother's impetuous entrance was due to coincidence. He was as certain as he could be that she had had her ear pinned to the door from the moment of his arrival, and catching sight of his father's face, he saw that he was not the only one who understood the duchess's motives. The duke was visibly annoyed by the interruption, but mixed with that emotion was another, warmer one, and a hint of resignation as well.

Thorne held his mother away and looked down into her plump, pretty face. There was anxiety in her hazel eyes, and pain as well. The latter emotion struck him with greater force than his father's displeasure had. He said gruffly, "It is not what you think, Mama. I have done nothing wrong this time."

"Oh, no, of course you did not, my darling. You could not!"

The duke snorted. "The devil he couldn't! He has done any number of disgraceful things these past ten years, and well you know it, madam. It will do no good to pretend otherwise."

The duchess said firmly, "Not disgraceful, my love. Josiah had never done anything to disgrace our name. To be sure, he has been naughty at times, even thoughtless, as for example when he encouraged that distasteful young woman last year to believe that he could provide her with a castle, and then sent her one made of spun sugar. But he had been merely funning all along, for we've no castle to give to anyone, and so she ought to have known.''

Since Thorne had assumed that his mother knew nothing about that particular episode, he was struck speechless. The duke had no such problem, however. ''The young woman this time, my dear, is no such unfortunate. She is a lady and an heiress who somehow has got the notion that a certain Baron Hopwood has offered for her. Since she seems entirely unaware that Baron Hopwood—''

''Oh, pish tush,'' the duchess exclaimed. ''How could anyone publish an announcement of that sort without discovering all there is to know about the gentleman in question? You cannot have thought, sir, for she is said to be an earl's daughter, so where is the earl in all of this? That is what I should like to know, for surely he cannot have allowed such an announcement to be sent in without taking a hand in the matter himself. You will learn, I make no doubt, that her father knows precisely what he is doing, and to whom he is doing it.''

''At present,'' the duke said, turning his chilly gaze upon his son, ''I wish only to learn how she became sufficiently acquainted with Baron Hopwood to think he means to wed her.''

''I doubt she ever did,'' the duchess retorted. ''I am persuaded that she created this farrago of nonsense out of whole cloth and has never so much as laid eyes upon poor Josiah.''

Thorne's temper had reacted instantly to his father's tone, but his mother's fierce defense brought a smile to his eyes if not to his lips, and he said much more calmly than one might have expected, ''I wish I could say she has not laid eyes upon me, Mama, but though I doubt she would recognize me if we came face to face—I am quite certain I would not recognize her—the fact is that we met briefly in October, and the circumstances were such that I thought it best to introduce myself as Hopwood.''

''Oh, October,'' the duchess said, nodding. ''When

you went to see about purchasing Mr. Haver's yacht. You went to a party, I daresay, and met the girl in passing. I have once or twice been tempted to introduce myself as Mrs. Nobody of Nowhere, but people nearly always know who I am without my saying anything.''

Thorne barely heard her, for a vision had leapt to his mind of a piquant face surrounded by a tangle of wet curls, of large, frightened eyes, a tip-tilted nose, and swollen, kissable lips. He could almost hear again Lady Gillian's surprisingly dignified voice, and he suspected he was being untruthful when he said he would not recognize her again. Firmly, however, he said, ''There was nothing in our meeting to suggest to anyone that we were ever likely to see each other again, let alone to suggest the formation of a more intimate relationship between us.''

''There, you see,'' the duchess said to the duke. '' 'Tis just as I said it was, my love, and you have been most unfair to take poor Josiah to task.''

The duke's stern gaze remained fixed upon his son as he said dryly, ''Despite his many other faults, I have never found 'poor Josiah' to be untruthful, so I am inclined to believe him, but that does not alter the present situation one whit. If she were some nobody's daughter, or if 'poor Josiah' had been a paragon of virtue all his days, no doubt the *Gazette* could merely print a second announcement, explaining that an error had been made. But neither option describes the case. Therefore, Josiah, since you have been at some pains to build your reprehensible reputation, you must now attend to its consequences with similar care.''

''Oh, I will attend to it, sir. Of that you may be certain. There is nothing about it that need concern you.''

''Make no mistake,'' the duke said harshly. ''I will have no more scandal attached to our name, nor will I allow you to ruin Lady Gillian's reputation. Even if she has brought this business upon herself, you must see to it that the tattlemongers discover nothing to twist their tongues in her direction. Do I make myself perfectly clear?''

''I cannot speak for the Lady Gillian, Father. If she

has created this tangle, I can scarcely be expected to protect her from its consequences. I will do what I can to keep the business quiet, however, and in less than a week from now, you will have the pleasure to read that she has cried off from her engagement.''

"You much mistake the matter if you think that alone would give me pleasure," the duke said.

The duchess said sharply, "But what do you want then, Langshire? I protest, sir, you confuse me.''

Thorne agreed. "I, too, am confused.''

"Then you have not thought the matter through," the duke said evenly. "If you did not lead this young woman astray— You needn't poker up like that, but I believe you might have done so unwittingly. There are few other ways in which this can have come to pass. Either she is an unconscionable liar or she has been coerced by someone who recognized a minor title. In the first instance, she deserves to be punished, but without undue publicity. In the latter case, she certainly does not deserve to suffer as the result of someone else's wickedness.''

Thorne shrugged. "In any case, I still do not see why she cannot simply be forced to cry off.''

The duchess, doing a swift turnabout, said, "Oh, but you must see that, my darling, for although her connections are excellent, she has never even been to town—at least, not that I know about. No one knows her, so everyone will believe the worst. Even if she is the one to cry off, people will assume either that you actually ended it or that she is both foolish and stupid to whistle your fortune and title down the wind. In any event, her reputation would suffer much more than your own.''

"Just so," the duke agreed, "and that I will not allow. Understand me, Josiah. You will sort out this business without displaying it before the public eye, or you will spend the rest of the year sorting out some rather tiresome estate business in Ireland. Perhaps, since you have once or twice in the past attempted to thrust your oar into running the estates, you will enjoy it, but since you have not yet managed to take the time to learn about them, I doubt it. Nevertheless, if you bungle this, you will go, and that, sir, is my final word on the subject.''

Thorne had managed to remain fairly calm throughout the ordeal, but the duke's final remarks aroused resentment that he had no acceptable way to vent, and thus inflamed his temper to such a state that by the time he departed for South Devon the following morning, neither his coachman nor his valet dared venture so much as a comment upon the excellence of the weather.

2

Carnaby Park, South Devon

THE EARL OF MARRICK'S eruption into the green parlor shortly after midday startled the room's four occupants so much that his lovely countess and his elder stepdaughter both exclaimed aloud, only to fall silent again when they saw the angry expression on his face. The silence lengthened while he stood glaring at them from the threshold, until the tension in the room grew nearly palpable. The earl was not a large man, being only of middle height with the form of one who has spent many hours in the hunting saddle, but his rage was awesome nonetheless. His complexion, customarily ruddy from so much time spent out of doors, was choleric now. His cheeks puffed in and out. His chest swelled.

Gillian, who had been writing letters, looked up from her work and waited patiently to hear what he would say, but Lady Marrick was not so forbearing. Collecting herself and setting aside the fashionable magazine she had ben perusing, she said with practiced hauteur, "Is something amiss, my dear sir?"

Marrick sputtered, turning his fiery gaze upon her in incredulity. "Amiss? You may well say so, madam. Amiss! What a word for it! I tell you, I could not believe what I read with my own eyes. Look at this!'' He waved the paper he carried.

''Is that the *Times*, then?'' Her beautiful blue eyes widened. ''How very prompt the second post has been today, to be sure.''

''It is not the *Times*, madam!'' he bellowed. ''The *Times* never arrives before three. Indeed, you may be thankful that it is not any London paper. For that small fact we may all be thankful!''

''I do not understand you, husband,'' Lady Marrick said, her voice rising and falling in a familiar chirping manner that Gillian instantly recognized as an imitation of an elderly dowager the countess had called upon several days before. ''If we are to be thankful, sir, then why are you distressed?''

''Distressed! Madam, I am not distressed. I am incensed!''

Knowing from experience that her stepmother would continue to question the earl in this manner until he either threatened to throttle her or stormed out without explaining himself to them at all, Gillian put down her pen and said gently, ''What is it, Papa? What has put you out so? Pray, tell us.''

''I am surprised you dare to ask, miss, for it is yourself, as you must know. Aye, you have put me out, that you have.''

''I? But what have I done?''

The earl strode toward her, waving a newspaper that she recognized as the South Devon *Gazette,* the weekly paper from the nearby town of Honiton. ''You dared to take part in clandestine behavior the likes of which no gently bred lady ought ever to be party to. Don't deny it! The proof is there beneath your nose, my girl, and I have learned precisely how it came about!''

The paper was certainly thrust beneath her nose, and Gillian managed only with an effort not to pull away from it. The terrier curled on the sofa beside her sat up abruptly and growled at the earl, but no one paid Marcus the least heed.

Gillian took the newspaper from her father's hand. Though it had undoubtedly been given to him as all his papers were, smoothly ironed by one of the footmen, it was well creased now. She tried to smooth it, to find the news that had upset Marrick.

"There!" The earl's bony finger stabbed at the item.

She read the announcement, and her eyes grew wide. She looked up again, red-faced but bewildered. "Papa, I knew nothing about this, I promise you."

Lady Marrick held out one slim, smooth, well-tended hand and said regally, "May I see that, please?"

Gillian turned to her and said, " 'Tis an announcement of my betrothal to Baron Hopwood, but I assure you—"

"Betrothal!" Twelve-year-old, flaxen-haired Clementina, who had been listening avidly from her place on the claw-footed settee in the window embrasure, clasped her small hands together at her chest. "Are you really betrothed, Gilly?"

"Hush, darling," the countess said sternly. "A lady does not shriek. But you cannot marry a mere baron, my dear Gillian, for as daughter of the Earl of Marrick and niece to Viscount Vellacott of Deane you must marry much higher. Of course, it is a great oversight that you have not had a proper Season before now, but I am persuaded that when we take you and Dorinda to London at the end of the month, you will make a good showing. Of course, you are not so well favored as my beautiful Dorinda, for with her golden curls and quite elegant figure she is a diamond of the first water, as I believe those in the first circles would say." She gazed complacently at her elder daughter, whose looks were nearly a mirror reflection of her own. Dorinda had returned to her tambour frame and, but for her scarlet cheeks, appeared to be oblivious to the accolade. "Surely," the countess continued, "there can be no prettier girl in the metropolis than she, but you will do well enough, Gillian, surely better than a mere baron. Why, barons must be a penny the dozen in London!"

"Madam," roared the earl, "will you be silent!"

Lady Marrick drew herself up and fixed him with a basilisk eye. "Do you address me, sir? Dare you take such an offensive tone with your own countess? I will not have it, and so I tell you most plainly. Have a care, sir, in how you speak to me."

He grimaced, making a hasty, dismissive gesture. "I meant no offense, but dash it, Estrid, I've never been so angry in all my life. How could the girl have done such a thing?"

"I am right here, Papa," Gillian said. "Pray, do not speak as if I had vanished. I feel already as if this whole business must be a bad dream from which I shall soon awaken. For weeks—no, 'tis months now—you all have made it clear that you did not even believe in my rescuer. I cannot imagine why you should be so quick now to think I would indulge in a clandestine relationship with him. I would not do so with any man, certainly not with one I had met only once—and in the dark, at that, so that I would most likely not even recognize him if I were to see him again. Moreover, I can assure you that I would never forget my position so much as to place my own betrothal announcement in any newspaper. Why, the very notion is absurd."

"Aye," said the earl with a growl, "and so I thought myself, which is why I sent one of the lads into Honiton to make inquiries at the newspaper off—"

Forgetting her warning to Clementina, Lady Marrick shrieked, "My lord, pray never say you did anything so indiscreet! Make inquiries? As well tell the world! Surely, you were not such a fool as to let them suspect there is anything out of the way."

"Hush, woman," the earl said, but his tone was more controlled than before. "I sent one of my own lads, and I told him precisely what to say. He rode in this morning and returned less than twenty minutes ago. As it happens, he knows a chap that writes for the paper, who told him the young lady herself handed in the announcement at the end of last week to be printed today. It was the talk of the place at the time. Never occurred to any of them that it wasn't God's own truth."

Gillian said, "But I never—"

"If it was handed in last week, why wait until today to print it?" Lady Marrick demanded, glaring her to silence.

"It's a weekly paper, that's why. Still, there's something dashed odd about the business, and that's plain fact."

Clementina said reasonably, "Why didn't you tell us, Gilly?"

The earl glared at the child. "Why ain't you in the schoolroom, for goodness' sake?"

Lady Marrick said, "Because I gave her governess a week's leave to visit her mama, that is why. Furthermore, she asks a very good question. Why did you not tell us, Gillian?"

Carefully, Gillian said, "I did not know anything about this, as I have already said. I told you all precisely what occurred that day last October. I have not seen Lord Hopwood since that evening, and since no one believed me when I described what happened then, I can imagine no good reason—"

"Is that why you did it, Gilly?" Dorinda asked sweetly. She had put down her tambour frame at last, and was regarding Gillian with wide-eyed, angelic wonder. "Is it because no one was taken in by your idiotic tale of a knight in shining armor arriving just in time to save you? I should think that being the reigning belle of all Devon would be sufficient for any young lady, that she would not need to play tricks to make herself interesting." She sighed. "I had hoped that someone might pay heed to me for once at Lady Halstead's party tonight, but I can see now that you will be the center of attention as always, since everyone will be agog to learn the details of your betrothal. I wonder what you will say to them. Will you confess 'tis all a hum?"

Clementina said, "Do not tease her, Dorrie. You must know Gilly would never do such a thing as this. Someone jealous of her popularity is having a game with her. I am certain of it."

Dorinda looked at her little sister as though she would debate the point, but when Clementina only smiled and shook her head, she fell silent and picked up her tambour frame again.

Lady Marrick said, "I believe Dorinda has the right of it. One cannot be surprised if poor Gillian, as small and dark as she is, does not suffer pangs of jealousy whenever she must be seen with her more beautiful sister. Still, it is not the thing for her to be putting announcements in the paper, and certainly not announcements about made-up barons.''

"He is not made up," Gillian said.

The earl glared at her. "I'd never have thought it of you, daughter," he said. "Not before you dreamed up that nonsense when we were at the castle, at all events. But since then—"

"To be sure, my lord," Estrid said with a sigh, "the poor girl has not been at all the same since our dear little John was born. Such a severe blow to her to lose her inheritance like that. One can understand that she might behave a trifle oddly."

"Well, I'd not have thought it of her," the earl said, glancing guiltily at Gillian. "And it ain't as if she forfeited her entire inheritance, Estrid. As I've told you, she still has what her mother left her."

"Oh, but what is a woman's wedding portion, sir? It can certainly be nothing compared to what poor Gillian has lost."

"Papa," Gillian said, "I have done nothing wrong, and I do not feel the least bit displaced by little John— or, at all events," she amended honestly, "certainly not enough to do all the things of which I presently stand accused."

"Come now," he protested. "To pretend that someone snatched you from the jaws of death was bad enough—"

Lady Marrick laughed behind her hand. "Really, my dear Gillian, you simply cannot expect anyone to believe you climbed one of those dreadful rocks jutting up by the cliff tops near the castle. Why, no gently bred lady could do such a thing, and certainly not with a dog clutched in her arms. Indeed, none would even make the attempt, not under any circumstance."

"Madam," Gillian said grimly, "I believe you underestimate the capabilities of anyone whose choice lies between improper behavior and the certainty that death must result from one's failure to attempt it."

Stiffening, Lady Marrick cast a compelling look at her husband.

Obedient to the look, the earl said, "You are impertinent, daughter. It will be as well for you if you seek your bedchamber until such time as I have got this business sorted out.''

"Oh, dear,'' Dorinda said sympathetically, "does that mean that Gilly will have to miss Lady Halstead's party this evening? I am sure all her friends will miss her sadly.''

"You will know nothing about it,'' the earl told her, "for you will not be there either. I see no good reason to provide the gossips with any more titbits than they've got already.''

The countess shook her head. "You go too fast, sir. This is none of Dorinda's doing, and you will not want to spoil her pleasure. Moreover, though I agree that Gillian is in no case to go into society tonight, particularly if she means to deny the truth of the matter—or even if she does not, for all that—it will spark much more gossip if none of us attends. You know we have sent our acceptances. The only excuse for us not to go now would be an indisposition or a drastic change in the weather. We shall simply inform her ladyship upon our arrival that Gillian quite unexpectedly found herself too ill to accompany us.''

Gillian had risen to her feet and was gathering her writing materials. "I will do whatever you command, sir, of course, but you ought to know that Hollingston is expected to return this afternoon to discuss what he has learned from Mr. Coke about his new seed. No doubt you will want to speak with him yourself.''

"No, I won't,'' the earl said. "Hollingston will know what he wants to do, and if you must put your oar in, someone can tell you when he arrives. But take yourself off now, and don't show your face to me again until you've come to your senses.''

Gillian retained her dignity until she had shut the parlor door behind her, but she had all she could do not to slam it. She could not, however, and well she knew it. Though in the past year she had frequently been made to feel as if she were alone in the midst of the large household, she knew, too, that it did not do to give in to her emotions. Still, she had done nothing wrong, and she had

an overwhelming need to talk to someone who would
believe her and offer comfort. She went to find Meggie.

Margaret Prynne had been her nurse when she was
small, and had advanced from that position to serve her
young mistress in whatever capacity was needed from
that time until the birth of the new heir. But with a baby
in the house again, Meggie had reverted to nurse, and
Gillian found her in the nursery wing.

Lady Marrick had spared no expense in the refurbish-
ing of several rooms on the third floor for the earl's first-
born son, and Meggie was found in the day nursery,
sitting in a comfortably cushioned rocking chair with
young John nestled in her capacious lap, contentedly
sucking his thumb. She looked up when Gillian entered
and smiled at her.

Gillian, deciding her erstwhile confidante was not
likely to notice that anything was amiss with her, smiled
back and said, "He looks vastly pleased with himself. I
take it, he does not miss Nurse Hammond in the least."

Meggie snorted. "That one! Why, she was worse than
the first. Pretending she could look after our precious
lamb and a husband and four children of her own as well.
The very idea! Whoever heard of such a thing? The first
one was able enough, but why her ladyship should want
a London-bred nurse for the young master is a mystery
to me, Miss Gilly, and that's the word with no bark on
it. And to take her to that outlandish castle, where she
must have known the poor woman would catch an ague
at the least— 'Tis no wonder she went running back to
town as fast as her skinny legs would carry her. I doubt
Miss Clementina's governess means to come back, either,
and if you've clapped eyes on the new butler, you'll agree
the mistress has no skill when it comes to choosing servants. A chestnut wig the man has on, instead of a proper
powdered one. And he drinks! I've never seen the like.
But was there something you was wanting, my dear, or
was you merely wishful to visit his wee lordship?"

"I just had not seen you for a while," Gillian said,
"but you are busy now. We can talk later just as well."

She turned away with a small sigh of disappointment,
but she had not reached the door before Meggie said qui-

etly, and in an altogether different tone, "He won't mind, you know, if you tell me what's troubling you. He's a good sort, the lad is."

Gillian looked back and smiled. "You are doing what you like best, Meggie, and enjoying it. I won't trouble you."

"So that's how it is, is it? You just come and sit down over here, missy, and we'll have no more nonsense. Where the lad is concerned, I aim to look after him until the mistress gets him a proper nurse, one who ain't so highfalutin she's got to have servants of her own to look after her, nor yet one whose responsibilities are spread all over Devon. But that don't mean I ain't still your own Meggie. Sit!"

Gillian grinned at her, wondering what Estrid would think could she hear the ever proper Miss Prynne speak so to her young mistress. "Very well, Meggie, but I must tell you first that I am in disgrace. You will be as shocked as I was to learn that my betrothal announcement appeared today in the Honiton newspaper."

"My goodness me! And just when did this astonishing event transpire, that you forgot to mention it to anyone in the house?"

"Just so," Gillian said. "I wonder that Papa believes I could have done such a thing and no one have known of it."

"Who, may I ask, is the fortunate young man named in this announcement?" Meggie asked, still rocking steadily.

"A certain Baron Hopwood of London."

"The gentleman who helped you when you got cut off by the tide, then." Meggie frowned.

"The very same. Merciful heavens," Gillian said suddenly, "do you know I never once until this very moment thought about what he will think of this turn of events? But perhaps he will not have occasion to see the paper."

"No reason he should, unless he lives near Honiton," Meggie said. "Does he?"

Gillian frowned. "To be truthful, I do not know where he lives. He was visiting that day at Braunton Burrows. He said he had sailed out of Bristol and taken shelter from the wind at Ilfracombe, but I do not recall that he ever mentioned his home. Maybe Hollingston will know something about him. Oh, Meggie, what a coil, but at least you do not think I placed that announcement myself. Papa and Estrid do. And so does Dorinda. Only Clementina believed me when I said I hadn't.''

"The dear, sweet lass," Meggie said. Her expression hardened a moment later, however. "Tell me precisely what was said by everyone else, my pet."

Gillian obliged her, and when she had finished, Meggie said, "I shouldn't be at all surprised if it was not Miss Dorinda who did it. Only think, pet. You did not, but some young woman did. Was Miss Dorinda not in Honiton at the end of last week with her mama, shopping for ribbons for her new party gown?''

"We all were there," Gillian said thoughtfully, "but I was not with them most of the day, because I had arranged to visit Grandfather's friend Mr. Burton, who had written to us of some wheat seed he had had from Mr. Coke of Norfolk, to replace his rye. English rye has been a dismal failure of late years, even here, and indeed, that is what made me think Hollingston might know something of Baron Hopwood, for Mr. Coke has been visiting Lord Percival Worth, who has a house at Braunton Burrows as well as his seat at South Molton, where Hollingston went last week to see if he might purchase some of that seed for us to try. But, Meggie," she added as her thoughts plunged down a new tangent, "Estrid would never allow Dorinda to visit a newspaper office!''

"No reason she should know. I'd not be at all surprised to learn that Miss Dorinda had given her mama the slip long enough to do whatever she liked. And you know the newspaper office in Honiton is just a step from the linen draper's. You just go and ask her, straight to her face, and watch her color up."

Gillian doubted that such a course would prove fruitful, and when she left Meggie sometime later, it was not with the intention of seeking out Dorinda. But she had no sooner returned to the second floor than she encountered Dorinda herself emerging from the parlor. The guilty look on Dorinda's face when she had shut the door behind her and turned to see Gillian was enough to make her wonder if Meggie was not right after all.

"I should like to talk to you, Dorinda," she said calmly.

"Well, I have no wish to talk to you. You are supposed to be in your bedchamber, and I daresay your papa would be very much displeased to learn that you had disobeyed him."

"Perhaps he would, though I doubt that he would be very much surprised," Gillian said amiably. "He has not been in the habit for many years of heeding whether I obey him or not. For the past four years, in fact, I have been my own mistress here."

"I know, and my mama says that is a very bad thing, that no young girl ought to begin thinking she can make decisions for herself, that she ought to know very well that important ones ought always to be made for her by persons who know best what is good for her. My mama says—"

"I am certain that your mama says a good many things," Gillian said, taking her arm in a firm grip, "but unless I miss my guess, you have no desire to learn what she would say if she were to learn that you are the one who placed that announcement in the South Devon *Gazette*."

"Why . . . why, how dare you!" But she looked guiltily over her shoulder, as if she wondered whether their voices could be overheard, and she did not resist when Gillian pulled her into the next room, a surprisingly plain chamber redecorated by the new countess in the Etruscan style that had become fashionable some years before, after the discovery of the ruins of Pompeii. No one had been more amazed than her ladyship to see the result of her command. Having read that many persons of high order had expressed a delight for the style, she had communicated her desire quite firmly to the gentleman she retained for such projects, and then had left him to his business. Since she had been confined shortly thereafter, it had not been until after the birth of young John that she had seen the results. But even though she had been heard to wonder more than once about what could have possessed otherwise sensible persons to prefer the starkness of such decoration to the clearly much more desirable brocades and velvets that bespoke great wealth, she had not said one word about changing the style of the room.

Gillian pushed the unprotesting Dorinda down upon one of the hard little benches that served as seating there, and said quietly, "You need not lie to me, Dorinda. I can see quite plainly that you must be responsible for this imbroglio."

Dorinda hunched a shoulder, then glared at her and replied, "I shall deny it if you accuse me, and no one will believe you against me if you do. Indeed, even if your papa does not believe me, he will pretend to so as not to annoy my mama."

"The point will not arise," Gillian told her, suppressing her distaste not only at Dorinda's words but at the unfortunate likelihood that the girl spoke the truth. "I am no talebearer, Dorinda, though I should certainly not object if your conscience pricked you to confess the truth. If you had any sense of honor, you would certainly speak up rather than allow someone else to suffer for your actions, but I do not think you can have any understanding whatever of honor."

Dorinda's large blue eyes seemed to grow even larger. "I do not know what you are talking about, Gillian. I should have to be feeble-minded to confess to anything of the sort, particularly when I took such pains to arrange the matter. You cannot have a notion of what it has been like for me. At home, my beauty was greatly admired. I had more beaux than any of my friends, and Papa was always joking me about them and promising me that when he took me to London for my come-out there would be no room for them all. But then Papa died, and his money and the London house all went to his cousin, and of course Mama's family are a pack of nobodies, so they could do nothing for us. Had we not been able to live in Papa's hunting box in Leicestershire and had your papa not so fortuitously fallen on our doorstep, I do not know where we should be. But for all that, I have had to put up with being cast in your shade and to know that certain unkind persons like your Uncle Marmaduke even go so far as to pretend that Mama and I do not exist. That man slips into the house whenever he likes but never stays to pay a proper call. I do not know how your papa can abide him. Mama says he's a libertine, and she says—''

"Your mama will not change my uncle, Dorinda. He cared a great deal for my mother, and though he has a general weakness for females, he does not like to see another in her place."

"I suppose you will tell him about this," Dorinda said sulkily, "and then he will think even worse of us."

"I have already said I will tell no one."

"I do not believe you. Why should you not tell? I would certainly tell everyone if you had done such a thing to me."

"That is one of the differences between us," Gillian said. "I had hoped that if you were responsible, you would own up to it once you knew you had been found out. Since you will not, I must decide what is best to do next."

Dorinda flushed at her tone, then said defensively, "I suppose you mean that I am of lower birth than you. I do not know why you go on so about it. If worse comes to the worst, you can always marry the man, *if* he does exist. Ah, now you color up, so it is just as I thought and you did make him up! So, miss high-and-mighty, you are not so perfect after all." She stood up, clearly pleased to think she had put Gillian in her place.

Gillian shook her head. "He is entirely real, Dorinda. If my color altered when you mentioned him, it is only because I cringe at the thought of the humiliation I shall suffer if he ever discovers what you have done. You had better understand now, too, that although my principles make it impossible for me to bear tales to your mama or to my papa about your behavior, those scruples will not prevent me from explaining to Hopwood just what you have done if the necessity to do so arises. You had very much better hope it does not."

Again Dorinda hunched a shoulder and scowled at her. "Oh, pooh, Gillian, you know perfectly well that there is no such person. I must say, if I had made up a knight in shining armor to rescue me from a watery grave, I should have made him an earl at the very least. Only a zany like you would make up a mere baron! I just hope your friends will see you more clearly now, and will pay heed to someone more worthy of their notice!'' And with that parting shot, she flounced from the room.

3

THE MARQUESS OF THORNE, peering out the windows of his traveling chaise, had been pleasantly surprised to see, even before the chaise rolled between the twin lodges guarding the entrance to Carnaby Park, that the rich, newly plowed fields and sheep-dotted pastureland surrounding it were well tended and prosperous-looking. The estate was set amidst well-timbered hills that nearly enclosed it on all sides but the south, which lay open to a beautiful bay of the English Channel. The views were magnificent, the weather extremely mild and salubrious.

Thorne's carriage passed a picturesque chain of mirror-like lakes, surrounded by velvety lawns, flower borders just beginning to show spring color, and great, towering stands of trees. Because of them, it was some time before he saw the house, but when it came into view, it proved to be an imposing three-story mansion resting on a slight rise, framed by the surrounding parkland, which set it off exquisitely.

His impression of Carnaby Castle had led him to suspect that Lady Gillian must have believed her plot would enrich her family coffers, but he was finding it necessary to alter that opinion a bit more with each passing mile. Carnaby Park was clearly the seat of a prosperous nobleman. The chit could have had no good cause to play such a trick as the one she had played on him.

From the near-side window of the carriage he could see a garden bounded by a crinkle-crankle wall, and at the upper end of the chain of lakes, near the house, stood a building with brick walls and a thatched roof that he thought must be an icehouse. Two other outbuildings, facing each other across the central lake, also caught his eye, but these were classically designed with semicircular porticos and pilasters, one clearly a temple of some sort, the other an orangery or conservatory.

The entrance to the house was screened by great Corinthian columns resting on rusticated arches and surmounted by a deep parapet. The architectural composition, in the Palladian tradition, was impressive, dignified, and extensive. Wings on either side of the central block increased the overall length, making a splendid display, and the drive was constructed in a circular manner to grant any visitor the full effect of the house on one side, the splendid view of the sea on the other.

The carriage drew to a halt before wide, shallow stone steps, and Thorne opened the door for himself but allowed the footman to let down the steps. Emerging, he turned to look back the way he had come. The garden view was superb, in the style he recognized as that of the great landscape architect Capability Brown, who had also been responsible for much of the landscape design at Langshire Hall, in Derbyshire. Realizing that the man who had commissioned this imposing place, and who kept it in such good trim in the present uncertain times, would likely prove to be a formidable opponent, Thorne decided he would have to tread warily until he more exactly understood his situation.

His footman had preceded him up the steps to knock at the great doors, and they opened as Thorne approached to reveal a portly man whose attire was that of a nobleman's butler but whose bright chestnut wig was not only unpowdered but was sitting decidedly askew, with its beribboned tail lying on his shoulder.

"What is it, my man?" the butler inquired of the footman in lofty accents, tilting his head back in order to look down his broad nose at the taller man. When his eye caught sight of the marquess, he snapped himself to a haughty posture that would have been impressive had he not stumbled backward in the attempt.

The footman caught his master's eye, but if he was tempted to express his opinion, in any way whatever, of a servant who dared to answer the door of a stately home in such condition as the butler so clearly enjoyed, the footman repressed the temptation, stepping aside as he announced the marquess.

The butler inclined his head. "Pray enter, my lord," he intoned. "I shall determine if her ladyship is at home."

"Do not disturb her ladyship," Thorne said calmly, stepping across the threshold onto the black-and-white tessellated marble floor of the two-story, neoclassic entrance hall. Handing his hat and cane to his footman, there being no other in attendance and the butler being apparently blind to their existence, he noted with approval the subtle harmony of the chamber, the walls and domed ceiling of which were decorated in shades of green with white details, forming an ideal background for the pillars and pilasters supporting the semicircular wood-railed gallery overhead. "I would speak with Lord Marrick."

The butler blinked at him. "His lordship?"

"Certainly, his lordship." Thorne was rapidly revising his opinion of his host, with the result that he was now just a little confused. "Where are your wits, man?"

The butler, responding to the sharp note of authority in the marquess's voice, bobbed his head, then clapped a hand to steady his wig and turned quickly, albeit unsteadily, away, saying, "I shall attempt to discover where he is to be found, my lord, if you will kindly await my return."

Thorne's rising temper was checked by the sound of a gasp from the gallery overhead, followed instantly by an indignant voice. "What are you about, Porson, to leave a gentleman waiting in the hall? I do believe you must be inebria— Oh!"

The marquess realized instantly that he had been extremely foolish to think for one moment that he might not recognize the Lady Gillian Carnaby. Had he not instantly known her face, he knew now that he would certainly have recognized her voice. There was a quality in it that was difficult to describe in words. It was lower than most women's voices, and very pleasant to the ear, even now when she was both annoyed and caught off her guard. But he also remembered her face.

What had been a thick tangle of wet hair the last time he saw her was now a cap of shining curls the color of a raven's wing, piled artfully atop her head and wisping softly about her piquant, rosy-cheeked face. Her gown was not particularly fashionable, being made of ordinary stuff, but the dusty-blue color suited her, for it very nearly matched her eyes. Realizing that he was staring, he collected himself and made a proper leg.

"Lord Hopwood? It is you, is it not? Oh, dear!"

The butler, straightening his wig and attempting to look up at her without toppling over backward, said in an overloud voice, "Not Hopewood, m'lady. This gentleman be the Marquess of Thorne, whose lordship I was just . . . that is, whose presence I was just going to announce to his lordship."

"A marquess? Here?" Another female appeared from behind Lady Gillian, this one a voluptuous woman in a mauve silk gown, which, like the turban swathed around her head, was more suitable for evening than for mid-afternoon wear. "The Marquess of Thorne?" she pronounced in haughty accents. "Good gracious, Porson, are you quite sure? I did not know we were acquainted with a Marquess of Thorne. Are you indeed he, sir?" She raised a gold-rimmed lorgnette to her eyes and peered at him through it, stirring both Thorne's indignation and his sense of humor.

"I am, madam," he said with a slight bow.

"You are not," Gillian exclaimed. "You are a baron!"

Lady Marrick snapped, "That will do, Gillian! You cannot know this gentleman. Moreover, I believe you are supposed to be retired to your bedchamber. Show his lordship into the drawing room, Porson. You may send that new footman there up to the green parlor to apprise the master of his lordship's presence, and I shall come at once to bear him company in the meantime. And tell that lad to powder his hair properly before he shows himself again in my presence," she added tartly.

Porson blinked at her. "Powder his hair, madam?"

"Yes, powder his hair. I do not know why you question me. I have given strict orders that all our servants are to be powdered. You, too, Porson. That dreadful wig will not do."

"But, madam—"

"Do not argue. Goodness, what an appearance you make, and before a marquess, for goodness' sake. His lordship must be wondering about our entire household by now, to be sure."

"He is not a marquess," Gillian said. "Porson is drunk, Estrid, as must be perfectly clear even to you, and he has mistaken his lordship's title. Oh dear, what a coil!"

"I told you to seek your bedchamber, girl, and I will thank you not to be giving orders in this house. I thought we had settled who is mistress here now, and who is not. You there," she called down to the footman, "what are you waiting for? Fetch your master to the drawing room as I commanded you to do."

Thorne, sternly repressing an urge to burst into laughter at the look on his man's face at being thus addressed, said, "I fear, madam, that Ferry does not know the way."

"What? Nonsense. Of course he knows."

Gillian, who had ignored the command to seek her bedchamber, was peering over the railing at the footman, and when Thorne's gaze encountered hers, he detected an unmistakable glint of laughter in her eyes. Without looking away from her, he said, "I fear that you mistake the matter, madam. Ferry is not your servant but mine. His locks are not powdered because I prefer them, like my own, in their natural state. And since he does not know this house, he cannot be expected to fetch your lord, though I would appreciate it if someone would do so."

Lady Marrick looked much taken aback at these words, and an awkward, though mercifully brief silence fell before Lady Gillian said, "Porson, go and find Mrs. Heathby, and tell her that Lady Marrick desires that she send one footman to fetch his lordship to the drawing room and another to attend us there. Several of them are no doubt lounging about in the kitchen. And, Porson, you are to remain in the kitchen yourself until someone sends for you. Pray, do not stand there gawking at me. Go.''

The man stumbled awkwardly away to the green baize door at the right rear of the hall, and Lady Marrick said grimly, ''You overstep yourself, Gillian. Porson is my servant, and I do not know what you think we shall do if he is to remain in the kitchen instead of seeing to his duties here. I suppose you expect his lordship to wait for someone else to take him to the drawing room. Or do you expect me to wait upon him myself.''

''No, ma'am, I will. I know that Porson is your man, but he must not be allowed to answer my father's door in that disgusting condition. As to his lordship, I have no objection to bearing him company until Papa arrives. You, of course, must do as you please.'' She turned toward the stairs.

''Gillian, do not be absurd. I am sure you are mistaken about Porson, and you have no more business to be entertaining gentlemen by yourself than you do to be ordering my servants about. But that is by the way. The plain and unfortunate fact is that you are not dressed for company.'' Smiling at Thorne in a coy way that he found perfectly terrifying, Estrid added, ''I cannot imagine what you must be thinking of us, sir.''

He did not think any point would be served by confessing that he had suddenly remembered the way Lady Gillian had snapped at him from her precarious perch on the rock, and the way she had retained her dignity even under such conditions as the ones under which they had first met, that therefore he had not been much surprised when she had so quickly recovered her composure after that first brief moment of recognizing him. He noted, too, that she had ignored the older woman's strictures on her gown and was descending the stairway with as much grace and poise as though she were dressed in the height of fashion. Thorne began to believe that she did think he was a baron.

Lady Marrick was not far behind her. Holding her skirt delicately in her right hand, she came down the stairs with much more stateliness than Lady Gillian. Indeed, Thorne thought, she carried herself with more dignity than the Duchess of Langshire ever displayed. The mental comparison of the lovely but haughty countess with his plump, warm-hearted mother made him smile.

Gillian smiled back at him and held out her hand, saying, "I must say, I am glad you have come, sir. I was at my wit's end, wondering what to do about this tangle. I had thought at first, you know, that I need only request the newspaper to declare that an error had been made, but I am not certain that that will answer the purpose. There is bound to be such a vast amount of speculation, you know, that will be embarrassing for both of us."

"Good gracious, Gillian," exclaimed Lady Marrick, "what nonsense are you talking now? Pray, do not heed her, sir. She has suffered a lack of parental control these past four years since her mama's death—for I am Marrick's second, as you may not know, and what with being confined so quickly after our marriage, I have not yet been in command of this household long enough to make my hand felt. You will forgive her, I am sure, for being so forward in her manners. Go back upstairs at once, Gillian."

"I am sorry to disoblige you, Estrid, but I am not going to leave. You see, this gentleman is no marquess but only Lord Hopwood, the very same Hopwood in whom you all refused to believe. Since he has clearly read that idiotic announcement in the Honiton paper, he must certainly want to speak to me."

"Hopwood!" Estrid's eyes narrowed speculatively as she gazed at Thorne. "Well, to be sure, I had not thought you could be a marquess, wearing only a plain dark coat and buckskins to pay an afternoon call at such a place as Carnaby Park. No ruffles to your cravat, and not a single bit of jewelry, either, now I come to notice. Just only that plain signet ring."

A stifled sound from the direction of his footman caught Thorne's attention, and he turned. But Ferry was no fool. His gaze was discreetly lowered. Thorne turned back and said, "This is scarcely a proper place for such a discussion as ours must be, madam. May I suggest that we all retire, as you suggested, to your drawing room. My man can certainly tend your door until someone comes to relieve him of the task, after which he can cool his heels here until I have need of him again." This last was added in a tone pointed enough to redden the footman's ears.

"Come this way, sir," Gillian said, leading him to the left rear of the hall, then through an anteroom decorated in pale green with black-and-white details, into a saloon decorated with trompe l'oeil designs of arabesques and other motifs in tones of green on the biscuit-colored walls, ceiling, door panels, and even the chimneypiece. The design was very elaborate, but the subdued tones provided an atmosphere of beauty and peace. From what little he had seen of the present Lady Marrick, Thorne was certain she had had nothing to do with the decoration, a fact that she promptly confirmed.

"A very old-fashioned room," she said when he paused to look at one design, painted to reflect the view from a window overlooking the Channel. It was so well done that for a moment he had thought there actually was a second prospect. Lady Marrick said, "Pray do not remark unkindly upon our lack of à la modality, my lord. I promise you, things will be altered very soon. I mean to order the very latest furniture for this room just as soon as we repair to London for the Season."

He made no comment, and a moment later found himself in the drawing room. There was nothing here to attract him, although he was certain that her ladyship must like the room much better than its predecessor, for it had been decorated with an eye to opulence. The predominating color was apple green, but with elaborate white-and-gold details, and the walls were decked with evenly spaced allegorical cameos painted in golden medallions.

"We shall soon have pink silk hung in here, my lord," Lady Marrick said complacently. "It will be just the thing to brighten the room a bit, as I am sure you will agree."

Gillian said, "I believe his lordship would prefer to discuss the matter that brought him here, ma'am."

"Yes, of course," Lady Marrick said, arranging her skirt with care and taking her seat upon a gilt-legged settee near the marble fireplace. She smiled again at Thorne. "To think we had no idea there really was a romance afoot, my lord. Our dear Gillian has been very quiet about you, you see, very quiet indeed. Perhaps one day she will explain her reasons to us."

Gillian's cheeks flamed, but before she could speak, Thorne said, "I should prefer, madam, to wait until Marrick joins us to begin so pointed a conversation, if you have no objection."

Gillian, still standing, said, "Please, sir, you must not think that—"

"Gillian," Lady Marrick said sharply, "what are you about to keep his lordship standing? Sit down at once, and do keep silent. He will think that you have no breeding at all."

"But—"

"Do sit down, Lady Gillian," Thorne said, smiling at her. "The matter will soon sort itself out, I assure you."

"Very well, sir," she said, sitting without further ado on a beechwood chair at the opposite side of the hearth from her stepmother, "but I hope you do not think this was my doing."

"I did think as much," he admitted, sitting in a matching chair. "I have had my doubts, however, from the first moment I entered the hall and saw you peering down at me."

"Very improper of her, to be sure," Estrid said, "but no doubt she was anxious to see you again. Now do explain, sir, for I have been thinking and thinking, and I do quite plainly recall your declaring yourself a marquess before. Why did you wish to have such a game with us, may I ask?"

"It was no game, madam," Thorne said, keeping his gaze firmly fixed upon Gillian and drawing pleasure from her dawning awareness and evident dismay. "I am indeed Josiah Hawtrey, Marquess of Thorne, though 'tis only an honorary styling at present, of course. My father is the Duke of Langshire."

"Merciful heavens," Gillian said. "Why did you call

yourself Hopwood then? An insignificant barony, you said."

Ruefully he said, "It is a minor title of my father's, another styling I have used from time to time when I preferred not to use my own. In my position, you see, it is sometimes better to . . ." His voice trailed off, for he found himself unnerved by her steady, interested gaze. And when she did not instantly prompt him, as so many young women would have done, but continued to gaze at him with that look of polite interest, he realized that he did not want to explain his reasons to her. They seemed suddenly dubious, even a little distasteful, though he had not thought them so before.

Lady Marrick said with a laugh, "I am sure we understand you very well, sir. In your exalted position, surely you do not want always to be plagued by the attentions of your inferiors. Anyone of sensitivity must understand you."

Gillian tilted her head to one side. "I think a gentleman ought always to be honest, especially with his inferiors."

With the laugh that was becoming more irritating to him by the minute, Lady Marrick said, "It must be plain to you, Marquess, that our Gillian has had little experience of the *beau monde*. She cannot be expected to comprehend the complexities of such a life as yours must be, what with every matchmaking mama in London no doubt urging her daughters on to plague you. Why, I just shudder to think of the parson's mousetraps that must have been set for such a promising catch as you must be."

Since this forthright speech made Thorne even more uncomfortable, if that was possible, than Gillian's pointed statement, he was relieved when Marrick chose that instant to enter the room.

"Could have knocked me over with a feather when the lad said we had a marquess in the house," he said, coming forward to greet Thorne, who rose instantly to his feet. "I thought Porson must be drunk again and had made the whole thing up. Haven't met you above two or three times, I think, and could scarcely have expected those meetings to sit long in your memory."

Thorne shook the hand held out to him, saying, "You are mistaken, sir. I remember you well as a bruising rider to the hounds and an excellent shot with a fowling piece. I believe we both enjoyed the shooting at Longford Hall last year, and if I am not mistaken, we sat at the same dinner table one night during the shearing party at Holkham two summers ago."

Marrick laughed. "If you remember who sat at your table that night, you were more sober than I thought, lad. It's true enough, but there must have been two hundred men at that dinner, just as there are for all Coke's shearing and shooting parties. Never knew such a man for hospitality."

"He is very kind, indeed," Thorne said.

Lady Marrick said, "I am certain that you will find the hospitality at Carnaby just as impressive, Marquess, though Mr. Coke's house is perhaps a trifle larger than ours."

"Thank you, ma'am, but I will not impose on you. The inn at Honiton will do well enough for the one night I mean to stay."

She said, "But you will displease me very much if you mean to stay at an inn, Marquess, and indeed, you must stay with us. 'Twould be thought very odd if you did not."

Marrick said, "Damme, Estrid, the man will stay where he likes. Welcome here, of course, but I cannot think why anyone would think it odd of him to stay at an inn. Very decent sort of place, the Lion is. And ain't you going to Lady Halstead's?"

"I shall send her our regrets," Lady Marrick said, casting the marquess another of her arch looks, "for you do not know the whole, my lord. Your foolish daughter's Baron Hopwood is none other than the dashing young man you see before you."

"Good God!" Marrick looked in bewilderment at Gillian. "Is that true, girl?"

"Apparently it is, Papa, though I assure you that I had no more awareness of his true identity than I had of that dreadful announcement. Clearly, the sooner a statement is printed disavowing the whole, the better it will be for all of us.''

Thorne, obeying Marrick's gesture to take his seat again, said, ''It will not be as easy as that, I fear.''

Lady Marrick said quickly, ''No, indeed, for it would make our foolish Gillian appear in a most unfortunate light.''

Marrick said testily, ''That cannot be helped. Serves the chit right for creating such a coil in the first place.''

''Papa, I did no such—''

Lady Marrick said, ''Pray do not continue to deny it, Gillian. It was very bad of you, but I am certain that if you own up to your actions, the marquess will forgive you. And if you must be embarrassed by a second announcement, it is all to the good, for it will teach you never to do such a thing again. I am thankful to say that my own daughters would never have been so indiscreet. You will not be the only sufferer, you know, for we must all be made to look nohow by your naughtiness. Indeed, I tell you now to your head that if Dorinda's Season in London is spoiled in the least by your wickedness, you will answer to me, and so you had better know from the outset.''

''Good God, Estrid,'' the earl snapped, ''do not be making such a piece of work about a matter that is easily put right. I will send an announcement to that fool paper, telling them they have got it all wrong.''

''But they will know there is more to the whole matter than that,'' Lady Marrick protested. ''Did you not say you were told that Gillian had handed in the notice herself?''

Surprised, Thorne looked at Gillian, easily recognizing the glint of anger in her eyes and wondering how she would defend herself. When she said nothing at all, and in fact avoided his gaze altogether, his curiosity was piqued.

The earl said gruffly, ''The fact is that the young woman who handed in the announcement was heavily veiled, but if it was not you,'' he added with an accusing glare at his daughter, ''then, damme, I should like to know who else it could have been.''

Gillian continued to avoid Thorne's steady gaze, and her face turned pink when she said, "I am sure it was meant to be a jest, Papa, merely to tease me. Very few people believed my tale of rescue, you will recall. No doubt someone who thought I had made it all up decided to teach me a lesson."

"I suppose you expect us to believe that," Lady Marrick said with a sneer, "but I can tell you, my dear Gillian, that it will not serve. It is much more likely that everyone in Devon will believe, as I do myself, that you meant to put yourself forward in a most unbecoming way, merely out of your displeasure at having to take second place to your papa's new heir. His lordship will, I know, forgive me for speaking so frankly, but I do not believe in letting young women get away with their foolishness so easily as your papa seems bent on doing."

"Now, see here, Estrid—" the earl began.

But Thorne had had enough. "Forgive me for interrupting you, sir, but the matter is much more serious than you have been led to believe. The fact is that that damned announcement found its way into the London *Gazette*. Evidently, someone on the Honiton paper who memorizes whole portions of Burke's *Peerage*, particularly those pertaining to dukes, sent the announcement, accompanied by his own deductions, to a relative on the *Gazette*. My reputation, I regret to say, is such that no one even paused to consider the possibility of error before printing the speculation that I had been playing fast and loose with a lady of quality. The fat is well and truly in the fire, you see, and a simple disclaimer printed in the Honiton paper will not, at this point, be enough to stop the scandalmongers."

A stunned silence followed his words. Thorne saw that Gillian had turned pale, and wondered what she was thinking. No more than Lady Marrick had he believed her suggestion that someone had placed the announcement merely for a jest, or out of vengeance. The way she had colored up led him to believe she knew much more about the matter than she was admitting. No doubt she left honesty to gentlemen—and their inferiors.

"Good God," the earl exclaimed, suddenly coming to

life again, "how could anyone in Devon have done such a thing?"

Thorne replied, "I am sure I cannot say." That the person in Honiton who had accepted the announcement had believed it was legitimate was unimportant as far as he was concerned, for no one knew better than he that newspapers would print what they thought people wanted to read, and just as news of the Marquess of Thorne was grist for the gossipmongers of London, so must news of Lady Gillian Carnaby be to the people of Devon. Of far more importance was his rapidly increasing willingness to obey his father's command to settle the thing without scandal. He had not cared much before, on his own account, except insofar as he found it unpleasant to stand in the duke's black books. Now he did care. He watched silently as the earl began to pace, muttering. Lady Marrick, for a wonder, had not spoken and seemed to be lost in her own thoughts, and Thorne was content to wait, to see what they would suggest. His thoughts were tumbling over themselves, and he tried to sort them out.

He had a strong notion that Lady Gillian disapproved of him. Her remark about gentlemanly honesty had told him much. More than that, it had made him squirm like a guilty schoolboy. He was not certain if he wanted more to punish her for daring to think badly of him, or to exert himself to prove her wrong. What he did know was that he was unwilling now to let the matter end with no more than another line or two in the newspapers, even if it could be ended as easily as that.

A relative of his who had had the good fortune to visit China had once told him, laughingly, that the Chinese believed that if a man saved another man's life, that life became his responsibility to the end of time. The relative had shaken his head, insisting that when one had exerted oneself to such a purpose, it was but poor payment to be saddled with the person forever afterward. That particular memory had never reared its head before, but now Thorne found himself wondering how Gillian would react if he were to repeat it to her. Something told him she would not find it amusing.

She was sitting silently, making no effort to speak her

thoughts aloud, and she was still alarmingly pale. Suddenly the notion of taking control of her life, of protecting her and ordering her as he chose, seemed rather intriguing. She was not in his usual style, and not beautiful. Even her stepmother cast her into the shade in that respect, but she had a charming countenance and those huge, expressive eyes, and her air of quiet dignity was impressive. He believed—indeed, he had seen the signs for himself—that there was fire beneath the cool exterior. It would be amusing, he thought, to stir those coals.

4

GILLIAN WONDERED WHY Thorne was so quiet. He was watching the three of them as though they were exhibits in a menagerie, and she did not like the speculative look in his eye. It looked very much as though he were considering the prospect of poking a lion with a stick through the bars of his cage. And Estrid was entirely too silent. Only her father was behaving normally, stomping about, muttering, because something unpleasant had intruded upon his pleasure.

Suddenly Estrid said, "My dear sir, I wish you would cease pacing about like that. It puts me off, and makes it quite impossible for me to think what is best to be done."

Marrick growled, "You need not think at all, madam. It's plain as a pikestaff what must be done. Gillian ought to be soundly thrashed for causing all this upset."

"Papa, please—"

"Oh, my goodness gracious," Dorinda said gaily from the doorway. "I did not know you was entertaining, Mama." She had changed to a frock of tea-green muslin gathered around the neckline and sleeves with lavender ribbon. The matching lavender sash was tied in a becoming bow just beneath her plump breasts, and she wore a lacy muslin scarf draped over her arms at the elbows. Her guinea-gold curls were confined beneath an undress cap of white crape trimmed with green and lavender ribbons and tiny yellow roses. And unless Gillian was much mistaken, she had applied more than a touch of rouge to her cheeks.

Gillian glanced at Thorne, getting quickly to his feet, and noted that his eyes had widened in appreciation of Dorinda's beauty. Looking away again, she hid a faint smile.

Lady Marrick said, "Come in, come in, child. Here is a fine surprise for you, for we are entertaining a real marquess. Make your curtsy, if you please." She turned complacently to Thorne, thus missing Dorinda's widening eyes and the deep flushing of her cheeks. She added, "Marquess, this is my daughter, Miss Ponderby, who is to make her come-out in London this Season."

Dorinda sank at once into a graceful curtsy, keeping her wide blue eyes fixed upon Thorne until she rose again, then lowering them so that her long, dusky lashes touched her glowing cheeks. "It is a pleasure to make your acquaintance, sir," she said. "Are you really a marquess?"

"I am," he said, smiling at her.

Dorinda looked sharply at Gillian, who gazed steadily back at her, then turned to her mother and blurted, "But I thought Annie said Lord Hopwood was here!"

Lady Marrick said repressively, "There seems to have been a misunderstanding, and Lord Hopwood is really the Marquess of Thorne, but it is not a proper subject for you to be discussing, my dear. Indeed, I am very much shocked that you should have been gossiping with your maid in such a common way."

"I wasn't! But a marquess! She just said—" Breaking off, looking around guiltily at the others, she flushed again and said, "Well, I wanted to see him for myself, don't you know, to see that he really existed. *You* know, Mama, we none of us believed Gilly." Turning to Thorne again, she said naively, "You will forgive me, won't you, sir?"

He made a leg. "To be sure, Miss Ponderby. A gentleman must always forgive when he is asked by a beautiful young woman to do so. I will forgive you, if you will forgive me my title."

She giggled, but Marrick said testily, "I don't know what you are about, Dorinda, but I suggest that you take yourself off again, and practice your music lesson or some such thing. You have no business to be putting yourself forward in such a way."

Lady Marrick said, "Pray, sir, do not scold her. It is no wonder she should be curious about him. I own, I am myself. There is more to this business than meets the eye, and there is no reason that dearest Dorinda ought not to stay now that she is here. It will be excellent practice for her to be present in the same room as a marquess. Sit down, my dear. We were merely talking about what ought to be done next, you know."

Gillian saw Thorne's lips twitch, and was not in the least reassured, for it was no comfort to think that he considered her stepmother an object of humor. In fact, the thought was a mortifying one, and it was mortifying, too, to have to sit quietly while her future was discussed as though she were no more than thin air. When the marquess's gaze drifted in her direction, she quickly lowered her lashes and looked at her hands, tightly folded in her lap. With an effort she relaxed them, watching the blood begin to flow back into fingers turned white by the strain of clasping them so tightly together.

As if from a distance, she heard Thorne's voice, deep and calm, the way it had been the day of the storm. "May I ask when you intend to travel to London, sir?"

Marrick's voice held a note of surprise. "Me? I don't mean to go there at all just yet. Still some mighty fine hunting to be had in the 'Shires, you know. Mighty fine."

Lady Marrick's tone revealed her displeasure when she said, "But of course you will go with us, my dear sir. Why, I have not even seen your house before! He delights in joking us, Marquess, but he knows that he must be in London for his daughters' come-out. We leave for the metropolis in a week's time, and the house is in Park Street, so that is where you will find us until the end of the Season. It is not far from my late husband's house in South Audley Street near Grosvenor Square, though it is not his house any longer, to be sure, for he died there and is buried in his family's plot in a nearby chapel churchyard. He was Sir Cedric Ponderby, you know, but the house is now his cousin's.''

When Estrid paused, Gillian looked up again and found that her stepmother was eyeing her critically. She straightened, aware that she was not behaving as well as she ought, but she did not speak and she did not look at Thorne again.

No one else commented, so Estrid went on, ''I cannot think what is best to be done, you know. This is a dreadful coil. To be sure, Marquess, it must be the result of something Gillian did—if she did not insert the notice herself, which of course is the likeliest explanation, and the one you no doubt believe. It was kind of you to pretend that you do not. However, as I was saying, it is most clear that either she did it or that one of the other young ladies did, so jealous they are, you know, of anyone who receives undue attention—and of course Gillian is popular amongst the young gentlemen of her set simply because they have all known her for donkey's years, so if—''

''Good God, madam,'' Marrick snapped, ''spare the man a litany of your thoughts. I have already told you what must be done.''

''Yes, you have,'' she said in measured tones, ''but the fact is, dear sir, that you did not think. Even the marquess perceives that little can be gained from a simple denial sent to the papers. If you want your daughter made the talk of London before ever she sets foot in the place, I can tell you that I do not. It will be bad enough for poor Dorinda to have to make her bow to people who have been stunned by her sister's odd betrothal to the marquess, but there's no laughing at dukes and marquesses, to be sure, and if Dorinda is known to be acquainted with Langshire and the marquess here, well, there's no saying but what it might do her a great deal of good, so long as there is no scandal attached to the relationship. There, that's the word with no bark on it, Marquess, but I dislike mincing matters.''

"As do I, madam," Thorne said.

Gillian heard a note in his voice that put her instantly in mind again of their first meeting, but it was not the pleasant note she had heard before. It was a pity, she thought, that he was angry. She wondered what it would have been like to have met him in London, without all this nonsense between them. Would she have liked him? Would he have given her a second glance? Would they even have met? He did not seem to be the sort of man who would exert himself to do what her father called "the fancy." She tried to imagine him at a cotillion ball like the one she had attended in Honiton at Christmas, and her imagination boggled. She had a notion that he was very much like her father in that respect, preferring gaming, hunting, and shooting to cotillions, routs, or concerts. He knew Mr. Coke of Norfolk, but it was clear enough that he looked upon that gentleman as a source of hospitality and entertainment, just as her father did.

These thoughts passed through her mind in the instant of silence after Thorne's reply to Estrid, for he continued almost at once, saying, "I asked about your intent, ma'am, because I believe I know what is best to be done. First, I will send a proper, formal notice to the London papers, announcing my betrothal to the Lady Gillian—"

"No!" Gillian cried, then clapped her hand over her mouth and looked guiltily at her father.

The earl glowered at her, but before he could speak, Thorne said pleasantly, "Did you wish to make an observation, my lady?"

She swallowed, wondering why on earth she had lost her customary poise. Clearly it had slipped away altogether, unnoticed, for now she was quaking inside like an inexperienced schoolgirl, something she had never really been at all. Thorne's note of kindness was almost too much for her to bear. She felt an ache at the back of her throat, and drew a steadying breath before she looked at him and said quietly, "I beg your pardon, sir. I ought not to have interrupted you, but I simply cannot sit quietly by while you decide on such a hazardous course. It would be deceitful, and dreadfully unfair to you."

Lady Marrick said, "Hush, Gillian. Let the man tell us what he intends to do, and do not make a fuss."

Thorne said, "Thank you, ma'am, but I did invite her to say what she liked, you know. You have recommended plain speaking, and I mean to take you at your word. I have no notion how this farrago got started. If I ever do find out, I promise you, the person responsible will soon understand his, or her, error, but in the meantime, I propose to deal simply with the accomplished fact. No harm must come to Lady Gillian's reputation, or to Miss Ponderby's." He smiled ruefully. "My own reputation will not suffer, which is the one thing in all this for which I do apologize. Were it not that my past behavior lends credence to nearly anything anyone might choose to say of me, we might be more quickly out of this. As it is, I want to put the best face possible on the business, which means a proper announcement. When you reach London, we will proceed as if there were truly a betrothal. Lady Gillian will be introduced to my parents, and my mother will see to it that she and Miss Ponderby are treated in the manner befitting connections of my family. That means Almack's, I suppose, and a host of dreary parties as well."

Dorinda, clapping her hands, said, "Oh, not dreary at all, sir. We shall adore every one of them!"

He smiled at her. "You have not met my mama's relations yet, Miss Ponderby. I promise you that a number of those engagements will be boring in the extreme. And the deuce of it is that I shall be expected to accompany you to all of them."

She giggled. "But I think that will be delightful, sir."

"Do you?"

Gillian said, rather more sharply than was her custom, "I cannot agree that this is at all necessary, my lord. Surely, there must be a simpler means to the same end."

"There may be," he said, smiling at her in nearly the same way that he had just been smiling at Dorinda, "but I do not know what that is. Do you?"

"No," she admitted, "but I do not like this way at all."

Marrick said testily, "Make the most of it, girl. It is

better than you deserve. And be thankful you are my daughter and not my son, for a good caning is what you'd get for landing us all in the suds like this.''

Thorne chuckled. ''If she were your son, sir, we'd not be discussing this business at all.''

Marrick, much struck, laughed and said, ''Well, that's a fact. Are you still for the inn, my lord, or will you stay and take potluck with us? I've a fine young foal I'd be glad to show you. Going to make a fine hunter, damme if he won't.''

Lady Marrick said, ''Of course he will stay. What would people say, having learned his true identity, if he were to stay at a common inn? Not at all suitable, I assure you. I will have the peach bedchamber prepared for you, Marquess.''

''You leave me nothing to say but thank you, ma'am.''

Marrick nodded. ''You do as you please, Estrid. Come along, my lord, there is no time like the present to see that foal.''

''Yes, I'll come,'' Thorne said, getting to his feet again. ''Just let me have a moment with my man, to tell him to collect my gear from the inn, and then I'll be with you. Do you dine early, ma'am? I've only the clothes on my back until Ferry returns.''

''We have ceased to keep country hours,'' Lady Marrick said grandly. ''I thought it best that the girls grow accustomed to proper town hours before they reach London, so you will have plenty of time, Marquess. We do certainly dress for dinner.''

''Aye,'' Marrick grumbled, ''and a damned lot of nonsense it is, to be putting on knee breeches and all that claptrap when a man only wants to eat his dinner and get back to more important matters. But there you are—women, God bless 'em.''

Thorne, on the point of following him, turned back and said, ''Lady Gillian, if it would be agreeable to you, I should like very much to have a chance to speak more with you about this. Perhaps you will be so kind as to take a turn around the garden with me after your father has shown me his foal.''

''Oh, I do not think—''

"To be sure, Marquess," Lady Marrick said, laughing, "she must learn not to hold you at such arm's length now, mustn't she? Don't be a pea-goose, Gillian, but do as you are bid. You will want to change out of that dreadful gown, however, so run along upstairs to your bedchamber, and ask Miss Prynne to give you a hand with your hair. She don't do as fine a head as a London dresser will do, but I believe in giving credit where it is due, and she does have a nice way with it. No, no, say nothing more, girl. I am quite certain the marquess don't want to hear your excuses, so just for once in your life, do as you are bid. I will send for you when he returns from the stables, and he will not want you to keep him kicking his heels, you know."

Gillian, her cheeks flaming, made a swift curtsy and left the room ahead of the gentlemen. Hurrying upstairs to find Meggie, she was conscious of a bewildering urge to laugh and cry all at once. One minute her spirits seemed to soar, the next to plummet. There was no understanding the feeling. Her temperament was not generally so volatile.

Passing through an anteroom into the east wing of the house, she went first to her own bedchamber to ring for a maidservant to help her. Knowing it would take the girl a few moments to respond, she hurried back toward the nursery wing, encountering Meggie on the point of coming to find her, and quickly explained that she required assistance.

"It's all over the house that you'd a visitor," Meggie said. "What's this about his being a marquess?"

"Oh, Meggie, you don't know the worst of it!" Gillian said, torn again between laughter and tears. "It is Baron Hopwood, only as it chances, he is really the Marquess of Thorne."

"Is he, indeed?" Meggie's brown eyes narrowed. "Chance is, I've heard that name before," she said. "Weren't he the one as your papa said was a rake of the very first stare? Orgies and such, as I recall, when his lordship was at Longford Hall last year for the shooting. What sort of rig was he running, daring to tell you he was only a baron?"

Gillian smiled and said, "He said he found it convenient to do so. Who knows the true reason? He does have an eye for a pretty woman, though. You ought to have seen him light up when Dorinda came in upon us. She was wearing that tea-green muslin that becomes her so well, with the lavender ribbons, and she had rouged her cheeks. He was bowled over at the knees, Meggie."

They had turned toward Gillian's bedchamber, but Meggie stopped again to demand, "And what business had that young miss to be going downstairs at all, let alone dressed up like a Christmas beef? A young woman not yet out certainly ought never to parade herself before the likes of him. And did you ask her, Miss Gillian, about that other business?"

Gillian sobered. "Yes, Meggie, but I do not want to say more about that just now. There is Mary, coming to help us. I am to put on a more proper gown than this one, to take a turn in the garden with his lordship. He wants to have a private word with me, and Estrid practically forced me to agree."

Meggie clicked her tongue. "That woman. I know I ought not to speak ill— You there, Mary," she said, interrupting herself with a grimace of annoyance, "don't stand there gaping. Get yourself in and fetch out Lady Gillian's pink sarcenet walking dress, and that light silk pelisse she had made to go with it. You know the one— with the poppy-red bows round the hem."

Gillian laughed, relaxing at last as they stepped into her cheerful yellow and white bedchamber. "You are absurd, Meggie. Talk of Christmas beef! That is a rig I had made for London, and I certainly cannot walk about the garden here in such a thing. Thorne would think me a lunatic. Moreover, those bows—not poppy-red, if you please, but coquelicot—would catch on every hedge we pass. I'll wear my yellow India muslin round gown, Mary, and the old chip-straw hat that we trimmed with yellow and green ribbons last week. That will do very well."

"You'll freeze, Miss Gillian." Meggie nodded toward the tall, yellow-velvet-draped window overlooking the sea view. "There's a wind blowing up from the Channel to-day."

"A fine warm breeze, Meggie, nothing to fret me. Now come, do my hair for me so that it won't blow all about my face."

Twenty minutes later, she peered critically at her full-length reflection in the mahogany-framed cheval glass and saw, gazing seriously back at her, a slight young woman with a puff of black curls framing the upper half of her face. The side and back hair that Meggie had so carefully smoothed and tucked was already wisping in a lamentably ungoverned manner. Gillian did not admire her sort of looks, and had she been asked, would have pointed out that her chin was too pointed for perfection, her neck too long and thin, and that her eyes were much too large for her small face. They were also sadly unpredictable. Though they had looked blue before she changed her gown, now with the bright light from the window and the yellow fabric, they were stony gray, the color enhanced by the black rings at the outer edges of her irises. The natural roses in her cheeks had returned, however, and she was not in the least distressed to see a fine dusting of freckles across her tip-tilted nose.

Meggie was not so tolerant. "Look there, Miss Gillian! Haven't I told you to wear a hat when you go out of doors? Now, you've gone and got all freckled again, and what her ladyship will say to that I'd as lief not have to think about."

"Then don't trouble your head, Meggie," Gillian said, grinning at her. She straightened the skirt of the gown and smoothed a sleeve. "That will do now, I think," she said.

Meggie shook her head. "And what if you was to need a handkerchief, missy? I cannot accustom myself to the fashion nowadays. One was used to carry one's necessities in a proper pocket tied round one's waist under a flounce or a pannier, but now— Well, I ask you! With these flimsy, nothing gowns, what is a female to do?"

Gillian laughed. "One keeps a handkerchief tucked under one's sash or up a sleeve, as well you know. As to anything else I might need to stroll in the garden, Meggie, I cannot think what it would be. Oh dear,'' she added when a scratching at the door reminded her that her time was nearly up. ''Do I look all right?''

''Aye, but put on your bonnet before you go. I'll tie the ribbons for you. And take your Norwich silk shawl if you won't take a pelisse.''

The maidservant who had scratched stepped inside and announced rather breathlessly, ''Her ladyship said as how his lordship were a-waiting and Lady Gillian should stir her stumps, begging her pardon, Mizz Prynne.''

''Address her ladyship, girl,'' Meggie said sharply.

''Never mind, Sal,'' Gillian said, smiling at her as she allowed Meggie to adjust her shawl fashionably over her arms. ''I'm just coming. How is your toothache today?''

''Oh, lawks, Miss Gillian, it be all better. Me old mum, she pulled it out last night. Just tied a string from m' tooth ter the door and give it a hard push. That were the end o' that.''

Hiding a shudder, Gillian congratulated her on her good news, gave herself a last look in the glass, and left the room, wondering why she should suddenly be trembling.

She saw Thorne waiting in the hall, but he heard her step on the stairs and met her at the arched doorway between the entrance hall and stair hall. ''That shawl won't do you much good hanging from your elbows like that,'' he said with a frown. ''There's a stiff breeze outside. Pull it up around your shoulders.''

Gillian smiled. ''I live here, sir,'' she reminded him, ''and I am not as fragile as you seem to think. I shan't blow away; neither shall I freeze.''

In response he reached both hands to her shawl and pulled it up, smoothing it across her shoulders. His warm hands sent a wave of shock through her, making it impossible for a moment or two for her to speak. By then he had put his right hand between her shoulder blades and was urging her toward the front door.

''I don't like that hat,'' he said in the same abrupt tone. ''It hides your face from me.''

She looked up at him, feeling a bubble of laughter in her throat. ''My shawl was worn very fashionably till you disarranged it, sir, and I'll have you know that this hat is thought to frame my face quite fetchingly.''

He grimaced ruefully. ''To someone with your own lack of inches it might do that, but to me it's as good as a mask. Can't you take the damned thing off? I want to talk to you, and I can't talk to someone I can't see.''

Shaking her head, she reached up and untied the ribbons, pulling the hat off without so much as a thought for her hair. Thorne smiled in approval, and since there was no one else in the hall, he opened the front door himself.

Standing at the top of the broad steps, they paused, and she heard his indrawn breath and knew he admired the view as much as she did. Before them the green lawn seemed to sweep all the way to the sea, framed by colorful borders and, at a distance, by the magnificent belts of timber that surrounded the other three sides of the house and grounds. Away to the right lay the chain of lakes, the conservatory, the temple, and the icehouse.

''There used to be deer everywhere in the park,'' she told him, ''but for some cause or other they all died two years ago. Now there are cattle. Papa paid them no heed, thinking they would behave as the deer had and keep a respectful distance, but they did not. I stepped out one afternoon to find a cow standing at the front door, as if she meant to demand admittance. I ordered the ha-ha dug then. You can see it there, that semicircular line just where the lawn seems to drop away to the sea. We are really almost eight miles away from the Channel, but the view is so clear that it seems a great deal closer than that.''

He hadn't said a word, and she told herself to stop babbling like a ninny, but she had a strong urge to keep talking, to keep from having to hear what he had to say to her. She did not doubt for a moment that he had demanded this interview in order to make his displeasure known to her. Remembering how sharp he could be, she braced herself and held her tongue.

His hand was still at her back, touching her lightly between her shoulder blades. He pressed harder, urging her toward the steps. ''Let us walk by the lakes,'' he said. "I want to see that arrangement a little closer to. Capability Brown designed this landscape, did he not?"

"Yes, sir," she said. "He and my grandfather. Grandpapa Carnaby had decided notions as to what the effect should be. I am told that he and Mr. Brown could be heard for miles, shouting at each other, when they disagreed upon some point or other. I have Mr. Brown's drawings of his earliest plans hanging on the wall of my bedchamber. If you like, I will show them to you."

"I'd like that. Landscape design interests me, and Brown did a good deal of the work at Langshire Hall too."

"Langshire Hall is your papa's seat, I suppose."

"It is. Langshire used to be a county all its own, a sort of bolster between Derbyshire and Nottinghamshire with its top just touching South Yorkshire, but it became part of Derbyshire under Charles the Second when the sixth Earl of Langshire's eldest son was executed for opposing Charles's Catholicism. On the accession of William and Mary, an act was passed pardoning him and his father was created duke by way of apology, but the county was never reorganized."

While he talked, he guided her down the steps and across the gravel drive to the path leading to the lakes. The path was bordered by low, neatly trimmed box hedges, and in some of the plots they outlined, new plants were beginning to show color.

"This climate appears to be very good for flowers," he said.

"And for crops," she said, smiling. "We are going to plant a new type of seed for wheat, sent to us by Mr. Coke of Norfolk. Since you have visited there, like Papa, you must know that he has tried many experiments to increase his yield."

When he chuckled, she looked at him in surprise, noting the way the sunlight gave his dark hair an auburn cast. "I did not intend to make a joke, sir."

"I am sure you did not," he said. "Can we sit in that temple over there?"

"Yes. Why did you laugh?"

"Because you must really be finding it difficult to think

of things to say to me if all you can talk about is Coke and his wheat. Crops are scarcely a ladies' topic of conversation.''

Grimacing, Gillian made no effort to tell him that she was very interested indeed, that she thought anyone with land to plant ought to be interested, what with food shortages everywhere and riots erupting in nearly every county over the price of bread. She knew only too well, however, that he was likely either to laugh at her or to ignore her. Gentlemen were less likely than ladies, in her experience, to take a serious interest in anything, and when they did, they assumed a superior attitude and claimed that it was impossible for the fair sex to have any true understanding of such things. She had long since come to understand that their pride was somehow touched, even threatened, when a female knew more about such matters than they did, but she felt a brief wave of disappointment at receiving such a reaction from Thorne. She could not have explained why, but she had hoped he would be different from other men.

''Cat got your tongue?''

''No, my lord, but I am not certain what you want to say to me, and I confess, I am in no real hurry to find out.''

They were nearing the little marble temple, which stood on a rise above the nearest lake. The temple was no more than a raised circular platform about fifteen feet in diameter with a domed roof supported by eight Corinthian columns, but from within, one had a view both of the lakes and of the Channel. They went up the steps in silence, and Thorne did not speak until she had seated herself on the marble bench in the center of the platform.

He said, ''I have been trying to think where to begin. I confess, my first intent, and that which kept me awake through most of a journey of a day and a half—''

''Goodness, Papa takes three days to go to London! He will not travel more than fifty miles in a day, and Estrid travels even more slowly. Did you drive all through the night, my lord?''

''I did not. My coachman, footman, and I took turns driving, and we racked up for a few hours at the Ship in

Mere. We left before dawn this morning to come on to Carnaby Park.''

"Goodness, do you always travel in such haste?''

"No. Under normal circumstances I would stay a day at Amport Park with Winchester, and a day or two each at Fonthill with Westminster and Stourhead with the Hoares. But I thought I had cause to make haste, my lady. At first I hoped to be in time to stop that announcement altogether, but then I realized that not only would it be impossible but that the damage had already been done by the notice in the London papers.''

"I did not know anything about that,'' she said with a sigh.

"It is my belief you had no idea about any of it.''

"Thank you, sir, for believing that. It is perfectly true. I am mortified by what has happened, but I must say that had you told me your proper title and come inside like a gentleman to meet Papa that evening, this would never have happened.''

"There is no doubt some truth in that. Would you like to tell me who was responsible for the whole? I think you know.''

She had meant to tell him. She had thought she would have to do so in order to convince him that she had not done the thing herself, and though she would have scorned to tell tales to Dorinda's doting parent, or even to her own father, she had been prepared to tell Thorne, certain—though again she could not have said why—that he would honor her request for discretion. But now that he had met Dorinda and seemed to admire her, it would be flying in the face of every principle of honor to betray her to him so brutally. Worse, it would look as if she were merely attempting to make him think badly of Dorinda.

Gillian turned toward him to try to explain, but his eyes crinkled at the corners just then—why had she not noted before how deeply blue they were?—and he said, "Don't try to cozen me, my lady. I don't take kindly to faradiddles.''

"I wouldn't lie!'' Indignant, she glared at him. "If one is to talk of faradiddles, sir, 'twas you who told one to me! I have never pretended to be other than who I am. Would you care to try to explain to me just why you pretended to be what my stepmama so grandly calls a *mere* baron?''

He grinned at her, and she saw a wicked glint of laughter in his eyes. "I would rather kiss you," he said, leaning forward and touching his lips to hers.

Gillian sat still, eyes wide, shocked to her toes. She scarcely dared to breathe. His lips were cool and touched hers lightly at first, but when she didn't move, they pressed harder, growing warmer and softer. She had never been kissed by anyone outside her family before, never in such a way as Thorne was kissing her now, and she wondered briefly, crazily, why his nose hadn't got in the way. It occurred to her that anyone walking nearby would see them, and she started at the thought and would have pulled back, but with his hand at her back again, resisting him seemed to demand too much effort.

His lips moved softly against hers, and hers responded. She would have sworn she had not meant them to. But as the thought crossed her mind, he was pressing harder, and his hand moved to her waist. Her body arched forward to meet his. Her breasts seemed to swell beneath her thin gown, and the feelings that swept through her were unlike any she had experienced before. A low moan began in her throat when she felt his other hand on her shoulder, but when it moved down her arm, perilously close to one aching breast, she jumped, pulling away.

Thorne let her go at once. He was smiling. "You are the first woman I've ever kissed who purred like a kitten," he said.

Involuntarily her right hand rose up to strike, but when he caught and held her gaze with a mocking gleam in his eyes, she let it fall again and said, "Is that how a rake of the first stare treats all the ladies he meets, my lord?''

5

THORNE KNEW HE had angered her, but he was not certain that one small kiss was the reason her eyes were blazing. He remembered thinking they were blue, but they were not. They were gray, like smooth stones, but not cold, not even in her anger.

He had behaved badly, and he knew he ought to apologize, but he knew, too, that he would kiss her again at the first opportunity. Her lips had been soft beneath his, and yielding. He had a strong desire to hold her in his arms again, to soothe her, protect her—or to do whatever else came to mind. He remembered the Chinese saying and collected himself. No doubt she stirred his lust, but giving in to it would never do.

He had an urge to tease her, but at the same time he wanted to give her comfort. He strove for middle ground. "I was not aware that you were interested in rakes," he said, "let alone those of such accomplishment as to number amongst the best."

She said calmly, "I was told that you fit that description, sir. I merely wondered if it is your habit to kiss every young lady who chances to find herself alone with you."

"It is not," he said, unreasonably annoyed that she should label him so. Getting to his feet, he said stiffly, "It is time to go back. I offer my apologies. My behavior was unseemly."

"Well, it was," she agreed, standing and shaking out her skirt, then picking up her hat from where it had fallen behind the bench. Holding it carelessly by its ribbons, she looked at him, her gaze direct and innocent. "You ought not to take such advantage of your greater strength, my lord. It is unfair.''

His temper flared. ''Now, see here,'' he said sharply, ''as I recall the matter, I didn't have to use an ounce of my strength.''

She flushed deeply and turned away. ''No,'' she muttered, hurrying toward the steps, ''that is perfectly true. I'm sorry.''

''Here, wait,'' he called, fearing she would run away back to the house. But she stopped on the path and turned back. To his astonishment, her eyes were twinkling.

''I hope you do not mean to scold me, sir. You were quite right to snub me just then, for I said just what I ought not to have said. I also behaved badly, and if it is all the same to you, I'd as lief not discuss the matter further. But it occurs to me now that you must have had cause to bring me here. If I flounce off in a heat of anger, we shall have to do this again.''

''Will you come back and sit down?''

The twinkle in her eyes deepened. ''I think not, if it does not displease you. We shall be far wiser to walk. Surely you are skilled enough to walk and talk at one and the same time.'' Her smile was delightful. He thought he had never seen teeth so even and white, or lips so damnably kissable.

''I asked you a question earlier,'' he said. ''You did not answer it.''

The look in her eyes became grave. ''I remember your question, sir,'' she said. ''You asked me if I would like to tell you who was responsible. I would prefer not to do so.''

''I want to know.'' He saw her flinch at his tone and knew he had sounded angrier than he meant to, but it vexed him that she would keep such information to herself. When she remained silent, he said more gently, ''It is my right, I think.''

She looked up at him, and her gaze was steady. ''I will not pretend that I do not know, sir, but it is a matter of honor. I should prefer not to bear tales of someone else. It will be better if the person admits to the error and better by far if we can end the business without a lot of folderol. I am grateful for your concern for my reputation, but since I really have none as yet, beyond the borders of Devon, I cannot believe I shall suffer unduly. I may be deemed a fickle woman, I suppose, but that can do me little harm.''

''You do not know the *beau monde*,'' he said. ''Its members like nothing better than to slice someone's character to ribbons. They feed on scandal, and unfortunately, I have, in my time, given them much fodder for their meals.'' He added bitterly, ''My name and position made me a natural target for them, of course, but I confess, I made little effort to be any sort of paragon.''

''Is it so difficult to be a marquess?'' she asked. ''I should think the title would have provided you with great advantages.''

The simple observation stirred an unexpected but familiar wave of resentment, and he struggled to maintain his calm. He had not realized that the old bitterness was so much alive within him. A swift vision formed of his house master at Eton, looming over him—the cane in his hand a long and limber one—telling a nine-year-old Thorne that he would show him a great advantage to being a marquess, for no doubt having been so smiled upon by God, he would not feel his well-earned punishment. The taunting had preceded a period of almost unendurable pain and humiliation, followed by blessed silence when he had been sent to his bed in disgrace. The incident was but one among many. His present state of limbo, that he was expected to wait patiently—and evidently with unmixed feelings—for his father to die before he would come into his own, was far harder to bear.

She was watching him, and he saw concern in her expression. Wanting to smooth it away, he said lightly, ''What could be difficult about being a marquess? As to putting an end to our betrothal, think no more about it, but trust me to know what is best, for you have not the experience of the world that I do. Believe me, once people have come to know you, they will not be so quick to condemn you when you do cry off. I think we ought to go back to the house, don't you? The wind is growing chilly.''

* * *

Gillian walked silently beside him back to the house, wondering where he had gone in his mind for those few brief seconds when the frozen look had seized his countenance. One moment he had been speaking in the tone most persons used when they were telling her something for her own good; the next moment he had seemed possessed by some ghost or private demon. Her curiosity to know what had caused such a look was overwhelming. Something troubled him, and she wanted to know what it was, but she knew that such curiosity was an unbecoming fault. One simply did not ask personal questions. Indeed, it had been her own overstepping of those bounds that had affected him.

At the house they found the entrance hall tended by a young footman in a powdered wig and bottle-green livery. "Merciful heavens," Gillian exclaimed, "I quite forgot about Porson. Do you suppose that awful man is still awaiting me in the kitchens?"

"What can you do about him?" Thorne asked.

She grimaced. "I do not know, precisely. If it were left to me, I should give him notice, but Estrid will fly into the boughs if I do, so I suppose I must not. Perhaps if I simply read him a scold, he will endeavor to behave better in future."

"Beggin' your pardon, my lady," the young footman said, "but Mr. Porson done left already. Said he knew when he was not wanted and would thank you to send his pay to him care of the Fox and Grape in Honiton, which is his brother-in-law's tavern."

Gillian looked at Thorne and saw her own amusement reflected in his eyes, but she was exasperated too. "That odious man," she said. "Now I shall have to see about hiring a new butler, and Estrid will be impossible to live with until we can find one to suit her. Fortunately, it is not yet three o'clock, so there is time to drive into Honiton to the registry office."

"I should be happy to drive you," he said.

She did not think that would be a good idea, for more than one reason. "You are most kind, sir, but I should prefer to drive myself. I—I have another errand to attend to as well, and I should not like to put you to any inconvenience.''

''It would be no inconvenience,'' he said.

''Well, but you must want to wait for your man to return with your gear, and you would not enjoy driving my gig. I am certain of that. It is old and rather fusty.''

''No, I would not enjoy that,'' he agreed, ''so it will be wiser all 'round if you put off this expedition until morning, when I can take you to Honiton in proper style.''

She grinned at him. ''In your traveling chaise with your coachman driving and your footman up behind? No, I thank you. Truly, sir, I have a number of small errands to see to before I go to the registry office, and I shall have to hurry if I am to be back in time to dress for dinner. I warn you, Estrid's notion of town hours is half past seven, which, I daresay, will seem early to you, for my cousin Lydia Vellacott has been to London twice, and she said she had dined as late as nine o'clock there.''

''I shall endeavor to conceal my dismay,'' he said.

The look he gave her told her he knew perfectly well that she was chattering in order to keep him from pressing her to let him drive her into town, but she didn't mind. As long as he yielded, she did not care what he thought. Not only did she want to attend to at least one of her errands in private, but she was sure that Hollingston must have returned by now, and she wanted to discover if he had brought the new seed.

''Gillian, my girl!'' cried a familiar masculine voice behind them. She turned with a grin to greet her favorite uncle, who was strolling toward them from the direction of the walled garden. He was a tall, dandified gentleman on the shady side of middle age, dressed with his usual flair in pale knee breeches, well-polished Hessians, and a dark coat. As he neared them, he raised a quizzing glass and peered at Thorne through it.

Gillian said, ''Uncle Marmaduke, I must make you known to our guest, the Marquess of Thorne. Sir, this is my uncle, the Honorable—well, most of the time—Marmaduke Vellacott.''

''What you need, lass, is to have your ears soundly

boxed,'' her uncle announced, hugging her and nodding to Thorne at the same time. "Must forgive me, m'lord," he said, his blue eyes twinkling, "but hugging my niece must always take precedence, and you don't look like a lad who will take offense."

Thorne smiled and said, "None at all, sir. It is a pleasure to meet you. At least, I don't think we've met before, have we?"

"You'd remember, lad, I promise you. I do know your father, however, so don't go asking him about me. I don't say the duke lies in his teeth, but what he'll say won't bear repeating."

Thorne chuckled, but Gillian said reprovingly, "You mustn't try to throw dust in his eyes, Uncle Marmaduke. If his grace of Langshire disapproves of you, it is probably because he has heard some disreputable tale about you and some poor misguided female. In any event, you ought not to be telling his son he lies in his teeth. What will he think of you? And where have you been, sir? You have not been to visit me in weeks."

"Oh, only over to Exeter," he said. "There's a devilish charming, delightfully wealthy widow there who rather fancies me. But never mind that. Tell me instead what the devil is going forward that I must read of your betrothal in the papers before I hear of it from you? And who the devil is this fellow Hopwood?"

Gillian felt a rush of heat to her cheeks, but said as calmly as she could, "Now, don't be vexed, sir, it is all a hum." She had never had occasion to tell him about her rescue, but she did so now, adding, "Hopwood is Thorne, only I did not know his true title, and whoever put the notice in the papers did not know it either. But someone on the paper recognized it and sent the notice on to the London papers. So we have a mess on our hands."

Vellacott gave her a sharp look and she feared he might demand to know more, but he did not. Instead he looked at Thorne and said, "Giving out false titles, lad? I daresay the duke didn't look any more kindly on that than he's looked upon some of my more enterprising adventures."

"No, sir," Thorne said, still smiling. "He did not. It has been decided, however, that for Lady Gillian's sake we will continue the charade for a time, long enough to silence the tabbies and allow her to become known in London. Then, of course, she will cry off."

"Ah, going to make a jilt of my niece, are you?"

Thorne's eyes narrowed. "It was thought the lesser of two evils, sir. The matter cannot be put to rest with a simple disclaimer, you know."

"Aye, that wouldn't do, but how the devil did you get yourself into this mess, girl? No, no, I don't want to know. Look here, I can't stay. Only came to discover the facts, and what with my widow keeping herself warm for me and all—"

"But you must stay to pay a proper visit, sir. You have already gravely offended Estrid, I fear."

"Have I?" Vellacott's demeanor hardened. "Daresay she'll survive it. Know she's generally safe in her bed-chamber at this hour, refreshing her wiles for the evening ahead, so I thought I'd pop in, but that's all, m'dear. Don't press me to stay."

"I shan't," Gillian said, "but only because I must drive into the registry office in Honiton to ask them to find us a new butler. Our last proved to be a drunkard and has gone."

"Dear me." But Vellacott grinned. "Appears as how your father's second wife is no better at picking servants than my second was. Always taken in by an attitude, Grace was, and never saw beneath the surface. Now, Millicent—that was my first," he added for Thorne's benefit, "she was a fine judge of men. Stands to reason, don't it? She picked me. But would you believe it, the second one filled our house with nidgets and twiddle-poops till there was no abiding it. Makes one almost glad she was took off by the influenza. Providence, that's what it was."

"Uncle Marmaduke, what a dreadful thing to say!"

He had the grace to look abashed, but said stoutly, "Well, she wasn't worth a hair of Millicent's head, and that's the truth of the matter. I'm for London soon," he added with a brighter look. "I shall go and talk to Millie at once. Always makes me feel better when I've had a word with her. I'll just pop down to the kitchens now without troubling anyone and see what Cook has to keep a man alive on the road.'' He turned and left them as suddenly as he had arrived.

Seeing Thorne's look of bewilderment, Gillian said, ''He has not accepted Papa's marriage yet, but he keeps a close eye on me. As for his talking to Millicent, you mustn't think he talks to spirits, sir, for it is no such thing, but my aunt was a charming woman and he misses her dreadfully even now, so he goes to the churchyard to visit her whenever he can.'' Turning to the interested footman, she said, ''Francis, take his lordship up to the peach bedchamber, if you please, and see that the door into his sitting room is left open for him and that the dressing room adjoining the bedchamber is prepared for his man, Ferry, to use. Ferry will want an iron and no doubt a few other sundries. You will know the sort of thing, but send one of the other lads to see to it. You must not leave the hall unattended for long.''

''Aye, m'lady.''

She held out a hand to Thorne. ''I enjoyed our walk, sir. Pray, do not be vexed with me for knowing my own mind. I am sorry if I seem to flout your wishes, particularly since I do understand that you are generally blameless in this matter, but I must be allowed to think things out for myself.''

He bowed over her hand, his own feeling warm and strong when he clasped hers. Smiling wryly as he straightened, he said, ''I will allow you what you please, my lady, up to a point.''

Something in his expression made her want to snatch her hand away, but she controlled the impulse and returned his smile politely. Leaving him, she turned at the half landing to look back, and she could see that he was still standing, watching her, while Francis waited patiently beside him for a sign that he was ready to be shown up to the peach bedchamber.

Gillian made haste, not bothering to call for assistance, but flinging on her red cloak—wonderfully refurbished by Meggie after its October ordeal—and hurrying back downstairs by the service stairs lest she encounter the marquess again. As she crossed the stable yard, she heard the clock ring the hour in the bell turret over the northern entrance. Hailing one of the grooms, she ordered him to bring out her gig and asked him if Hollingston had returned. Receiving an affirmative reply, she went on to the steward's room, located in the stable wing to the right of the clock tower.

Mr. Hollingston, a barrel-chested, auburn-haired man with some fifty-five years to his credit, got up from behind a large, cluttered desk with a broad smile of welcome on his face. "A good day to you, m'lady. I'd have wagered I'd see your bright face before sundown, and it's good news I've got for you too."

"Do you, Hollingston? How wonderful! Did you speak to Mr. Coke himself? I warned you not to let yourself be fobbed off by a mere minion of his."

"No trouble about that, m'lady. A fine man Mr. Coke is, a right pleasant gentleman, and bound to help anyone wanting to establish a wheat crop, or any other for all that. He spoke to me as if I were a nob m'self."

"Well, I should hope so," Gillian said, "when you had gone all that way to meet with him."

"Oh, as to that, it were only to South Molton, for you know, m'lady, he were a-staying wi' m'lord Percival, and he's bound to be there a week or more yet by what he was tellin' me."

Gillian nodded. It had been the fact that Coke of Norfolk was known to be visiting Lord Percival Worth at South Molton that had spurred her to send Hollingston to meet with him. She had not dared write Coke herself, fearing that he would only laugh at such a letter from a female, but she had thought he would be perfectly willing to discuss crops with Hollingston. The thought reminded her that she had meant to ask him about Thorne.

"Hollingston, do you know of a Baron Hopwood?"

"No, m'lady."

"Perhaps you know the Marquess of Thorne."

Hollingston grimaced. "Not to say know, precisely, but I've heard of that one." He regarded her searchingly. "Not a man your grandfather Vellacott would have approved of, if you'll pardon my taking the liberty to say so, Miss Gillian.''

"I see. Well, did you get any seed?''

"Aye, a bit to try and more to follow as soon as them at Holkham send it. Says it'll come straight off last year's crop, and a bounteous crop it were. Bound to feed all his own people and a right good few others as well. Says if everyone would plant like he does, there'd be no shortages and an end to the fussing. And Mr. Coke says the seed's to go into the ground just as soon as it arrives. In Norfolk they'll be waiting nigh until May, so as to be sure the last frost is gone, but he says we can be doing it here now, and I agree with the man. We saw scarce a drop of frost the entire winter hereabouts. Odd to think that not two years ago we had snow!''

Delighted by the news, she said, "Our people will be in good trim then, Hollingston. Be sure you let our tenants know they can have seed for their own gardens, and as much of the flour as they need, once it has been milled. 'Tis a pity it takes so long to grow the stuff. I daresay things will be a lot worse by then. We are already hearing of so much unrest.''

"Aye, and Lord Percival said there's a law in London now that, because of the shortage, bakers can no longer sell new bread, not until after it's been sitting twenty-four hours. They think people don't eat as much bread when it's day-old as they do when it's warm from the oven, and they say the law will spread elsewhere, too, and there's even been talk of famine, he said. Seems an exaggeration, but there's no denying provisions are scarce, m'lady. We'll be set right enough at Carnaby, however.''

She stayed talking for a few minutes more, then took her leave. Finding her gig waiting, she took her whip from the groom, allowed him to help her to the seat, then dismissed him. Remembering without concern that Estrid had insisted that she must never go to Honiton without her groom, she whipped up the horses and drove at a spanking pace through the stable-yard gate. She didn't want a groom or anyone else with her on this trip.

* * *

From the window of the peach bedchamber, Thorne watched her drive away without so much as a groom to attend her. What, he wondered, could her father be thinking about to give the wench so much freedom? She had no business to be let out on her own, certainly not to drive the highroad into Honiton. What if something occurred? What if one of her horses went lame? Both looked like fine, healthy animals, a pair he would not—from what he could make of them at this distance—scorn to have in his own stable, but even so, something could go wrong. Though he winced at the wicked pace she set, driving through the narrow brick archway, he could see that she had room to spare. Had she been one of his own friends—Corbin, for example, who could drive to an inch and was, like himself, a member of the Four Horse Club—he would not have thought it such a great feat. But for a woman to do such a thing was remarkable. Or foolhardy. And from what he had seen of Lady Gillian Carnaby to date, he was as willing to bet on the latter as the former.

He wondered why she had spurned his company. She might at least have tried to arrange something for his entertainment while she was gone, since her stepmother had not troubled to do so. Everyone in the place seemed to think only of his or her own comfort and nothing else. But thinking of Lady Marrick reminded him that he would have to take care to stay out of her way. He didn't think he could stomach any more of her platitudes for a while.

He had concluded that Lady Gillian was the person most responsible for the smooth running of Carnaby Park and thought it amazing that she was allowed so much license. Clearly the only one who challenged her authority was Lady Marrick, who had made at least a few token attempts to wrest the reins from her, but it was clear, too, that the countess was inexperienced and, if anything, merely a hindrance. Vellacott scarcely paused at Carnaby long enough to hang his hat, and Marrick did not seem to take the slightest interest in the place. But Gillian was entirely too young to shoulder such a burden. To be sure, she seemed to enjoy it, but she would soon be at loggerheads with Lady Marrick if she kept on as she was doing now.

Staring down into the stable yard, and thinking it a mighty poor view to give a guest when there was such a fine one from the south front, he found himself wondering if he would be subjected to a scene when Lady Marrick discovered that her butler had taken leave and that her stepdaughter had presumed to hire a new one without consulting her. And why the devil hadn't Gillian simply sent a man into Honiton to ask a representative of the registry to call upon her stepmother at his earliest convenience?

To the best of Thorne's knowledge, though he had never had cause before to give the matter much thought, few persons looking to engage servants actually set foot in a registry office. He certainly had never done so, and the duke's steward was so puffed up in his own esteem that he would deem such a visit far beneath his dignity. That thought stirred several new ones. She had been in an almighty hurry, almost as if she meant to act before her courage failed. No, he was being fanciful now. He shook himself and turned to ring for hot water. He could at least wash his face and hands before Ferry returned with his gear.

Another half hour passed before his man hurried into the bedchamber, followed by two footmen carrying various articles of luggage. Ferry waited only until the others had set down their burdens as he directed them before saying, "Hakson's taken the carriage round to the stables, my lord. I beg pardon for being so long, but we was detained by Lord Crawley at the inn."

"Crawley! What the devil is he doing there?"

Ferry said with admirable calm, "Seems he and my lords Corbin and Dawlish all wanted a look at the Lady Gillian, sir."

"May the devil fly away with them!" Thorne exclaimed.

"They said if they did not hear from you before five, they would come along here to inquire for you. I did my best, sir, but Lord Crawley damned my eyes, and Lord Corbin got that sleepy look he gets—you know the one—

and said he couldn't for the life of him think why you wouldn't be wishful to see them after they'd driven so far and at such a wicked pace and all. He said—''

"Oh, I can imagine what he said, but you needn't repeat his prattle," Thorne said, grimacing. "I'll see them, all right. Order me a horse, Ferry. I saw some prime cattle in the stable when his lordship showed me that foal of his. Tell them I want a good one, but fetch out fresh buckskins first, and while I'm gone, see about a decent rig for dinner, something I can hustle into without a lot of bother when I get back."

"Aye, m'lord," Ferry said with a sigh as he hurried to obey. " 'Tis a pity you won't take more care, though. How I'm ever to get a good place as a gentleman's valet, I'm sure I don't know. And Cherriton back in London no doubt biting his fingernails to nubs for worrying about how poorly I'm turning you out."

Thorne smiled at the thought of his valet. "He will know you are doing your best, Ferry. Now stop chattering and order up that horse. I can get into my own buckskins and jacket."

If he was not ready by the time Ferry returned, he was nearly so, and required but a few touches to finish. Then, clapping his hat to his head, Thorne hurried downstairs and out the front door to find one of the stable lads leading a fine-looking bay gelding up and down the drive.

Taking the reins with a smile and flinging himself into the saddle, he touched the gelding's flank with his heels and was off. The animal's forward action was excellent, and it soon settled into a distance-eating pace. Thorne did not ask himself why he was in such a hurry to confront his cousin and their two friends. He just knew he wanted to get to Honiton as quickly as possible. The six miles were accomplished in well under an hour, and he was pleased to see when he drew rein before the Lion that the gelding seemed to have a good number of miles left in him.

Dismounting, he threw the reins to a boy who hurried to meet him and tossed him a coin from his pocket, giving orders to walk the gelding so it wouldn't get chilled. Then, taking the steps two at a time, he entered the inn.

The first persons he saw were Dawlish, Corbin, and Crawley, all sprawled at their ease in the common room to the left of the entrance hall, their feet stretched out before them, glasses of wine or ale near at hand.

Corbin saw him first and drawled, "How now, why the long face, my lad? You don't look at all pleased to see us."

"I'm not at all pleased. What the devil do you mean by following me down here?"

Corbin's face fell ludicrously. "Damme, but you cannot know the wicked pace they insisted I set or you would not wish to distress me by asking such an insensitive question. Why, not only was I forced to drive—for entrust my cattle to a coachman in such a case, I would not—but I have been jostled about so much that my wig near came off, and to make matters worse, the ale in this house is tainted. I believe the damned fellow must have added water to it. Dreadful stuff!"

"So dreadful," Crawley said, grinning, "that both he and Mongrel have found it necessary to drink three mugs of the stuff in the past half hour alone. They will soon be flat, so say what you like to us quickly, or they will miss the best of it."

"Aye," Corbin agreed morosely, "and I wager I'll have a brutal head in the morning, due to the villainous adulteration of the spirits of this house. How came you to rack up here, Josh?"

"I won't, as it happens. I am to stay at Carnaby."

"Aye, so your man told us," Dawlish said. He had been watching Thorne silently, and a trifle warily.

"I shall speak to Ferry about that," Thorne said grimly.

"Now, don't go flying into the boughs, coz," Dawlish said. "We didn't come entirely on your affair, you know. Well, not altogether, at all accounts. There was Crawler as well. At outs with his lady and pockets entirely to let." He lowered his voice, glanced right and left, then murmured, "Bailiffs."

Thorne raised his eyebrows. "Tipstaffs after you, Crawler?"

Crawley shrugged. "It hasn't come to that, of course—

can't clap up a peer. But I confess that when Mongrel said he and Corbin thought a little drive to Devon might benefit them, I agreed in an instant. Not only ain't the dibs in tune at present, but my darling Gwendolyn has fallen under the spell of a blasted Scotsman. I thought my absence might induce a bit of proud desperation in the wench. Or better yet . . . any heiresses about, Josh—that you haven't already snabbled, that is?''

"How much do you need?" Thorne demanded with resignation.

"More than you'd be willing to give me," Crawley answered instantly. "It's no good, Josh. My pockets are to let, that's all. Shall we go away again? Mongrel always wants to help, you know, but I think we are a trifle *de trop*. Are we?''

"Infinitely. Did you expect merely to ride up to the house and announce that you had come to look over my betrothed wife?''

"Nothing so no-account as that, dear boy," Corbin assured him. "I'll have you know that I have relations in the neighborhood—well, in Devon, anyway. To be truthful, they reside near Plymouth. I'll confess that I haven't visited there since I was in short coats, and that I thought Plymouth was a deal closer to Honiton than it is, but there you are. Well, how was a fellow to remember that Devon was such a damned big county. Take a week to ride around it, I should think. Truth is, we had nothing better to do and didn't want to be fobbed off later with more of your nonsense, so we thought we'd come along and see for ourselves. After all, it's the first one of your recent jaunts where we'd a notion where you were bound. So tell us about Lady Gillian Carnaby and this utterly unexpected betrothal of yours.''

Thorne grimaced and, gathering his thoughts, moved away toward one of two small windows overlooking the street.

"Ring for another pitcher of ale, Crawler," Dawlish said. "Can see he wants to wet his whistle, can't you? Now, no need to poker up like that, coz," he added hastily. "We mean no harm.''

Thorne shot him an oblique glance. "I do know that,

but I'm in a a deuce of a pickle, Perry, and I'm going to need my wits about me to get out of it without hurting anyone else. I can't tell you everything, because I don't know it all yet, but you can take it from me that there are more than a few innocent people involved. The damned betrothal will have to stand until I can sort it out, so I'll ask the three of you to have the goodness to hold your tongues on the matter until I decide what to do.''

"Don't the chit want to marry you?" Dawlish demanded, his speech slurring a little on the words.

"No, of course she doesn't. She didn't— Good God!" A flash of red in the street had caught his eye, and he turned in time to see a scarlet cloak disappear through a doorway opposite the inn. "Here, landlord," he snapped to the man just entering in response to Crawley's ring, "what's that building yonder?"

"Yonder, my lord?" The man wiped his hands on the white cloth he had tucked into the waist of his breeches, and moved a little to peer through the window. "Ah, now that would be the offices of the South Devon *Gazette*, sir."

"Would it indeed?" Thorne said grimly. "Forgive me, gentlemen, but I must leave you. I shall return when I can. In the meantime, be good enough to stay right here, if you please."

Corbin said a little plaintively, "Well, I like that. Not so much as a taste of the ale, and—"

But Thorne heard no more. His temper rising rapidly, he went back through the little entryway, out the door, and across the street, paying no heed to the fact that he had stepped right into the path of a farm wagon. Ignoring the curses of its driver, he kept his gaze on the door he wanted. A moment later, he threw it open and strode into the newspaper office.

6

GILLIAN HAD NEVER been inside a newspaper office before and found the smell of ink and the sounds of the place fascinating. There was a great deal of banging going on in the nether regions, and when a thin, pock-scarred young man stepped to the wooden counter separating the back of the room from the tiny entryway and spoke to her, she was unable to hear him clearly, but she found his look of polite inquiry suddenly rather daunting.

When she had imagined the scene to herself, it had seemed a simple matter to place a notice declaring that the announcement of an engagement between Lady Gillian Carnaby and Baron Hopwood had been made in error. It was quite another matter now. Even without being able to hear all the young man said to her, she had a horrid notion from his air of deference that he had recognized her, and she was cursing herself for not having had the foresight—as clearly Dorinda had had—of wearing a veil.

The office door banged back on its hinges, crashing against the wall behind her, and Gillian whirled in dismay to see Thorne striding into the office. Seeing instantly that he was in a blazing fury, she felt her breath catch in her throat, and she had to fight an instinct to put up her hands to fend him off.

"I thought I'd run you to earth here," Thorne said in what she thought was an amazingly light tone as he turned to catch the door and close it, just as if he hadn't thrust it into the wall only seconds before. He smiled at the lad behind the counter and said in a voice raised above the noise from the back of the office, "Fearful wind. Sorry about the door. I saw my cousin come in here and thought

I'd come in to lend her a hand with her notice. Though why," he added, smiling indulgently at Gillian, "she would want to place an advertisement for a new butler in your newspaper when there is a perfectly good registry office right here in town, I haven't the least notion."

The youth smiled at Gillian and said, "He makes an excellent point, ma'am. Our next edition won't appear for a sennight, for we just had one out today. And in a sennight, like as not, the registry office could find you a dozen butlers."

"Goodness me," she said, smiling back at him, resigned to the fact that her notion, little though it had had to do with butlers, had been a poor one, "I shouldn't know what to do with a dozen butlers, but I shall take your advice. If they do not find someone suitable before the week is out, I will return."

"Excellent," Thorne said, putting his hand firmly between her shoulder blades and urging her inexorably toward the door. Looking back as he opened it for her, he said, "Thank you for your good advice, lad."

Gillian had the odd notion that she was being hurried to a tumbril, if not straight to a guillotine. Certainly, if Thorne had anything to say about it, her head would soon be separated from her shoulders. He was urging her along at such a pace that if she was not careful, she would trip over her skirt and fall flat on her face in the street. But if she resisted him, she would create another, even less desirable scene to entertain the people of Honiton. She could feel the energy of Thorne's temper crackling in the air around them and wondered how long it would be before it exploded. The three gentlemen on the front step of the inn across the way were clearly expecting something of the sort to happen. They regarded her with the sort of interest one associated with spectators at a mill, or at a beheading—not that she had had any experience with such events, of course.

"The devil!" Thorne muttered beneath his breath.

She looked up at him. "What is it, sir?"

"I have much to say to you, Lady Gillian, but even you do not deserve to hear it before an audience like that one."

"You know those three gentlemen?"

"I regret to say I do, though I doubt I should use so polite a term as 'gentlemen' for them at present. Where is your gig?"

"I left it in charge of a boy near the registry office in the next street," she said, eyeing him, then adding with what she hoped would be taken for airy assurance, "I'll just go collect it and be on my way back to the Park."

The hand at her back moved to her upper arm, gripping it as though he feared she might bolt. Sighing in resignation, she said, "You need not bruise me. I shan't go if you dislike it."

"We are going to have a talk," he muttered.

The three gentlemen were coming toward them, so when Thorne released her, Gillian gathered herself to face them. They doffed their hats, and she could see by the amusement in their faces that they were greatly enjoying themselves, although the shortest of the three, a portly gentleman with a youthful but rather vague countenance, seemed to walk with caution. She was not certain whether that was habit or if he was wary of Thorne's temper.

The second man, a taller, harsh-visaged gentleman with a lean, muscular form, was dressed comfortably, like Thorne, but the third was much more debonair. In his tight double-breasted, dark green coat with its skimpy tails, huge puffed shoulders, and a double row of flat gold buttons down the front, he looked quite the town beau. His lapels were cut in a wide zigzag shape to show off a shirt collar so high that it brushed his cheeks and a stiff lace-edged cravat tied in a fat bow. A fashionable two inches of red satin waistcoat could be seen below the front edge of his coat, covering the waistband of his dashing yellow tights. He wore tall Hessian boots with red silk tassels, and carried a gold-rimmed quizzing glass on a black velvet ribbon.

He was the first to speak, saying in a cultivated drawl, "There you are, my lad. Wondered what had become of you." Raising the glass, he peered briefly at Gillian, then added, "Daresay you will desire to present us to this young woman. Can't say we've had the pleasure. Good day to you, ma'am.''

The youngest man raised his quizzing glass too, blinked at her through it, and said, ''By Jove, yes. A fine ma'am, day.''

''Good day, sirs,'' she said, keeping her countenance with difficulty, for she had no doubt now that both gentlemen, and very likely the third as well, were a trifle the worse for drink.

Thorne said caustically, ''Put that damned glass in your pocket, Perry, or I will feed it to you.''

Sobering rapidly, the gentleman attempted to obey, but the quizzing glass appeared to be too large for the fob pocket into which he tried to slip it. After a second attempt he pushed it up under his coat and said, ''There, Josh, that'll do, won't it? No need to put yourself in a pucker. Only came out to do the polite, and you still ain't introduced us.'' Turning back to Gillian, he said, ''Must excuse 'im, ma'am. Got no manners. Brought up to think everyone else had to have 'em instead, on account of he's going to be a duke one day. Went to his head, don't you know? Allow me. Thorne's cousin, Peregrine Dawlish, at your service. And these two gentlemen . . .'' He gestured toward the other two. ''Chap on the right is Andrew Corbin—Lord Corbin, that is. You can remember him because, except for Thorne, he's the biggest. And the other's Crawley. Excellent man. Nottinghamshire family. Daresay you've heard of 'em.''

Gillian looked expectantly at Thorne, but he remained stubbornly silent. ''Your cousin is right, sir,'' she said. ''You ought to have presented them to me, you know. Am I to make myself known to them, or do you mean to do it?''

His lips twisted wryly. ''Thought you liked to do things on your own, my dear. I won't pretend that was not a matter I had hoped shortly to discuss with you, but you will perhaps comprehend why I did not immediately leap to do the honors.''

Crawley chuckled. ''I can see that he has not been treating you well, ma'am, so let me assure you that we are pretty certain you must be Lady Gillian Carnaby. Of course, if you are not, I am immediately made to look the worst sort of an ass, so I do hope you will take pity on me and say that you are, regardless.''

Gillian smiled at him and then at the other men in turn and said politely, ''I am certainly Gillian Carnaby. Did you come all this way in search of his lordship? You must have many things to say to him.'' She turned to Thorne. ''No doubt, my lord, you will want to remain in town to dine with your friends.''

''Not so fast, my dear,'' he said smoothly, gripping her arm again. ''Corbin, did you drive down in your phaeton?''

''Certainly I did,'' the beau replied. ''Didn't I tell you before? Rattled here at such a pace that I feared I'd put us in a ditch. Phaeton's not large enough for three grown men either. I had to come without my valet, Josiah. Devilish inconvenient!''

''Don't expect me to sympathize,'' Thorne said. ''I want your rig. I know your team's not fully rested, but it's a short way and I won't spring 'em. Lady Gillian has a gig in the next street, being watched over by some urchin. See if you can induce him to entrust it to your care for the present. There is also my horse, yonder. Look after him. I am going to drive her home.''

''But that is not necessary, my lord,'' Gillian protested. ''I can drive myself perfectly well, and you must want to visit with your friends. How you think I shall recover my gig later if we leave it here now, I don't know. Or the gelding.''

Dawlish, smiling, said, ''Don't mean to push in where we ain't wanted, m'lady, but there is a simple solution to that problem. Can understand that Josh would not want to leave you on your own to travel these roads, but he wouldn't want to be seen escorting a mere gig, let alone driving one. Too much beneath his dignity, to be sure.'' For once he ignored the withering glance shot him by his cousin and continued, ''No reason he can't drive you if he likes. I should be only too happy to ride his horse back, and I daresay Crawley can handle the gig without any bother or loss of dignity. The only question is whether Corbin can be induced to ride in such a lowly vehicle.

But perhaps he will choose to remain behind at the inn instead.''

"Corbin begs leave to say he will not," the beau drawled. "I'll wager I'm as curious . . . that is, I daresay her ladyship will be glad of our escort too. Bound to," he added in a gently confiding tone, shooting a sidelong glance at Thorne.

"Exactly my point," Dawlish agreed. "Stands to reason that if Josh is put out—which even a nodcock could see he is—she'd as lief have us around to keep him from jawing at her, which, if you want my opinion, is the true reason he don't want to drive a noisy gig or ride alongside her whilst she drives it.''

Feeling the hand that gripped her arm tighten painfully, Gillian said swiftly, "I shall be delighted to be so well escorted, gentlemen, and you must, all of you, stay to dine at Carnaby Park. My father and his wife will want to make your acquaintance.'' And what Estrid would think of three extra gentlemen arriving to grace her table without so much as an hour's notice, Gillian decided not to think about.

The three gentlemen accepted with a promptness that made her bite her lip to keep from laughing, and she was sure she heard a grinding sound from Thorne's teeth. She looked at him, expecting to see the anger in his expression that she had seen before. Instead she saw a decided twinkle in his eyes.

"Piqued, repiqued, and capoted," he murmured for her ears alone, "but don't think that you have escaped hearing what I want to say to you, for you have not.''

She was given no opportunity to reply. Corbin shouted for a groom to bring his carriage, gave the boy holding Thorne's horse a coin to collect the gig, and it was not very long before their little cavalcade was ready to depart. Gillian discovered that the phaeton was a light one rigged for speed rather than comfort, and drawn by a magnificent team of matched bays. They were soon bowling rapidly along the highroad. Looking at her companion, Gillian saw that his lips were set in a straight line, and his gaze was focused upon the road. His skill was evident in the confident way he managed the ribbons, however, and after watching for several moments, she relaxed, waiting for him to speak.

He remained silent, concentrating on the team and on the road ahead of them. Observing that the others had begun to fall behind, Gillian looked at him again and said, "Trying to lose them, my lord?"

He glanced at her, then looked over his shoulder. "I haven't driven Corbin's bays before," he said. "I've driven his chestnuts, but I think this team is even finer."

"Just trying their paces, in fact." She grinned at him and was pleased to see the twinkle return to his eyes in response.

He slowed the pace a little before he said, "The others will catch up in a few moments." Then he added abruptly, "I thought we had agreed that our betrothal would stand for a time."

"Well, in truth, sir, you decided that it would," she said. "We did not agree to much of anything that I can recall. Indeed, I told you right up to the last that I thought you were mistaken to drag the business out any more than was absolutely necessary."

He was silent again, and she found herself hoping that she hadn't banished the twinkle. His eyes were so deeply blue and his lashes so dark that the twinkle was quite remarkable, and she wanted to see it again. But his attention was back on the road when he said, "I suppose I did make the decision, and I still think it was the right one. Just what did you think you were going to do at that newspaper office?"

She grimaced. "I had the oddest fantasy, sir, that I could simply walk in there, say that a mistake had been made, and ask them to print a correction. It was not simple at all. I became quite tongue-tied and hadn't the least notion what to say. I hate to admit this to you, but I was never so glad to see anyone in my life as when you burst through that door."

"I do not burst through doors. I open them and walk through."

"You were in a blazing fury."

"I was not. I was in complete control."

She smiled. "Do you know, I think you are quite right

about that. I certainly have never before seen anyone who looked as angry as you did who could then manage to speak as lightly as you spoke. But I am not mistaken about the fury.''

Again he fell silent, but when she said nothing more, he turned to her at last with a rueful smile and said, ''No, you are not mistaken. There are times I'd like to throttle Mongrel—my cousin Dawlish, that is—but he does have an aggravating way of nicking the nick from time to time, and he knew I was vexed. Babbling on about manners and such was his way of rebuking me. I've been known to react in a quite reprehensible way to his prating, and he's got a healthy respect for my temper, but he is no coward and frequently speaks without concern for his own well-being—just wanting to be helpful. Safe enough for him when others are around, of course. I have learned to hide my feelings reasonably well when I must, for it has been brought home to me more than once that it is not only the gentlemanly thing to do, but often the wisest. My father is something of a Tartar.''

Gillian grimaced. ''What does he think of all this, sir?''

''He is the reason I came down here with any willingness whatsoever to be reasonable about it. It is by his command that the whole thing is to be settled without scandal. He has threatened to pack me off to Ireland if it is not.''

''And you would go?''

''I doubt I would be given any choice in the matter. His methods are what one would call peremptory.''

''I think you must be very much like him,'' Gillian said.

He stared at her. ''I am not!''

''Well, it would not be surprising, for most men are like their fathers, just as women are like their mothers. One learns from what one sees, I expect. But you are something of a Tartar in your own way, you know. I have experienced it myself, and you pointed out that your own cousin has a healthy respect for your temper. The others do, too, I think. They were watching you rather closely, even whilst they teased you. Did they really drive all the way from London merely to see what I look like?''

"They did." His jaw tightened again, and she knew he was not pleased to be reminded of the fact.

"Why are you angry now?"

"I'm not."

"Don't be childish, sir. You know you are still vexed with me if not with them. Wouldn't it be a good deal more sensible merely to say what you wish to say when you wish to say it?''

"I didn't want to speak before; I wanted to shake you."

"There, that's much better, but you could not shake me in the newspaper office, of course, or in the High Street. It simply isn't done. Although a man did sell his wife in the market square last week," she added thoughtfully, "and one was used to believe that that wasn't done either. One of our grooms told me the fellow led her right through town on a rope halter."

Thorne laughed. "Sounds like a sensible chap to me."

She considered the point for a moment, then said, "I do not think it can have been at all sensible, for surely the Church does not recognize a change of ownership as a legal marriage."

He said, "Are you trying to pick a quarrel with me?"

She chuckled. "No, certainly not, though it would serve you right if I did, for I am certain now that you made me angry on purpose that day on the north coast. It did me a great deal of good at the time, of course, and really, I do wish you would lose your temper now if you are going to lose it, and be done with it. It is difficult to go on pretending that I am not quaking in my boots waiting to hear what you will say to me."

"I don't believe you ever quake."

"Well, but you do not know me very well, do you?"

"On the contrary, I think I am coming to know you very well indeed. I distinctly recall now that when the waves were nipping at your toes, even when I did make you angry—and, yes, I did do it on purpose—you did not seem to be at all frightened of me."

"Well, that shows just how mistaken you can be, for I was paralyzed with fear. In that horrid moment when you swung me off the rock, I shut my eyes and prayed, certain I was only moments from meeting my Maker.'' When he still looked disbelieving, she gave it up and said, ''Are you still vexed with me, sir?''

''Will you attempt to deny our betrothal again?''

''No, I quite see now that such a course will not answer.''

''Good. If you are prepared to be reasonable, there is no more to be said.''

''But there is. I can see that placing an announcement in the South Devon paper will not answer, particularly since the news has found its way to London, but I still can see no good reason to continue the charade once we reach the city. Surely I can cry off at once then. This pretense is what I do not like.''

He looked directly at her, his expression implacable. ''Let me make myself plain; there can be no pretense about it. As far as I am concerned, and as far as you or anyone in London will be concerned, you are my affianced wife, with all the rights and privileges of that position, and you are under no obligation to cry off unless you wish to do so, now or ever. I will make the usual arrangements with your father, regarding settlements and dowry, and everything will go forward just as it would have had we met any other way and had a marriage arranged between us.''

''But that is dreadful!'' she cried.

''Do you really think so?'' he asked in a gentler tone. ''You have encouraged me to speak freely, so I will tell you that I find I am rapidly becoming accustomed to the notion.''

The warm look she saw in his eyes just then startled her, but she felt no responsive warmth in herself. On the contrary, a distinct shiver shot up her spine when she remembered what Meggie had said about him, and what her uncle had said. Thorne was a rake of the first stare, a man accustomed to charming ladies and bending their will to suit his own. No doubt he thought he had only to smile at her to make her submit to his every wish and decree. That must be how it had always been for him, for was that not the very nature of a rake? One could not be successful in the posture if one did not possess the skills with which to charm one's victims. He would learn his error, she thought. In the meantime, it was better to see him smile than frown, even if one suspected that his warmth was no more than masculine lust. His displeasure had made her a great deal more uncomfortable.

As much to divert her own thoughts as to make a point, she said, "There is no need to arrange matters with my father. It would be needless bother, since nothing can come of it later."

"There is a small matter of the law," he said. Again she received that direct look. "I must protect myself as well as you, for a betrothal is a binding link between two people, and when one is a man in my position, he would be a fool not to put the details down on paper. Moreover, a proper settlement ought to be made that protects you even if you cry off. I think you do not understand the pinch you could find yourself in when you do. There should be some small compensation for that."

"But that is not at all necessary!" she cried, truly distressed. "You are not at fault, sir. If it had been one of your friends who had been so misguided as to play this trick upon us, then perhaps you might be forgiven for taking some of the burden unto yourself; but since it was not—"

"Yes?" he prompted with a glint of mockery in his eyes. "Do you mean to tell me the truth at last, then?"

"No," she said hastily. "Pray, believe me, sir, that I must not do that. But I do mean to insist that you do nothing so foolhardy as to settle money on me. Indeed, I do not need it, and I should find that a most untenable position."

"You do not understand," he said gently. "I do it not for you so much as to protect myself. Even if you cry off, all you would have to do to sue me for breach of promise would be to suggest that you had done so under duress—"

"I would never do such a thing," she said sharply. Anger and mortification nearly overwhelmed her. She could not bear it that he should think such a thing of her.

"Don't be nonsensical," he retorted. "It has nothing

to do with whether you would or would not. It has to do only with being sensible. My father would have my head carried to him on a platter if I did not take such a simple precaution, and your father," he added grimly, "ought to be just as determined to see that you are properly protected as well."

"But I do not need any such protection!"

"Nonsense. I heard your stepmother just as plainly as you did, and I would have understood your position even without her help. The birth of your little brother puts you right out of the heiress stakes, my girl. Until his birth you were Marrick's sole heir. That can no longer be the case."

"But I am anything but destitute, sir. It is not my position to speak about such things, I know, but it is only right to tell you that I inherited my mother's fortune. She was a Vellacott of Deane, you know, and inherited nearly everything that was not entailed. My fortune is in trust, of course, and will remain so until I am twenty-five, but I have an independent income. You must have wondered why my stepmother does not awe me as she certainly would if I were completely without means of my own, like most girls are. Grandfather set up the trust so Mother would not be entirely dependent upon my father and so that he could not waste her fortune, had he been of that mind. He would not have done so, of course. He loved her very much. You have met my Uncle Marmaduke. The present Viscount Vellacott of Deane, his elder brother, is a sour, grasping sort of man. My grandfather did not like either of them very much, which is why the bulk of his fortune went to Mama. Grandfather said she was the only Vellacott he knew who was not a parasite."

"Pleasant fellow," Thorne said. "I prophesy that you will enjoy great success in London once the news gets out, and that Crawley will soon become my chief rival for your hand."

She smiled. "The prospect does not precisely recommend itself, I confess. Not so much about Lord Crawley, but about London. Will I be a success only because of my fortune?"

"I no doubt sound like a cad to say so," he said, "but

in fact you might have three warts hanging off the end of your nose, and with such a fortune as I suspect you are describing, you would still be proclaimed the prize of the Season.''

"Dear me. And Lord Crawley will lead the pack?''

He nodded. "He is suffering the pangs of an unrequited love at the moment. He fell top over tail for Gwendolyn, Lady Darcy, a widow of excellent figure and enormous fortune. But of late it appears that she might cast her handkerchief in quite another direction, leaving Crawley to face his bankers and the bailiffs.''

"Has he no family to assist him?''

"Only his mother and a pretty sister desirous of making her come-out this year. His father died last year, leaving him acres of encumbered estates and little with which to support them. His attempts to fund himself at the gaming tables have met with so little success that he decided to marry an heiress instead.''

She chuckled. "He seems nicer than that.''

"He is. He was one of my best friends at school, a truly stout fellow who took up the cudgels more than once on my behalf. You might not think it to see me now, but I was small for my age as a child, and since my father thought I'd do better not to be coddled, I often found myself in the briars. I grew, as you see, and learned to defend myself, but in the meantime there were some unpleasant moments. Other than Corbin, there's no one I'd rather have in a tight corner with me, even now, than Crawley.''

Though Gillian could not imagine the dandified Corbin in a tight corner with anyone, she saw no reason to say so, and found herself feeling very cordial toward Thorne's friends. She encouraged him to tell her more about his school days, and he did so, but since the tales were generally comical, with himself as the butt, she learned nothing more of note about him or his friends before they reached Carnaby Park.

She sent word at once to Mrs. Heathby, the housekeeper, that there would be three more gentlemen at the table, and then took her guests to the drawing room to present them to Lady Marrick.

To her surprise, Estrid expressed great pleasure at learning that they were to dine at Carnaby, welcoming Dawlish, Corbin, and Crawley as if she were truly delighted to meet them. Gillian discovered the reason when everyone gathered in the saloon before dinner and Dorinda appeared last of all, wearing a pink muslin Etruscan robe trimmed with white satin ribbon and brown cord, which was far more appropriate for a London ball than a country dining table. The gown was extremely becoming to Dorinda, however, and its very low white satin bodice, trimmed with delicate lace, drew the eye directly to her plump bosom.

Gillian had changed into a gown she often wore, of white sarcenet trimmed with coquelicot velvet. It was becoming, but she knew that Dorinda, with her rosy complexion, deep blue eyes, and golden curls, quite cast her into the shade. She could see as much from the gentlemen's expressions. Thorne's eyes had widened noticeably, and the apparently unflappable Corbin stood like a post with his mouth hanging open. Dawlish had instantly raised his quizzing glass, and Crawley made a profound leg.

Corbin murmured, "Magnificent. Why did no one tell us?"

Lady Marrick chuckled. "Dorinda is as pretty as a princess, is she not? My sweet, allow me to present you to lords Dawlish, Crawley, and Corbin. My daughter, Miss Ponderby, gentlemen."

Dorinda made her curtsy, peeping up at the men from beneath her lashes in a manner that made her stepsister yearn to slap her, but Gillian knew the gentlemen would find no fault.

Before Dorinda's entrance, Crawley had been looking around the saloon with visible appreciation, and so Gillian, remembering what Thorne had told her about his friend, was not surprised now when Crawley stepped forward first to greet Dorinda.

"We have been told, Miss Ponderby, that you are soon to travel to London. May I presume to ask how soon that will be?"

Smiling, Dorinda rose and said, "Very soon, sir. I believe we depart within the week."

"Then we must certainly hurry back to London," he said.

"Good gracious, why, sir?"

"Why, so as to be first in line on your doorstep when you arrive," he replied, twinkling. "It would not do to let any of the others be before us, would it?"

Dorinda blushed adorably, and Lady Marrick said, "Don't be putting ideas into her head, if you please. Not that they won't be beating down our door, for they will, but here is Marrick now, so I daresay they will be announcing dinner any minute."

The evening passed pleasantly, for Dorinda, basking in the light of approval, was on her best behavior, and the gentlemen were witty and delightful company. Gillian enjoyed herself and when she discovered that the men had not been joking about their intent to return at once, and that Thorne meant to go with them, she realized she was going to miss them. She looked forward more than she had expected to the forthcoming journey to London.

7

NEARLY A FORTNIGHT LATER, after a long and tedious journey, the family arrived in London in the midst of a rainstorm, and Lady Marrick's first comments regarding Vellacott House in Park Street, Mayfair, were caustic ones.

"This is it? Good gracious, my lord, it is no more than fifty feet wide, and the entrance not the least bit impressive! I thought you had told me the house was designed by Robert Adam, but I know for a fact that his style is still very much admired by fashionable people."

Due to the rain that had begun to pelt down upon them as they crossed the river Thames at Staines, Marrick had for the last several hours been crowded with three women, a child, and a small terrier into a traveling carriage meant to carry no more than four persons, and he was not in a charitable mood. Shifting Clementina on his lap and looking out to see what was keeping the footman, he said sharply, "This is certainly Vellacott House, madam. It may be only fifty feet wide, but I assure you it is at least two hundred feet from front to back, and as to who built it, I can tell you that my father-in-law hired only the best people, whoever they were. The inside is better, I promise you."

Gillian said calmly, "Indeed it is, ma'am, for my mother once told me that Mr. Adam always favored a modest exterior so as to achieve more of an impact on the visitor with the inside. Grandfather Vellacott used to say that Vellacott House reminded him of a French hotel, which is what the French nobles call their mansions, you know. He had seen many of them on his Grand Tour, and he told Mr. Adam he was determined to achieve the same sequence of grand apartments that the French admired. I have not been here in some years, but I remember the house is magnificent. Good heavens," she added, peering through the rain at the figure coming down the wide, shallow steps with a large black umbrella held above his head to meet them, "is that one of our footmen? His wig is on crooked. I do wish you had let Hollingston see to the hiring of the servants here, Estrid. I don't think that man looks at all suitable. His livery is too tight too."

Estrid sniffed. "I'll thank you to keep your nose out of my affairs, miss. I wrote to tell the caretaker that we should be here today and told him to find at least one footman to wait on us until I could see to the hiring of our other servants. We shall need a new governess for Clementina too," she added, "since the last one never returned from visiting her mama."

"Good God, madam!" Marrick exclaimed, avoiding Gillian's steady gaze. "Do you mean to tell me we have no servants here?"

"I mean no such thing," she said tartly. "We have

brought a number of our own with us from the Park, have we not, sir? As to a butler and a housekeeper, I am sure the people who have been looking after the house can do that well enough, so you needn't fly into a pelter. I shall see to all the rest tomorrow."

"I shall dine at my club," Marrick said with a growl.

"You must do as you like, of course," Lady Marrick said.

Gillian understood her father's dismay, and wished she had made an effort to see to the business of the servants herself. Not that she would have had to do anything more than tell Hollingston to attend to it, but for some reason Estrid had an aversion to telling the steward to do anything whatever.

The footman held his open umbrella over the earl and Lady Marrick, and everyone else followed as best they could, laughing when the rain struck them, shrieking when cold droplets slithered down inside their clothing. Inside, Gillian nearly ran full tilt into her stepmother, who had stopped to gaze about her.

"This is more the thing, certainly," her ladyship said.

From black-and-white marble floor to vaulted ceiling, the large square hall was arranged in a gold-and-white pattern of advancing and receding surfaces, of columns, pilasters, alcoves, and niches. Classical coolness underscored the opulent splendor for which Adam was justly famous, and Estrid was impressed.

"Where are our rooms, my love?" she asked Marrick.

"My dressing room and cabinet are beyond that stair hall before you," he said. "Dining room, then the library and my rooms. A private stair from my dressing room leads to our bedchamber on the next floor. Your dressing room is off that, and there are three drawing rooms there as well. Down here, through the anteroom beyond the two marble columns, you will find a parlor and a small terrace garden. A larger garden lies at the rear, beyond the stables."

"And the girls' rooms?"

"The floor above ours. Servants' rooms above that."

She nodded. "I shall look over the whole house tomorrow. Today we must get settled, however, for I daresay the knocker will begin to clatter just as soon as anyone learns we are in town. The marquess, at least, knows precisely when to expect us.'' She turned to the waiting footman. ''Mrs. Parish is expecting to serve our dinner this evening, is she not?''

''Aye, mum, but it ain't what Aunt Sairie be accustomed to, she says, and she don't be willing to do it but the one, mebbe two nights, is all.''

Gillian said, ''What is your name, please?''

''I be Alfred, an' it please ye, miss.''

''I am to be addressed as your ladyship, as is Lady Marrick.'' She gestured toward the others. ''This is Miss Ponderby, and this is Miss Clementina. Please see that you remember their names.''

''Aye, your ladyship.''

''Excellent. Now, Alfred, be so good as to inform Mrs. Parish that we have arrived, and when the second carriage arrives, you and Mr. Parish can help our servants bring in the baggage. You will have to show all of them except my father's man and my woman where they are to go.'' When Alfred had gone, she turned to her father and said, ''Papa, before you go to your club, perhaps you will be kind enough to show Estrid her rooms, and then when her woman arrives, she can order a bath to refresh herself after her journey. Dorinda and Clemmie and I will find our own rooms. Though I haven't been here in years, I remember that mine is at the front, so I expect I can find it, and when Meggie arrives, she can take care of all three of us. The other coach cannot be far behind. Even as heavily laden as it was, it cannot have traveled much more slowly today than we did.''

Marrick glanced at his wife, but when, for once, she made no objection to Gillian's high-handed methods, he agreed to show her upstairs, leaving Gillian to deal with her stepsisters.

Clementina, shown to a charming room overlooking the terrace garden, said, ''This is a splendid house, Gilly. Our papa's house in South Audley Street was not nearly as nice as this.''

''South Audley Street is quite near here, I believe,'' Gillian said. ''At least I know it is in Mayfair, because

Uncle Marmaduke has a house there, and I remember his saying that the only things that recommended the place were that it was in Mayfair and just a step from the South Audley Street Chapel. We attended services at the chapel once years ago when I was here with my parents.''

Dorinda seemed pleased with her room, too, and once Meggie, the earl's valet, and her ladyship's maidservant and personal footman arrived, they were quickly settled in. Gillian waited only until she was certain her father was no longer in the house before she went in search of Estrid, finding her in the elegant dressing room that had once been Gillian's mother's, seated at the dressing table while her maid arranged her hair. The room was redolent of verbena, Estrid's favorite scent.

Repressing a pang of resentment at the sight of the voluptuous blond woman, swathed in gauzy lace, sitting at the dressing table that had belonged to Gillian's petite, dark-haired mother, she said, ''May I speak privately with you, please?''

Estrid dismissed her maid. ''What is it, Gillian? You must be able to see that I took your advice and have had a bath, so I am very much occupied just now.''

''Yes, ma'am,'' Gillian said, ''I do see that, and that is why I wish you will allow me to see to the matter of new servants for you. Truly, Estrid,'' she added before the woman could protest, ''I do not mean to put myself forward in an unbecoming way, but I do know what will suit Papa—and what is more, so will his man of affairs here in London. I do not propose to interview people on my own, I assure you. That would never do. But neither would it do for you, ma'am. It would only put Papa's back up to have a stream of applicants marching up the steps to Vellacott House.''

It was clear that Estrid had not envisioned such a possibility, for she turned quite pale. She did not give in, however. ''I do not know your father's man of affairs in London,'' she said. ''I do not trust your papa's Hollingston to hire people I like, so how do I know I can trust this other man?''

Keeping a strong grip on her patience, Gillian said, ''Because he has always attended to such matters for us, ma'am. Had you put the matter in Hollingston's hands whilst we were still in Devon, he would have directed Mr. Squires to see to the complete staffing of Vellacott House before ever we arrived, which would have been much more comfortable for all of us.''

Estrid seemed to be considering her words, and for a long moment it appeared that she would agree, but suddenly her countenance hardened and she said, ''I see what it is. You mean to attend to the whole business and then inform your papa that I could not do it, after all. Well, I will not have it. You will see, miss, that I, too, have my man of affairs in London. I am quite certain that Sir Cedric's man, Weston, will act for me, and now that you have told me how to set about it, I shall do so.''

There was nothing more to be said, for experience had taught Gillian that nothing would be gained by debate. She had been as diplomatic as she knew how, but when she left Estrid's dressing room and went through the opulent chamber known simply as the third drawing room, to the grand stair hall, she was lost in her own thoughts. Descending the stairs, intending to seek out Mrs. Parish and do what she could to soothe the woman's feelings and assure her that she would soon have the necessary help to run the house, she paid no heed to the murmur of voices from the entrance hall until she was about to turn toward the nether regions, when she perceived at last that a visitor had arrived.

Normally, she would not have stepped into the hall but would have waited for the footman to seek her out. However, she recognized the marquess's deep voice, and without so much as a thought for proprieties, hurried into the hall to greet him.

''How very pleasant, sir,'' she said, holding out her hands to him. ''We had not expected to see you here as soon as this.''

Thorne turned at the sound of her voice and took both her hands in his, squeezing them warmly. With a smile that warned her at once that he meant to exert himself to be charming, he said, ''You appear to have survived your journey well.''

''Oh, it was dreadful,'' she said, laughing as she conceded, if only to herself, that whatever his motives, she was very glad to see him. "Estrid detests traveling, and Papa prefers to ride his horse, so we traveled no more than thirty miles a day and generally not so many as that. And today it rained, so Papa had to sit with us, because he had arranged for only two carriages and refused to hire another even though Clemmie and I said we would not mind traveling with Marcus in a job chaise. By the time we arrived, the mood in our carriage was a trifle tense."

He chuckled. "I can imagine how it was. Was that wonderful specimen of the serving class at hand to help you from the carriage?" he asked, nodding in the direction of the door through which the footman had already disappeared.

"Don't criticize Alfred," she said, lifting her chin. "The poor fellow is Mrs. Parish's nephew and was dragged into service against his will. Estrid decided to wait until she arrived in London to hire servants, and like a ninny, I did not think to look into the matter whilst we were still at home, assuming at the time, you know, that she would simply put the whole business into Hollingston's hands, as anyone else would have done."

"Do we continue this fascinating conversation here, or is there perhaps a more comfortable room at hand?" he asked gently. "I inquire with some trepidation, I confess, since it occurs to me that every other room may still be under holland covers."

She grinned. "If that was meant as a rebuke, sir, it falls short of the mark. I have not seen for myself whether the parlor is still in holland covers, but I know for a fact that the drawing rooms are as tidy as can be, so I must assume the parlor is as well. Mrs. Parish is an excellent caretaker, but she does not presume to be a proper housekeeper, and is very much out of her element when the house is occupied. You may perhaps think that I ought to have brought our housekeeper from Carnaby—"

"I think no such thing," he said, putting a hand firmly on her shoulder and turning her toward the anteroom. "Can we be private if we go this way?"

"The parlor is through here, certainly," she said, "but

perhaps you would prefer to go up to one of the upstairs drawing rooms. That is where guests generally are taken.''

"Will I meet your stepmama up there?"

"I should think so."

"Then the parlor will do nicely." Urging her through the anteroom, he paused briefly on the threshold to look around the pleasant parlor, which was pale blue and gold with dark blue velvet curtains and white moldings. He said, "Now perhaps you will explain to me why your mind is so filled with household business that you cannot even be depended upon to see that your visitors are not kept standing in the hall."

She tilted her head. "Are you vexed, sir? I cannot think why you should be. You do not appear to be the sort of man who takes offense at being kept standing for a few moments."

"We will leave my 'sort' out of this discussion, if you please. Do you intend to answer my question?"

She sat down in an armchair upholstered in blue-and-silver brocade near the tall windows overlooking the terrace garden, and gestured to him to take its twin. "I suppose my head is stuffed with household matters just now," she admitted. "It was always my mother who looked after everything, you see, and after her death, before Papa married Estrid, I became accustomed to doing so—in Devon, at least. Indeed, I have retained a good deal of control there, for it was my heritage, after all, and Estrid is not at all consistent in her wish to take the reins, but does so in fits and starts. Of course, she was in the family way soon after their marriage and was often ill, so she did not care about anything much. And when she was confined, she left it all to me. I know I should not be talking about her this way—"

"Don't be foolish," he said.

She smiled at him. "I daresay you do think it foolish—men don't concern themselves with such things, in my experience."

"Nor, in mine, do women concern themselves with estate matters," he said with a wry grimace. "And sons do not either. I think I envy you your father's lack of interest. Whenever I have the temerity to offer a suggestion, it gets short shrift.''

"Oh, that is too bad, for you ought to know everything about what will one day be yours. Mama always insisted—'' Breaking off at the sight of his frown, she added quickly, "But of course it was different with us, for Papa took no interest, but I am in a quandary now, I can tell you, for Estrid insists that she means to hire the new servants herself, and she cannot have a notion of what that will entail. She did say she would put it all in the hands of her late husband's man of affairs, but I daresay that will annoy Papa just as much as if she were to parade all the applicants through his hall. And to be perfectly frank, I do not care for the notion of my servants being hired by a stranger.''

Gently he said, "I do not think you can have much to say about it, however, so why do you not go upstairs, put on your hat and gloves, and let me take you for a drive in the park? The rain has stopped, and the whole of London is sparkling clean.''

She wanted to explain how much she did have to say, but she knew he most likely took no more interest in her problems than her father or any other man would have taken, so she grinned at him and said, "You can have less notion of females than I thought you had, sir, if you think that a hat and gloves will prepare me for my first appearance in public. Not when there must be many persons as anxious to see me, after that scandalous announcement, as your friends were. I hope you don't mind kicking your heels for at least twenty minutes. I intend to make a stir.''

He smiled. "I can wait.''

"Perhaps you would prefer now to go upstairs.''

"Not at all. I shall sit quietly here and contemplate your garden. Someone has taken excellent care of it.''

"That would be Mrs. Parish, I expect. She says she has naturally green fingers and cannot help potting about. It is very pretty, though, isn't it?''

He gestured toward the door. "Go. My patience is not inexhaustible, I assure you.''

Grinning, she turned and fled.

Upstairs, she rang for Meggie, changed her clothes quickly, then took a few moments to dash off a short letter. Giving it to Meggie, she said, "Ask Parish to take that 'round to Mr. Squires's office in Clifford Street at once, will you? And warn Mrs. Parish that there might be a gentleman staying to dine. I'm driving out with Lord Thorne, and if he wishes to dine with us later, I want her to be prepared for him."

"I'll attend to it, Miss Gillian. I've already told her I'd give her a hand with the cooking if she needs it, and told her it was quite all right if she wants to have her niece in to act as scullery maid. But if there's to be gentlemen for dinner, we shall have to have a savory and a sweet. Now, I'm a fair hand with pastry, but we will want a couple of lads to help with the washing up, I'm thinking."

"Meggie, you do whatever you think right," Gillian said. "I am very grateful to you for offering to help Mrs. Parish. It is none of your affair, I know, but it is ever so comfortable to know I can rely upon you. I am trying very hard not to step on Lady Marrick's toes, but this situation is intolerable and must not be allowed to continue. It would be dreadful if word of it got out, and Dorinda made her come-out only to be tormented by every jokesmith in town, or worse, thought ineligible simply because we were known to be making shift for proper help. I have informed Mr. Squires of the exact nature of the problem and have asked him to deal with the late Sir Cedric Ponderby's man if that is possible. If we can manage it neatly enough, her ladyship need never know she did not make all the decisions."

"She don't know the true facts, Miss Gillian. 'Tis as plain as the nose on your face that she don't."

Gillian sighed. "I know, Meggie, and that is what makes the business so hard to put right. How I wish Papa were a forthright man and not the sort who prefers peace at any price, for it makes things very difficult for the rest of us. First there was all the nonsense about the castle, merely because he never bothered to explain beforehand what condition it was in, and now this."

"Well, to my mind, it's going to set the cat amongst the pigeons, right enough, when her ladyship finds out."

Shaking out her skirts, Gillian said briskly, "We will not fret about that now, however. Lord Thorne warned me that he is not a man of infinite patience. Not," she added with a chuckle, "that I needed any such warning. Do what you must, Meggie, to see that a proper dinner is put on the table tonight, and leave me to deal with the rest."

Downstairs, she found the marquess in rapt contemplation of the garden. He had opened one of the tall French doors and now sat sprawling in the same chair drawn up to the open doorway. He seemed to be listening contentedly to a pair of birds chirping from an apple tree. The sun was shining brightly now, and lazy clouds of steam rose from the damp leaves of the shrubs. Gillian could smell moist-earth odors mixed with the scent of new blossoms on a potted rose bush on the terrace.

Thorne turned, saw her, and got to his feet. "You will certainly make a stir," he said appreciatively. "I like that rig. Red becomes you."

She turned around, giving him the full effect of her white dress and coquelicot spencer. Her wide-brimmed chip-straw bonnet was likewise trimmed with flowers and ribbons in the fiery color, and her gloves and the silk cords of her indispensable were as well. "And red kid half boots," she said, putting one foot forward so that he might admire them.

He was staring at her face, however. "Your eyes are gray," he said. "I thought they were blue the first time I saw you, but they change with whatever you wear, don't they?"

She nodded, staring back at him, trying to decipher his expression.

He was silent, still looking into her eyes, much as if he expected them to turn color while he watched, and Gillian stood very still, feeling his gaze as though he touched her, feeling her body respond to it as though the touch were a caress. She was suddenly very much aware of the fact that there was no one else in the room. The whole house was oddly silent. She could hear his breathing, and she knew suddenly that if she did not break the silence, he would kiss her. She tried to think of something to say, but no words would come.

When he bent toward her, she licked her lips nervously but made no effort to evade him. He put one hand behind her head, pulling her gently toward him, watching her, his expression challenging her, seeming to mock her inability to resist him. His face came nearer, nearer, until his lips touched hers. In that instant a shock of electricity leapt between them, shooting through her body to her fingers and toes, before he pulled her tightly against him and his mouth took possession of hers. He kissed her hard, then set her back on her heels and smiled.

That smile seemed to her to mock the ease with which she had yielded to him, and without thought she slapped him as hard as she could, leaving a fiery imprint on his cheek.

With what she suspected was a deplorable lack of sensitivity to her outrage, Thorne caught the offending hand, smiled wickedly at her again, and pulled her back into his arms. He moved the hand he held behind her, holding it gently against her waist and pressing her closer. "Naughty," he murmured, kissing her again. This time his tongue touched the line between her lips, soliciting entrance, and her mouth gave way, opening, allowing his tongue to enter and explore. Never had Gillian done such a thing or experienced such feelings as she was feeling now. She knew she ought to struggle to free herself—and did not doubt for a minute that he would let her go if she did—but she seemed to have no command over her baser instincts. Her breasts swelled, tingling, yearning to be touched. Her lips responded to his, and her breathing came in near sobs. He still held her hand behind her, and when his other hand moved to her waist, then lower, teasing her senses as it moved up again, easing around to the side of her breast, she knew she was allowing liberties that ought never to be allowed a man to whom she was not married, but she could not seem to stop him. She shivered, trembling, when his fingertips brushed against the tip of her right breast.

Thorne kissed the tip of her nose and released her. "Want to slap me again?" he asked gently.

Feeling heat suffuse her face, Gillian forced herself not to look away and said, "I cannot think what induced me to strike you, sir. I have never done such a thing to anyone before."

Thorne had the grace to look a little ashamed of himself, but before he could speak, Clemmie said from the doorway, "Oh, there you are, Gilly! Dorinda said to find you and discover how we are expected to amuse ourselves before dinner. Hello, sir," she added, making a hasty curtsy. "I did not know Gilly had a visitor. I hope you will forgive me dashing in like this. Why are you so red, Gilly? Are you feeling quite the thing?"

"How do you do, Miss Clementina?" Thorne said, recovering himself. "You run up and tell Miss Ponderby I have come to take her and the Lady Gillian for a drive in Hyde Park. She may have fifteen minutes to find her hat and gloves and meet us in the hall. I would offer to take you as well," he added kindly, "but my curricle will be crowded as it is. Another day, perhaps."

"Oh, you needn't take me, sir," Clementina said. "Mama says I may do as I please in London, so I mean to ask Step-papa to provide me with a tutor who knows all about the city. I want to see everything, of course, but I needn't trouble anyone else."

"You terrify me," Thorne said.

When the child had gone, he looked sternly at Gillian. "Surely that woman does not really intend for her child to look after herself or to be looked after by a male! It mustn't be thought of. Not here in London at all events."

"No, sir," Gillian said demurely. "One never knows how disrespectfully a young lady might be treated once she steps outside the safety of her own parlor."

"Now, see here, my girl, you asked for that!"

"Did I, sir?" She opened her eyes wide, much the way she had frequently seen Dorinda do.

To her surprise, Thorne chuckled. "You did and you know it, but I admit in all fairness that a true gentleman would not have taken advantage. The difficulty is, of course, that I am not a gentleman. Moreover, my reputation is well known to you now, and so you ought to have taken greater care.''

"Very true," Gillian agreed, "but I had not expected to be so easily affected by your methods. I know it comes of your having so much practice that you know exactly how to take the trick, but still it is the most astonishing thing! No doubt I shall recognize the symptoms next time, and in any case, I can safely promise that I will not slap you again, sir.''

"See that you don't," he retorted a little gruffly. "I cannot be held accountable for my actions when violence is employed against me." There was a small silence before he added in a quite different tone, "I am sorry about inviting Miss Ponderby to go with us. I don't know what got into me.''

Gillian was certain she knew precisely what had gotten into him, but she had more pride than to admit, even to herself, that she did not welcome Dorinda's company. And so it was that fifteen minutes later, the three of them set off for Hyde Park in the marquess's curricle. Most of the *beau monde* had turned out to enjoy the change in the weather, and numbers of people strolled, walked, or drove in the park at that fashionable hour. Thorne pointed out young Lord Petersham in his chocolate-colored carriage with its chocolate-colored horses, and the Countess of Jersey in her barouche, and a host of other members of the elite of London society. And in turn the young ladies with the marquess drew more than their share of attention.

They drove along the carriage drive beside Rotten Row, and Gillian soon discovered that the word had gone around that she was Thorne's intended bride. Some people waved, others stared rudely at her, and still others drew alongside to engage them in conversation. Since the sole purpose of such conversations seemed to be to discover just how she had managed to entrap one of the greatest prizes on the Marriage Mart, she was never so glad to be interrupted in all her life as when lords Crawley and Corbin rode up beside the carriage, and Lord Crawley rather abruptly cut off a simpering miss and her mama to inquire if the young ladies had had a pleasant journey to London.

The woman, who had been coyly attempting to discover the details of Gillian's antecedents, lifted a tortoiseshell-rimmed lorgnette to protuberant eyes and glared terrifyingly at Crawley, but he was oblivious.

"Thought you said you were coming up to town in a week," he said. "Must be a fortnight by now."

Gillian looked at Thorne. "His lordship knew when we expected to arrive," she said. "We were on the road for quite a time, because my stepmother dislikes long days of traveling."

Crawley turned to Thorne accusingly. "Trying to keep them all to yourself, Josh? A fine way to treat your friends!"

"Had I known you were so interested, Crawler, I'd have sent you a detailed accounting," the marquess said. "Must you drive on, Lady Sudeley? Ah, yes, there is another carriage trying to pass us. Dreadful woman," he added when Lady Sudeley and her daughter had driven on. Then, to Gillian, he said, "If that cursed announcement has spared me more of that sort of thing, it's the one thing about it that can make me damned grateful."

Gillian glanced at Dorinda, who had been chatting amiably with Lord Corbin and apparently had not heard Thorne, which, Gillian thought, was just as well. She turned the subject, deciding once more that the sooner her unexpected betrothal was ended, the better it would be for them all.

8

THE LONDON SOCIAL SEASON was in full swing, and Gillian soon learned that Almack's Assembly Rooms were

to open the following Wednesday night for the first subscription ball. She received a graceful note from the
Duchess of Langshire two days after their arrival, apologizing for not being immediately at hand to meet her,
due to the fact that she and the duke had been invited to
Oatlands, and providing assembly vouchers for Gillian
and Dorinda, and for Lady Marrick as their chaperon.
Without such vouchers, Gillian knew, no young lady—or
gentleman, for that matter—could enter Almack's sacred
precincts. Of more interest to her, however, was the second part of the duchess's note, informing her that invi-
tations would soon be dispatched for a ball at Langshire
House in honor of her betrothal to Thorne.

Reading the missive, Gillian began to feel as she
thought a fly must feel once it had been caught in a web,
when the spider began to spin more silk to entwine it.
Struggle though she might, she could not seem to stop
the process that had begun. But she was no fly, she told
herself. Something would have to be done. She began by
looking for Dorinda.

"Look," she said, handing Dorinda the duchess's note
when she found her in the sunny morning room on the
second floor.

Dorinda looked up when she finished reading the note.
"On Friday next? But what is wrong? Had we some other
engagement that evening? Surely nothing can be so important as this? Do you think Corbin will call today? He
is amusing, is he not?"

"Never mind Corbin, Dorinda. I cannot let this charade continue. I am not betrothed to Thorne, and it is
wrong to pretend that I am."

"But of course you are betrothed to him. He said so
himself. I am quite certain that he did."

"It's your doing, you wretched girl. You know perfectly well that this mad arrangement is entirely your
fault."

Dorinda hunched a shoulder pettishly. "Well, so what
if it is? It has all worked out for the best, has it not? You
will be a duchess one day, Gillian, which is not at all
what I intended, so I do not know why you persist in
flinging it in my face. Do you like this bonnet?" she

asked, holding up a fetching leghorn hat with lavender ribbons. "I purchased it yesterday because I thought it the very thing to wear with my purple silk pelisse, but Corbin said the pink one I had on the day before was prettier and that I ought not to have wasted my money. He said—"

"Dorinda, I do not care a fig what Corbin said. Will you pay attention to what I am telling you? I have no wish to become a duchess, and I wish you would stop pretending that you have done something wonderful by putting me in this dreadful predicament."

"Oh, pooh, Gillian, there is no predicament. To be sure, if Thorne had made a fuss, things might have got out of hand, but he did not. And since you did not tell him at once that it was any of my doing, you can scarcely tell him so now. Goodness, if he likes you, thinking you were the one who put the notice in the paper, I cannot think what you have to trouble yourself about."

"He does not think I did it."

"What?" Dorinda stared at her. "You did not tell him the truth, I hope!"

"No."

"But if he does not know that, and does not think you are to blame, then why is he allowing the betrothal to go forward?"

"Because he is a gentleman, Dorinda." No more than she would betray Dorinda to Thorne would she betray him to her by telling her that he was obeying the duke's commands. "Thorne says it is for the lady to cry off, but he would not allow me to do so until we had been in London long enough for people to come to know me for myself. He said it would do my reputation no good to be known only as the woman he had thrown over."

"But how could they think that if you cried off?"

"Being known as a jilt is no recommendation," Gillian said wryly. "Moreover, he said that without knowing me, no one would believe I had cried off. I daresay they would assume the notice was some sort of snare to entrap him and that he had eluded it."

"Oh, Corbin said he and the others all thought it was something of that sort at first," Dorinda said airily, "but now he thinks it's a case with him. In fact, Corbin said—"

"Look here, Dorinda," Gillian said, seeing nothing was to be gained by trying to explain Thorne's motives to her, "are you attempting to add Corbin to your string? He is very handsome, to be sure, and he dresses well and looks very well in the saddle—"

"Oh, pooh, I do not care about that. But someone said he is not easily snared, so I thought I would try my hand at it. He is not nearly wealthy enough to suit me. At least, I do not think he can be. Except for his pretty clothes, he does not behave as if he had money, carping over the cost of trifles as he does and telling one where things may be had for less. As if one cared."

"I am sure I do not know what his prospects are," Gillian said repressively, "and it is not a suitable subject for you to dwell upon in any case, Dorinda."

"Oh, pooh to that. I must have money, Gillian. You know I must. I intend to marry a country house, at least, and I daresay your papa will see to it that I have a proper dowry. Even Mama does not suggest that he will do more than that, not now that little John is to inherit everything, at all events."

"Dorinda, it is very improper for you to talk of such matters," Gillian said. "Your dowry will no doubt come from your own papa's estate, so it is proper for your mama to deal with it, and your father's man of affairs, Mr. Weston," she added, remembering the existence of that gentleman.

"Oh, there is only a pittance from my papa," Dorinda said lightly. "His money mostly went with the title and the estate to some paltry cousin we've never met. That is why it was so out of reason fortunate that your papa came to grief upon our doorstep and then chanced to fall in love with Mama. I don't know where we should be now if he had not done so."

Gillian gave up trying to make her understand that she should not talk about such things or depend upon Lord Marrick for a large dowry. She doubted that it had crossed her father's mind that Dorinda might expect a dowry. No doubt Estrid planned to discuss it with him at some date or other, but Gillian doubted that the subject had yet come up between them.

She wanted to talk about her own predicament, but although lords Crawley, Dawlish, and Corbin paid calls that afternoon, she was inclined to confide in none of them. It was apparent that both Crawley and Corbin had both come to pay their respects to Dorinda, and that Dawlish had merely come in their train. When the other two become engaged in a spirited debate with Dorinda over which of two plays currently enjoying popular favor might be the better one, Dawlish took the opportunity to speak to her.

"I must tell you," he said, regarding her in his open way as he drew up a stool near her feet and sat down upon it, "that I am becoming daily more confused, and it ain't a state that sits well with me. You may tell me to go to the devil—daresay you'll want to—but we were with Josh the night he saw the announcement—fact is, I showed it to him—and I know the damned thing—begging your pardon—came as a shock to him. I know, too, that my uncle was fit to chew nails over any new scandal, so I've a strong notion Josh has been doing his best to keep on his good side. I'm also damned sure—again begging your pardon—that you didn't place that notice yourself. What I mean to say is, you're a lady, ma'am, not just by birth but by nature, and I'd like to help. I can't ask Josh—he'd knock me flat—but if you didn't . . ."

"Don't ask me about it, either, my lord," Gillian said gently when he paused. "I refused to tell Thorne if I knew the guilty party, so don't think I will tell you. I thank you for your kindness, though. It means a great deal to me. I think his lordship is fortunate indeed in at least one of his relations."

Dawlish colored up to his eyebrows. "D-Dash it all, ma'am," he said, "you'll have me stuttering like a schoolboy if you prate that stuff to me. Damned nonsense, that's what it is, begging your pardon again, of course. Mean to say, however, that if the seas get rough in the coming days, you can always count on your humble servant. Anything I can do, anything at all . . ." His voice trailed away, and he tugged at the knot of his cravat as though the neckcloth were too tight. "Only want to help, truly."

She was grateful both for his concern and for his openness. What a difference, she thought, to know someone who, unlike most people she knew, was not afraid to say what he thought. Estrid spoke in platitudes. Dorinda never had a thought beyond her own person and refused to discuss any topic that was important to anyone else. And as for the earl, one might as well try to discuss the current food shortages with a gatepost as to try to get him to talk about anything other than hunting or his latest wager.

Just then the butler announced Thorne, and Gillian scarcely noted that the new butler was the first she had seen in a while who seemed to know his business. Thorne had drawn everyone's attention, though he came in like any other caller. He wore a dark blue coat, biscuit-colored breeches, and glossy Hessians, and in one hand he carried a slim blue book, which he gave to Gillian when he had greeted the others.

"It is a new guidebook of London," he said, nodding when Dawlish murmured that he would join the others. "I thought Clementina might like to have it for her explorations. At least, I am assuming that she has continued with her plan." He ended on a note of inquiry, but there was a twinkle in his eyes.

"Oh, yes," Gillian said, "she is out even now, but you need not concern yourself. I took the . . . that is," she amended hastily, "most fortunately a governess has already been found for her—a most capable and responsible young woman who came highly recommended. Her name is Maud Casey, and she knows London well."

"I see," he said, giving her a rather sharp look. "Where have they gone today?"

"To see the beasts at the Tower menagerie," she said. "Quite unexceptional. Indeed, I should like to have gone with them."

"Surely Almack's will offer you the same sort of amusement," he said, glancing at the others, who had broken off their conversation only long enough to acknowledge his presence before returning to their lively debate.

Gillian chuckled, relieved that he had not pressed her about the governess. Miss Casey, cousin to the estimable Mr. Squires, had thus indeed come highly recommended, but Gillian had had the notion before that Thorne disapproved when she took a hand in such matters. She said, "Will Almack's be as bad as that?"

"Worse," he said. "Nothing fit to drink or to eat, and a roomful of people staring at you who are being stared at by others in return. 'Tis a damnable bore."

"Devilish thing, boredom," Dawlish said at his elbow. "Don't glare at me, Josh. I just came to take my leave."

"What, Peregrine, going away so soon?"

"Well, you don't want me, and they don't want me, and I ain't about to start adoring that angel from across a room. I ain't the type, but both those fellows are besotted, Josh. It's painful to watch. And what Crawler thinks to accomplish by casting lures in that direction, I'm sure I can't say. Unless I miss my guess, she ain't one with the gelt, and he needs an heiress, don't he? Here's his sister Belinda come to London, no doubt costing him a pretty penny, and he can't attend to her and put his estate right without he gets some money, now can he?"

"No, he can't, but his mother franks his sister, not he, so you button your lip, my lad. This is not the place to be prattling of another man's affairs."

"Don't suppose it is," Dawlish said. "If it were, I'd ask you if my uncle knows the whole truth about this business yet."

Thorne gave him a look, which Dawlish met steadily for a moment before he looked away, saying, "Oh, very well. No need to fly into the boughs. I dashed well don't want to have to count my limbs to be sure I've still got them all, merely for the sake of asking a home question. Will I see you later at Brooks's?"

"If you like," Thorne said.

When Dawlish had gone, Gillian said, "Sir, we must talk."

"Good God, not you too!"

Indignantly she said, "I hope I have the right to speak to you about a subject so nearly affecting me, sir. 'Tis a pity that more people are not as forthright as Lord Dawlish."

"Well, you'd change your tune pretty quickly," he said, "if everyone were to speak only the truth."

"I would not. I think such a state of affairs would be vastly refreshing!"

"Well, it wouldn't. How would you like to be told that your hair looks odd or that the color of your gown don't suit you?"

"I shouldn't like it at all." She hesitated. "Does my hair look odd, sir? I thought it looked rather good today."

"Of course it looks good," he said impatiently. "It always looks fine to me. But that don't mean it looks fine to everyone. Do you think it necessary for everyone to tell you just how they think it looks? Or perhaps you think you'd like to hear all the things *I'd* say to you if common courtesy didn't stand in the way," he said ruthlessly.

"Just what sort of things do you mean, sir?"

"Suppose I demand to know the whole truth about Clementina's governess," he snapped.

She knew by the look on his face that her expression had given her away.

He nodded. "Care to give me a round tale?"

Involuntarily she glanced at the others, who were still chatting, paying no heed to her. Even so, she shook her head. "There is much in what you say about too much candor, sir. I will explain it all later if you like, but what I want to discuss now is the very kind note I had from your mother, informing me that she has arranged to hold a ball in honor of our betrothal. Surely you must see that it will not do, sir."

"Nonsense, there must be a ball. It's expected."

"My lord, I must know the answer to the question your cousin asked you. Do your parents know the truth about us?"

"My dear girl, I don't even know the truth about us."

She bit her lip. "Oh, dear, here I am bewailing the fact that people do not speak out, when I have been anything but frank with you. I meant only that people should speak more about their feelings, not that one ought to reveal confidential matters that must be kept to oneself. Dear me, what a tangle!"

"Get your hat," he said abruptly.

"I beg your pardon?"

"You heard me. I came to take you to meet my mother. And my father, too, may God help us, and if I don't take you at once I am likely to throttle you."

"I thought they were out of town."

"They are back. Get your hat."

She was about to tell him not only that she did not like his attitude but that she could not simply get up and leave Dorinda alone with two gentlemen callers, when Lady Marrick came in, sparing her the necessity.

Her ladyship was not in a cheerful temper, however. "That new butler is the most dismal creature," she said. "I was kept standing at the door much too long just now. I was only out and about—seeing Mayfair, you know—and then to be kept standing! I must write to Weston at once and tell him the man is unsuitable."

Gillian, thinking it very unlike Estrid to explain where she had been, looked at her in surprise and said, "But Blalock is thoroughly suitable. Why, he knows his business perfectly and comes very highly recommended."

"I do not like him. He looks down his nose at everyone. Makes a person feel like a maw-worm. Ah, how do you do, my lords?" she said to the other gentlemen, who, having just noted her entrance, had leapt to their feet. "No, no, sit down again, do. Were you going out, Gillian?"

"Thorne is going to take me to meet his mama and papa."

"How kind, but you must not go in that dress. Whatever will the duchess think if you are not better rigged out than that?"

Gillian looked at her yellow-and-white spotted muslin, then back at Estrid. "This dress is fine," she said. "I shall wear my yellow pelisse and the bonnet with yellow ribbons to match.''

''Well, you must do as you please, I suppose, though I should have thought you would want to wear something finer to impress a duchess, my dear. But there, I daresay you know what you are about, and girlish modesty must always be becoming. You run along now to tidy your hair and fetch your things. His lordship can have a comfortable coze with me whilst you are away.''

Thinking Thorne was being well served, Gillian cast him a mischievous glance. When he returned it with a grim one, she said quickly that she would make haste. When she returned, she discovered that her father had come in during her absence, and was being informed of Estrid's dislike of the new butler.

Glancing behind her to be sure the man in question was not within hearing, Gillian shut the doors to the drawing room just as the earl said he thought the fellow was perfectly adequate. ''Just so, Papa,'' she said. ''He is certainly better than the last specimen chosen to grace the halls at Carnaby Park.''

''Well, I do not like him,'' Estrid said, ''so he must go. Clementina's governess seems pleasant enough, but I am not certain about the housekeeper, and I cannot understand it, for I specifically told Weston I wanted people who were not so puffed up in their own esteem as those one so frequently sees amongst upper servants. I asked him to look out for a new nurse as well, you know, because dear little John and his nursery maid will arrive soon, and we will require a proper one for him.''

The earl fastened upon the first name she mentioned. ''Who the devil is Weston?'' he demanded.

Estrid stiffened. ''Why, he is my late husband's man of affairs, sir. I asked him to hire more servants for us.''

''Well, why the devil didn't you send round to ask Squires to undertake the arrangements? Fellow knows what *I* like, and it's his business to be looking into such matters.''

Gillian, conscious of the fact that Thorne was looking not at the earl or Estrid but at her, took care to avoid his gaze. She hoped her father and stepmother would take their conversation elsewhere, and soon.

Estrid said sharply, "I suppose I can ask whomever I choose to select *my* servants for *my* house!"

The earl turned red. "You would do better to be guided by me, my love," he growled. "I suppose, if you cannot like the man—" He glanced at Gillian. "No harm in looking about a bit for another butler, I suppose."

"No harm at all, sir," she said, "except that it is patently unfair to Blalock to dismiss him when he has done nothing wrong. If he is a trifle high in the instep, I am certain one need only speak to him about it. He is no doubt feeling his way in a new establishment, but if Estrid finds after a week or so that she still cannot tolerate him, of course he must be replaced."

"Good God, Marrick," Estrid said sharply, "what purpose can be served by discussing the matter with Gillian?" When Crawley cleared his throat, she blushed and exclaimed, "How dreadful of us to be debating such matters when we have visitors, but you know we have seen so much of you gentlemen of late that I have come to think you as quite part of the family. Marrick and I can sort this out later. Do run along now, Gillian."

Gillian looked at her father but could not catch his eye, so when Thorne touched her shoulder, she said, "Very well, sir, I am quite ready to go."

He did not reply, and she became aware of a gravity in his expression that she had never seen there before. He did not attempt to speak to her privately, however, and when they emerged from the house, she saw that his phaeton was in the charge of a small, wiry man of the type known to the fashionable as a tiger. This worthy, having been introduced to her as Tim Cooley, stood at the leader's heads until the marquess had lifted her into the carriage and climbed in himself, taking up the reins. When Thorne called to him to release them, the man did so and nimbly swung up behind them as the carriage swept past him. Thus, there could be no private conversation during the journey to Langshire House, and when they arrived, passing between the tall iron gates and rolling to a halt at the front entrance, servants emerged at once to attend them and more were found in the front hall.

"Where will I find her grace?" Thorne asked the porter.

"In the yellow sitting room, my lord. Jonathan will announce you."

"No need," Thorne said. "This way, my lady."

As they crossed the black-and-white marble floor, Gillian noticed that above them a railed gallery went around all four sides of the hall and that the floor was raised at the far end. Impulsively she turned to him and said, "A dais, my lord? I did not know people—even dukes—still had such things."

He smiled, the first time since they had left Vellacott House. "This hall is what's left of the medieval portion of the house, but the raised floor is here only because the room was enlarged during the last century, and the room next to this one had a higher floor." He gestured toward the nearest wall. "That paneling dates from the same period, the family arms are carved into the chairs yonder, and the paintings on either side of the chimneypiece are by Hoppner and Sir Joshua Reynolds. The dashing chap on the right is my grandfather, the lady his second wife, who was my grandmother."

"Does your father open his house to the public?" Gillian inquired sweetly. "You sound as if you'd had practice taking visitors around."

He shook his head, urging her into the stair hall, where the handsome staircase was found to be one in which the balustrade was composed of carved and pierced panels, ornamented with gilded scrollwork. Gillian said, "How very handsome, to be sure, but it must take a great deal of work to keep it so fine."

"I suppose it does," he said, "but you needn't concern yourself with the housekeeping here, you know."

There was a note in his voice that warned her not to take up the subject, so she remarked instead upon the beauty of the doorways leading off the stair landing, all topped with broken pediments framing busts of famous men of the past. Thorne and Gillian passed beneath Julius Caesar into a sunny apartment, where wide oriel windows hung with yellow velvet curtains provided a view of a broad green, flower-bordered lawn sweeping downhill to the river Thames.

The duchess's sitting room was furnished with an elaborately scrolled and gilded suite, consisting of a sofa and six chairs upholstered with yellow satin and decorated with couched red cord in a pattern repeated in the footstools and fire screen. The walls were painted to resemble ancient tapestries, and a number of brightly colored Turkey carpets overlapped one another to cover most of the highly polished oak floor.

Gillian noted the furnishings in the brief instant before her attention was claimed by the room's sole occupant, a little round lady wreathed in smiles who got up at once to greet them.

"Josiah, my darling, how very nice!" she exclaimed, rushing forward to hug him. "Did I know you were coming? But I cannot have known, or I should have been standing at the gallery window watching for your arrival. And you must be Lady Gillian," she added, emerging from her son's hearty embrace to hold out a soft, plump little hand to Gillian.

"I am," Gillian said, taking the duchess's hand and making her curtsy, wondering if she had dipped low enough. But this fascinating little lady didn't seem to pay any heed at all.

Instead she was already pressing them both to sit down, saying to Gillian as she did so, "I want to hear all about you, my dear. Josiah has told me that you never put that ridiculous notice in the paper at all, and I quite see that you are not at all the sort to have done any such thing, and—Oh, you needn't look daggers at me, my love," she said to her son with a chuckle, "for I promise I shan't ask her who did do it. Josiah thinks you know, Gillian dear, but I quite agree that you must not tell him if you do not quite like to do so. And now that that is all settled, do tell me, what sort of things do you like, and what do you dislike? I do hope you like children."

"Mama!"

The duchess turned a blandly innocent gaze upon him. "Yes, my dear? But why should she not like children?"

Gillian, trying to suppress her amusement before the duchess's hazel eyes turned her way again, encountered Thorne's rueful gaze instead.

"You can't say I didn't warn you about the misuses of candor," he said.

She looked him straight in the eye. "There can be nothing wrong with candor, sir, if it is acceptable to both sides." Then, before he could reply to that statement, she turned to the duchess and said, "May I speak as plainly, ma'am?"

"Yes, certainly, my dear, though I do hope you don't mean to tell me you do dislike children. That would be a pity."

"No, ma'am, I like children very much and would like to have any number of them someday. However, I must know—since his lordship appears to have told you the truth about our ridiculous betrothal—why you have decided to give a ball in its honor. He must have told you that I mean to cry off just as soon as I can do so without creating too much of a stir."

"Nonsense," the duchess said.

"Nonsense?"

"Certainly. You cannot do it."

Gillian began to feel a trifle dizzy. "I cannot cry off? But of course I can." She looked at Thorne in bewilderment.

But it was the duchess who responded with one of her delightful chuckles. "Not without making a stir. That simply cannot be done, my dear, not when you are betrothed to my son. You cannot have thought the matter through carefully, or you would see the difficulty for yourself. Everything he does provides grist for the gossip mills. It is what so frequently has set him at odds with his father, but as I often have to remind my husband, it is not fair to blame Josiah for the mere fact that he lives in the public eye. People must always be curious about dukes and their sons. And in truth, my dears, I am scarcely breaking any confidence to tell you that his grace had very much the same difficulty with his own papa."

"So he did, my love," declared a voice not unlike Thorne's from the doorway behind Gillian, "but I believe

I would prefer that you not describe those difficulties to all and sundry.''

Realizing who it must be, Gillian got to her feet and turned to face the Duke of Langshire, making a very deep curtsy at once, for there could be no confusion about what one ought to do in this instance. His grace was almost as tall as his son, and his bearing was as regal as she imagined the Prince of Wales's must be, if not his majesty the king. When she looked up, Langshire was standing directly before her, holding out a long, thin hand.

She put hers in it and arose to find him smiling at her. She saw at once that while the twinkle in Thorne's eyes had come from his vivacious mama, the smile was exactly like his father's.

''Do you know,'' the duke said, looking her up and down in a way that ought to have disturbed her but didn't in the least, ''I believe I can easily accustom myself to you as a daughter-in-law—if you can bring yourself to take my son in hand.''

Seeing the flash of anger in Thorne's eyes, Gillian said quietly, ''It cannot be, sir. This whole charade is rapidly acquiring the characteristics of a farce, and I simply cannot be comfortable with it. It is not right that your son be forced to acknowledge me in this way.''

''It is perfectly right,'' the duke retorted, casting an oblique look at his son. ''Reaping the harvest of one's own sowing is always meet and right.''

''But I do not want to be thought a consequence to anyone's misbehavior, your grace,'' Gillian protested.

The duke smiled at her again. ''Nor shall you, my dear, for to win your hand must be a reward rather than a consequence, and a far greater reward than that scapegrace deserves. You may tell your father to call upon me at his convenience.''

Casting a swift glance at Thorne, Gillian saw that his face was flushed and knew he was containing his anger with difficulty. She said quietly, ''Your grace, pray do not think me insolent, but my father will not force me to do what I dislike.''

Langshire looked down his long nose at her. ''Dear

me, must you be forced to wed my son? I knew he was difficult, but not so intolerable as that. Surely, his rank alone must recommend him.''

"He is not intolerable at all," she said, fighting a sudden urge to burst into tears. "But what would people say?"

"That Thorne has done very well to win the hand of the Vellacott heiress. Did you think it was such a secret, my dear? Your situation must soon be very well known here in London."

"Must it, Father?" Thorne snapped. "I promise you, I did not know it. In fact, I am not so sure, for once, that you do."

Langshire said, "Don't be insolent, Josiah. I understand it well enough. There will be the settlements to arrange, of course, but your bride will bring you a very pretty fortune."

"You don't understand, your grace," Gillian said, forcing herself to look away from Thorne. "Even if we were to wed, there would be no need to settle money on me."

"Nonsense, my dear, I am certain that your father and your trustees will agree that you must have adequate pin money, and I can assure you that you will not find my son ungenerous."

Gillian fought to hold her tongue, knowing it was no proper business of hers to discuss the matter further. If the duke was determined to pursue it, he would soon discover the truth. But she could not bear the look of resentment in Thorne's eyes.

Thorne gave her no chance to recover. "You claim to admire plain speaking, my lady," he said grimly. "Perhaps you will tell me, plainly, just how your fortune is fixed. No, no, don't turn away. Answer me. If it will make it easier, I have concluded that you own the house in Park Street. Do you also own Carnaby Park? You seem to call most of the tunes there as well."

"Only a portion of the Park lands are mine," Gillian said. She turned to the duke. "He is right, your grace. I must tell you at once that it is beyond the power of my trustees to do as you propose. My grandfather Vellacott arranged matters through a Court of Equity to ensure that my mother would retain control of her fortune when she married my father, including the right to bequeath it where she would. Thus, you see, though my trustees oversee matters, they are more answerable to me than I to them.''

"I see," the duke said. He turned to his son with a rueful smile. "I suppose that now you will be expecting me to make you an allowance commensurate with your wife's independence."

"Your generosity has never come into question, sir," Thorne said in that same tone of suppressed fury, "but I think you will agree now that we must allow Lady Gillian to do as she chooses."

There was little to be said after that, and Gillian soon found herself back in the carriage, heading for Park Street with a grim, silent driver. On the doorstep, Thorne said, "When I think that earlier today I came within ames ace of making a fool of myself, thinking your father gave you entirely too much say in his affairs and nearly telling you I'd not stand for the same sort of nonsense once we were married, I suppose I must look upon this turn of events in a rather more favorable light, mustn't I?"

"Had you not taken it upon yourself from the outset to make every decision without first discussing the details with those concerned," she told him roundly, "many things might have been different. But I think, now that I have met your father, that you make a practice of making judgments without discovering all the facts." With that Parthian shot, she took advantage of the fact that the door opened just then, and whisked herself inside.

Thorne made no attempt to follow her, and she went upstairs feeling utterly miserable, certain she had lost something very special but not entirely certain why she should feel that way, since she had never had it in the first place. The next day, she sent a request to Mr. Squires to notify the *Times* that the Earl of Marrick was announcing, with regret, the termination of his daughter's betrothal to the Marquess of Thorne.

9

Before the notice could appear in the *Times*, Gillian wrote to the Duchess of Langshire. She did her best to apologize for ruining her grace's ball but could think of nothing whatever to say to explain her action in a way that might be acceptable to Thorne's mother. Indeed, she could think of nothing whatever to write that would explain her desire to put an end to her relationship with the marquess. As it was, she had to blot not only the ink on the page, but a number of her own tears as well.

The fact was that she had no wish to thrust Thorne out of her life. He had come to mean a great deal to her. But it would not do. Perhaps if they had met in an ordinary way, it might have been different, but even then, she thought, he would have resented her unconventional fortune and her habit of authority. No doubt, she had made the right decision.

Having dispatched her letter, Gillian braced herself for her family's reaction, which was not long in coming. The following morning, as she was arranging new flowers in the crystal vase she had filled with her pretty pebbles from North Devon, the earl stormed into the morning room, waving his copy of the London *Times*. Gillian was alone in the room, for neither Dorinda nor Lady Marrick had come down to breakfast yet, and Clementina had already gone off on a new adventure with her governess.

"What do you know about this, my girl?" Marrick demanded.

Carefully setting down the knife with which she had been trimming the stems of her flowers, she said, "I did not know it would be in so soon, Papa. That is, if you are referring to the notice ending my so-called betrothal.''

"I am, indeed. 'The Earl of Marrick wishes to announce,' it says right here. Damned odd I don't remember announcing, ain't it? But maybe not so odd at that, for I didn't recall it before either. Can't call my soul my own anymore, damme if I can!"

"Papa—"

"Don't 'Papa' me, my girl," he snapped. "It is time and more that you began to show proper respect, just as Estrid says you should. I'm your father, Gillian—by God, I am—and you must learn to heed my wishes or rue the consequences."

"Very well, sir. Pray, tell me what it is that you wish."

"If that ain't just like you! Taking a fellow up on something when you know good and well what I meant."

"No, sir," she said, "I do not. I know that you told me when you remarried that you would explain the details of my inheritance to your wife in your own good time and that it was no business of mine to speak about it. I obeyed your command. I have even accepted your excuses for putting off telling her, but I found myself in an embarrassing position yesterday as a result, because Lord Thorne was not aware of my circumstances, and when his father began to talk about settlements—"

"No doubt planned to come down generous, too," the earl declared, "but now what have you done, I should like to know, to cry off this way? Where have your wits gone begging, girl?"

"Papa, you cannot think I would willingly accept any kind of settlement from the duke. My fortune is sufficient to anyone's wants, and it is protected for me and for any children I might have. No one can change that, as you must know very well, for Mama once told me that you— or perhaps it was Grandpapa Carnaby—tried to challenge Grandfather Vellacott's arrangement in a Court of Chancery and found that it could not be done. It was a matter of Equity, she said, rather than Common Law. I did not precisely understand it all, but she said that Mr. Squires would explain the matter more clearly to me one day if I desired him to do so."

"No doubt he will," the earl growled, "but it is not for you to be explaining that business or any other to my wife or to the duke. I don't suppose it occurred to you that at least a part of that settlement you scorned to discuss might have come my way."

"But you are very well to pass, sir," she exclaimed. "You forget that, thanks to Mama's training and Hollingston's, I am as well acquainted with your income as with my own. You put me in an untenable position. I know I owe you filial duty, and I want to obey your wishes, but I cannot simply stand aside and pretend I have neither interest nor voice in the matter. Nor could I allow Thorne to believe for one minute longer that he would simply take control of my fortune if we married. It is horrid enough to think that he might have been amenable to the whole business merely on account of my money. But I suspect," she added with a sigh, "that that was indeed the case. He told me once that I might have a wart on my nose and still be a great success."

"Good God, girl, he's going to be a duke one day. You don't suppose he would have considered your feelings for an instant without there being something to gain for himself in that mad betrothal if he risked acknowledging it. He's a rake, for God's sake, a gamester with an eye for a pretty female, but he ain't stupid! You're easy enough on the eyes, but if you think any man's going to see you for dust once he's got your fortune in his sights, you're more of a peagoose than I thought you were."

"Then I would suggest, sir," she said with icy calm, "that the sooner you make my true circumstances known to the entire world, the better it will be for everyone. I have no intention of marrying where I cannot find affection, or of allowing any man to marry me who thinks he will control my fortune."

"Which just goes to show," the earl retorted, turning on his heel, "what a fool the law is to have allowed any female to control her own money! Well, I just hope you don't cut off your nose to spite your face, girl. You may take it from me that any man who accepts a woman who holds the purse strings is a fool."

"Did you never love my mother then, sir?" she asked
sadly.

"Of course I loved her. Don't be nonsensical. But
thanks to that fool arrangement of Vellacott's, the Vellacott lands will never become part of Carnaby Park now,
will they?"

For the first time Gillian thought she understood him.
He was an impulsive man who loved the chase and found
excitement in the turn of a card, but he was not a man of
foresight. Nor was he a particularly affectionate man, and
it occurred to her now that he had undoubtedly married
his present wife because he had wanted to possess her
physically and could think of no other way to persuade
her. But having married her and had a son with her, he
had destroyed his chance to retain the prosperous Vellacott lands with his own. Only if Gillian inherited both
Carnaby and Vellacott fortunes could the estate remain
an entity. John's birth made him instant heir to the Carnaby share. She could not doubt, seeing Marrick now,
that proud though he was of his son, he was sorry for the
loss of those acres that belonged to her.

She was alone again with her flowers for several minutes, and then, to her astonishment, her uncle strolled
into the room.

"Uncle Marmaduke! I did not know you were in London."

"Did you not?" he asked, ringing for the footman before he took a seat at the table. "I've had to let my cook
go. Dreadful dinner last night. I came to have breakfast,
if you don't mind."

"Of course not," she said, sitting down opposite him,
"but I must warn you that Estrid has not yet come down
to breakfast."

"No matter," he said, "not here, at all events." When
the footman entered he proceeded to discuss in detail his
choices for a hearty breakfast, and when the man had
gone again, he grinned at Gillian and said, "Found the
Widow Torrance was getting to be a bit of a handful, if
you can believe it, so I came along to town to look over
the new crop on the Marriage Mart. They'll be too young
to have decent experience, of course, but a man likes to

refresh his memory from time to time. Arrived last night for dinner, and went for a stroll afterward to the churchyard to pay my respects to Millicent and have a friendly chat. What a woman she was! Pity I married that Grace creature after her. Nearly spoiled my taste for feminine company. But Grace has been gone for years now, too, and things are looking up. Found a fine bit of muslin right there in the churchyard, if you can believe it.''

"Good heavens! But you must have been there rather late, sir. What was a woman doing there at such an hour?"

"Oh, it was after eleven, to be sure, and very dark," he said with a mischievous smile. "As to what she was doing, I expect her purpose was the same as my own. I did take the liberty of suggesting that she ought not to be abroad at such an hour, but she was a bit coy and wouldn't talk much at first."

"Do you know her name?"

"No, but she's a lady, though not of the first circles. Could tell by her speech, you know. Daresay I frightened her witless. Pitch-black out, and I had on my long cloak and a wide-brimmed hat. Must have seemed like the devil himself rising up before her. I was careful to keep my distance and to keep my voice to a murmur so as not to terrify her more, and I fancy I had her tame as a dove by the time we parted, though to be sure she never saw my face, and we did not exchange names. She was clearly embarrassed to have been so startled, and I felt it would be better to maintain a certain air of mystery for the future."

"Then you will meet her there again?" Gillian was amused, and grateful, too, to be distracted from her problems for a time.

"Oh, aye," he said carelessly, "unless more enticing game appears. What plans have you for the future? Have you been to Almack's yet? To balls? Who is doing what?"

"I am afraid I am a little in disgrace just now, sir," she said, smiling at him. "I have cried off from my betrothal."

"Good for you," he said. "Much better to look them all over before you make up your mind to one lad."

"Well, you will be the only one to take that position, I fear," she said. "Papa is utterly enraged with me."

"Naturally. You know—and tell me to go wash my head if you like—but when I saw the pair of you, I thought you liked him."

Gillian was silent for a moment, fearing her feelings would overflow into a speech she might regret. But Vellacott simply sat and stared at her until she felt her cheeks grow hot. She was spared for a moment by the return of the footman with her uncle's breakfast, but he had no sooner left the room again than Vellacott told her to cut loose and tell him a round tale.

"I do like him," she said, "but I do not want him to feel he must marry me. Not for propriety's sake, or my own. If he loved me it would be different, but I do not think he can, for when he discovered the facts of my inheritance, he became unreasonably angry, and after he drove me back here from Langshire House, he said some cutting things, though I'm afraid I did too."

"Nothing unreasonable about that," Vellacott mumbled around a mouthful of coddled eggs and ham. "Daresay the fellow don't like the notion of a female managing her own affairs. Most men don't. Seems a pity, though. He looked to be the sort who might put a bridle on you, lass. You could stand one."

She smiled a little wryly at that. "Do you think so, sir? I confess, I cannot find it in myself to agree with you."

"Daresay you can't, but it's fact nonetheless. I don't mean you need a man telling you when you may breathe. Nor do you want one who will snap your head off every time you chance to disagree with him. But you do need a man who can curb your more willful starts by appealing to your better nature. You've a good mind in that stubborn head of yours, and you've a dashed good heart. But you've carried more of a burden than you should have to carry, my dear, and that's plain fact. Your papa don't like taking responsibility as long as there's anyone else about willing to take it for him. 'Twould be a pity for you to find yourself shackled to a lad of the same cut. I thought Thorne was different, but if he can't stomach your fortune being arranged the way it is, you count yourself well out of a bad bargain.''

''There never was a good bargain,'' she said sadly. ''I do think that if we had met in a normal way, things might have been different, but since that was not the case—''

''And just what was the case, if I might ask?''

Before Gillian could reply, the door opened and Estrid said, ''Mercy, Gillian, did I hear a man's voice in here? I know it cannot be your father, for he left—'' She broke off, staring at Mr. Vellacott, who was in turn staring right back at her. ''And who are you, sir, if I might ask? Good gracious, Gillian!''

Vellacott got smoothly to his feet and made her a bow. His eyes were dancing, but he did not so far forget the proprieties as to introduce himself, so Gillian did the honors.

Estrid chose to be gracious, saying playfully, ''You have been avoiding us, sir. My lord is most put out with you, and I protest, you were never at Carnaby but what you slipped away like a ghost without so much as pausing to pay us a proper call.''

''To my own disservice, madam,'' Vellacott said, making her a deeper leg than before. ''No one chanced to mention that Marrick had found himself such a beautiful lady. I assure you, had I known, I should have made a nuisance of myself by visiting you upon every possible occasion.''

Laughing and clearly pleased, Estrid took her seat and begged him to sit down again and finish his breakfast, but Gillian, startled by his affability toward one whom he had stigmatized more than once in ways she would not think to repeat to anyone, looked narrowly at him. He met the look blandly.

Estrid turned to Gillian and said, ''Little John will arrive today, I believe, for I have had word that they stopped for the night in Brentford. I confess, I look forward to seeing him. I know it is not the fashion to interest oneself in one's children, but I have always found it difficult to release them entirely to servants. No doubt,'' she added rather more tartly, ''you will condemn my middle-class behavior, but before you do, let me tell you that your father has already told me that you have been stupid enough to whistle a dukedom down the wind, so don't expect me to heed any paltry condemnation you might care to make of me.''

"But I do not condemn you, Estrid. On the contrary, I honor your feelings, for I intend to be exactly the same. No doubt I will annoy my servants, for I will not want to miss a single day with my children. And I, too, look forward to John's arrival.''

Estrid looked at her suspiciously, but though she seemed about to contradict her, she glanced at Vellacott and did not, saying instead, "Well, then, perhaps you will honor my feelings in another matter, and understand why I have sent to Weston to arrange for a more congenial butler and housekeeper.''

"Oh dear, you shouldn't have done that," Gillian said, the words coming without a thought about how they would be received.

"I beg your pardon," Estrid said in freezing accents. "Just what do you think you mean by such an improper comment, miss? As I said before, in my own house I can certainly choose my own servants without requesting a by-your-leave from you!''

Marmaduke Vellacott choked on his eggs, snatched up his napkin, and clapped it across his mouth, his eyes wide with repressed merriment and brimming with tears from his coughing.

Gillian jumped up and began to pound him on the back.

"Raise his arms above his head," Estrid recommended in an acerbic tone, "and then perhaps you will be good enough to explain to me just what brought on this ridiculous fit of his.''

"He must have swallowed the wrong way," Gillian said, pounding all the harder in hopes that her irrepressible uncle would hold his tongue. She pounded in vain, however.

"Enough!" he cried. "You will murder me with all that pounding, girl." Coughing one more time, then clearing his throat, he wiped his lips and said to Estrid, "You do know that this place is called Vellacott House, do you not?''

She glared at him. ''And what is that to say to anything? It may once have been part of your family's holdings, sir, but my husband owns it now, since, as I must suppose, it was part of his first wife's dowry.''

''You may suppose what you like,'' he said, his mischievous eyes agleam. ''Fact is that Gillian here owns the place, not your precious husband. He's perfectly well to pass, of course, but his fortune don't match the Vellacott fortune. Fact is, my dear Lady Marrick, you and I are here as your stepdaughter's guests.''

Estrid looked at Gillian. ''Is he speaking the truth?''

''Yes, ma'am, I inherited the house from my mother.''

''Good God, why did no one tell me?''

''It was not my place to do so, ma'am. My father insisted that he would tell you himself. And I daresay he would have done so had you come to London before this, but from one cause and another you did not,'' she ended rather lamely.

Estrid's eyes narrowed. ''What else has he failed to tell me? Do you also own that dreadful castle and Carnaby Park?''

''No, ma'am, both are part of the Carnaby estate. I do own much of the land surrounding the Park, however. Hollingston—''

''Good God, he is your man! That is why he always behaves toward me as if I were something to be stepped upon.''

''If he has, ma'am, he must not do so again. He is not precisely my man, but Grandfather Vellacott did send him to Carnaby when my mother and father were married, because it was thought that the estates would be joined one day, and Grandfather wanted a steward who knew his business. The Vellacott part was my mother's then—her portion of the Vellacott estate—and since I was her only child, her entire fortune came to me by the same trust in which it had been passed to her. Grandfather did not want the lands passed to someone who was not of his blood.''

Estrid's face was white. Vellacott had returned his attention to his breakfast, but amusement still lingered in his eyes, and Gillian was sorry to see it there. She did not like Estrid much, but she found she could feel pity for her.

"Good God, what is to do now?" Estrid muttered.

"Why, nothing," Gillian told her. "Pray do not think anything has changed, ma'am. As I see it, you have as much right to be here as I have myself, and while I must confess that I have been guilty of a certain amount of duplicity in the matter of the servants, which is why I was aghast when you said you had written to Mr. Weston, that can all be put right and, I hope, arranged to your satisfaction. I have no desire to upset you, and if Blalock continues to do so, he will be replaced. I do ask for your cooperation, however. We cannot be continually changing and exchanging servants if we wish to live in any comfort. I think we would do better to see if Blalock cannot improve his ways before we simply thrust him out of the house."

"You must do as you please, of course," Estrid said, but Gillian saw that her stepmother was truly mortified, and had a strong and most unfilial desire to box Marrick's ears.

Her day did not improve. Next she had to contend with Dorinda, who soon learned from her mother that Gillian had cried off from her betrothal. It was apparent, however, that Estrid had not seen fit to explain any matters of finance with her, and for that Gillian was grateful.

"How could you do such a stupid thing as to cry off?" Dorinda demanded. "Thorne is going to be a duke, Gillian!"

"I know he is," Gillian replied with as much patience as she could muster, "but that really has very little to do with the matter at hand. The fact is that the man never asked me to marry him. He agreed to honor your idiotic betrothal announcement only after he saw that I was no prankster but as much a victim as he was himself, and that was very kind, even noble. I could not take advantage of that kindness."

"Well, I should not be that stupid if such an advantage ever came my way," Dorinda said. "A dukedom! Good God."

Even Clemmie shook her head when she learned about

it, an event that took place when the family adjourned to the third drawing room after dinner. Vellacott, who, being without a cook, had apparently decided to accept his brother-in-law's marriage, had joined them for the meal. Clemmie said, "But you care for him, Gilly. Anyone can see that. And he cares for you too."

Glad there was no greater audience to hear that declaration, Gillian replied, "Lord Thorne was just being kind, Clemmie, that is all. No man likes to be forced into matrimony."

"Well, I think whoever put that dreadful announcement into the papers ought to be flogged in the market square," Clemmie said roundly. "It was a dreadful thing to have done."

Involuntarily, Gillian glanced at Dorinda and saw that her cheeks were flaming as she bent her head over the needlework in her lap. Looking back, she encountered her uncle's shrewd gaze but ignored it and said in what she hoped was the same calm way she had spoken before, "I should not wish such a dreadful punishment on anyone, Clemmie. People usually learn from their mistakes, you know, and do not repeat them."

What Clemmie, or anyone else, might have said to that, Gillian would never know, for at that moment the drawing room doors were flung open and the footman announced in stentorian tones, "The Marquess of Thorne!"

Startled, Gillian turned toward the door, wishing one moment that she had decided to wear a gown more becoming to her than the rather insipid pale-green muslin she had chosen, and the next that she were somewhere else altogether. Thorne's eyes were blazing with fury, and she was as certain as she could be that she could count on no one in the room to protect her.

The footman, having accomplished his duty, disappeared, but the marquess came no farther into the room, making only the barest response demanded by courtesy to the greetings from the others before he said abruptly, "I want to talk to you, Gillian."

Not wanting in the least to hear what he had to say to her, she said calmly, "Do come in and sit down, sir.

Perhaps you would care for a glass of Papa's sherry. It is a very fine mountain variety, is that not so, Papa?''

"Aye, but he don't want it. Not by the look of him."

"More likely wants brandy," Vellacott said sapiently.

Thorne shot him a look from under his brows, then said, "I would prefer it if you will come to another room with me, Lady Gillian. I want to speak privately to you, but I will say what I came to say right here if you force me to do so."

She got to her feet at once. "I will come with you, sir."

Estrid said, "I am not by any means certain that that is quite the thing, you know, for the pair of you to be alone as you will be. Perhaps it will be better—"

But Gillian heard no more, for no sooner had she neared the doorway than Thorne took her by the arm and whisked her through it, shutting it behind them. "Where?" he demanded.

She glanced at him, saw no softening in his hard eyes, and said in a faint voice, "The parlor where we talked before, I think. We are less likely to be heard there."

"Good, for I may do some shouting," he snapped.

His grip was tight enough to make her fear he would leave bruises, but she did not think he meant to hurt her, and when his hand relaxed more than once during their hurried walk down the stairs, she knew he was aware of his strength and that his grip tightened more by reflex than by intent.

Several branches of candles had been lighted in the little parlor, and their golden glow flickered warmly on the furniture. The curtains had been drawn to shut out any view of the garden, but Thorne evinced no interest in the surroundings. His attention was riveted on Gillian. Once inside the room, he thrust her away from him almost as though he feared to remain too near her, and snapped the door shut behind him.

"Now, my girl," he said, "perhaps you will be good enough to explain this idiocy to me."

Struggling to compose herself, she said, "I don't know what you mean, sir. There is nothing to explain."

"Oh, is there not? Did you not think that I might be

interested to learn from some source other than a newspaper that my betrothal was at an end? Or do you believe
that the only proper way to communicate such news is
through the London *Times*?"

"But I did tell you! I told you yesterday, and before
that, too, that I meant to cry off as soon as possible, and
yesterday your own mother said it would make no difference when I did it, that the result would be the same.
And you said I must do as I chose, Thorne, you know
you did! I know you were angry that I had not told you
about my fortune, and even angrier to learn that my husband will have no control of it, but—"

"The devil take your fortune!" he exclaimed. "Do
you think I care a farthing for it?"

"Well, of course you do," she retorted. "You would
not dare to deny your feelings, either, if you had been
able to see your face when the matter was made plain to
you."

"Oh, I don't deny I was angry. Damned frustrated,
too, but I do not expect you to understand my feelings,
nor do I attempt to excuse myself to you on their account."

"But you should!" she cried. "Don't you understand,
sir, if only you would say what you think when you think
it, things would be so much clearer. It is all the pretense,
all the games people play, that makes for this sort of
trouble. How can I, or anyone else, understand what
makes you angry if you do not tell us?"

"You don't know what you're talking about," he
snapped. "You keep prating about candor and speaking
one's mind, but in face, my girl, you neither practice the
arts yourself nor like it when someone speaks plainly to
you. Suppose I were to tell you right now that I *want* to
marry you? What would you say?"

"I would say that you were lying in your teeth," she
retorted. "You could not possibly want to marry me and
behave as you are right now. And that, my lord, is plain
speaking."

"Oh, no, it is not! Plain speaking is when I tell you
that you have grown so great in your own conceit that
you believe only what you choose to believe. You do not

see your own faults, only those of other people. And while you are quick to take control when you see a lack, you do not take the time to consider anyone else's feelings before you do. Oh, yes, I see that you remember saying much the same thing to me and believe I am merely flinging words in your teeth, but only look how you managed the business of hiring servants for this house, even Clementina's governess, who was no concern of yours. You overstepped yourself there, my girl, but you behaved throughout as if only you knew what was right to be done. Now, how is that for plain speaking?''

She stared at him, shocked to silence. Then anger took over, filling her, quickening her breathing, and sending hot flames to her cheeks. Gritting her teeth in an attempt to hold her tongue long enough to think, she glared at him, struggling to control herself. But when that gleam of mockery she disliked so much flashed into his eyes, she lost control. "You do not know what you are talking about," she said. "You, of all people, a spoiled son of a duke, brought up to think yourself the grandest among the grand. Who do you think you are, Marquess? You think that title of yours gives you the right to do as you please and to order others as you choose! And when someone does something *not* by your command, you come the great lord over them. Well, you are not so great, sir. You will not command me. Why, you scarcely know me, so how can you make such dreadful accusations? And what do you think you are doing now?'' The look in his eyes as he advanced sent a tremor up her spine. "Stay back, Thorne!''

"I do know you, Gillian.''

"No! I warn you, I will not—''

But she could say no more, for he had snatched her into his arms, given her a shake, and silenced her with his lips. His anger turned swiftly to a passion she could not withstand, for it left her breathless, and the heat of his lips against hers came as such a shock to her that she did not even try to struggle to free herself. The heat of his kiss seemed to radiate through her entire body, kindling her nerves to life and putting every word she had wanted to say to him straight out of her head.

His hands were clutching her upper arms and suddenly he thrust her away from him, releasing her, then standing and glaring at her almost, she thought, as if he hated her.

She stared back at him, raising the back of one fist to her lips, pressing it against them as if she could thus cool them. Instead it merely strengthened the memory of his lips against hers. She felt tears in her eyes and wanted to brush them away, but she couldn't seem to move at all.

At last Thorne said grimly, "You've got physical courage, Gillian. I can certainly attest to that. But you lack the courage of your convictions. I can prove you don't know what you're talking about, that in fact you despise the only person you know who truly does always speak plainly to you."

"I don't! Who?"

"Your stepmother."

The tears spilled over then, but they left him unmoved, and when she brushed them away he was gone.

10

GILLIAN TRIED NOT to think about Thorne and succeeded for as much as an hour at a time in diverting her thoughts to other matters. She discovered that she had become overnight an object of extreme curiosity to the *beau monde,* and she had all she could do to smile and make polite conversation when it was necessary. Since she had assumed that the Langshire ball had been canceled, she was not at all prepared to learn the following week from Lord Dawlish that although the duchess had postponed it a week, she had decided to go ahead with the ball. Nor was Gillian glad to learn when she received her invitation

the very next day that both Estrid and Dorinda expected
her to attend it with them.

"But of course you must go, Gillian," Dorinda exclaimed the afternoon before the ball. "If you do not, I
shall have to spend the entire evening explaining to people why you did not, and goodness knows what I can say
to them!"

"There can be no question of your not going," Estrid
said flatly. "As you see, the invitation contains not the
least mention of any betrothal, so there can be no good
reason for you to offend her grace by refusing to attend."

"I have no wish to offend her," Gillian said, striving
to remain calm, "but surely you must see that to attend
would be an intolerable strain for me, ma'am."

"Not at all," Estrid said. "You pride yourself on your
breeding, miss. Let us see some of it now, if you please."

With the memory of Thorne's upbraiding still perfectly
fresh in her mind, the rebuke struck home in a painful
way, and when she received a kind note from the duchess, assuring her that her presence was desired and that
all care would be taken to ensure her tranquillity and to
disarm any gossipmongers, Gillian knew that only a person of extreme ill-breeding would refuse to go.

The week passed all too swiftly, for there were any
number of activities to fill the time. She did not see
Thorne, but she saw Corbin, Crawley, and Dawlish. All
three paid frequent calls, clearly intent upon raising her
spirits but diplomatically silent about Thorne. Dorinda
mentioned him frequently enough, bemoaning the fact
that they did not see him, but Estrid did not speak of him
at all. Indeed, the countess seemed to be in a world of
her own. She was clearly enjoying her sojourn in the city,
and twice that week was known to have gone out again
after they had all returned to the house for the night. As
for the earl, they saw little of him, for he spent most of
his time at his club.

The night of the ball, Gillian stood quietly while Meggie helped her don her dress, a delicious confection of
white crape, draped with an Indian sash that was richly
embroidered in purple and gold and drawn up at the left
with gold tasseled cording. Her bodice and train were

likewise embroidered with purple and gold, and Meggie arranged her hair in braids and loose curls, ornamented with three gilded feathers on a narrow white satin band. But even knowing that she was looking her best did nothing to quell the butterflies flitting wildly in Gillian's stomach.

There was nothing to distress her in her reception at Langshire House. The duke and duchess and their son each greeted her in the same manner as they greeted their other friends. Why she should find it impossible to look Thorne in the eye she could not imagine. And why she should be irritated when without so much as a glance at her he led another damsel out for the first dance she did not know either. She did not want to create a stir by dancing with him herself, but discovering that the damsel in question was his cousin Dawlish's sister, who had recently announced her forthcoming marriage to an eminently suitable young man, did nothing to assuage Gillian's annoyance. Nor did it help to see that his next partner was Belinda Crawley, for Crawley's sister was an exceptionally pretty girl, and Gillian was glad to see her claimed at once afterward by the wealthy Lord Dacres.

The Langshire ball vied in brilliancy and numbers with any given that Season. The company consisted of above two hundred persons, including such notables as the Prince of Wales and Mr. Charles James Fox, notable politician and incurable gossip; and, at the conclusion of the third dance, five supper rooms were thrown open to reveal tables displaying a profusion of every delicacy in season. After supper, the dances would be resumed, to continue until nearly five o'clock in the morning.

Gillian danced every dance, but she did not enjoy herself much and found it difficult to pretend to be in good spirits. She smiled obediently when Dawlish told her an amusing story, and responded appropriately each time she was asked to dance, but she had all she could do to keep her gaze from drifting in the wake of a tall, dark-haired man who seemed to dance in turn with all the prettiest young women in the room, including her stepsister. Corbin was not there, but Crawley appeared just after the supper rooms were thrown open to invite her to take supper with him, and she was nearly betrayed into looking around before she agreed.

He smiled. "Don't say no, I beg you. I have my heart set upon dining in your company. Moreover, my mama will insist that I take my sister down if you do not take pity on me, and that would destroy a reputation I have been at great pains to create."

That drew a smile from her. "Would it indeed, sir? I think you must be trying to bamboozle me, for I saw you approach my sister Dorinda before you came to me."

He smiled. "I hadn't a chance with her, however, for Corbin was before me, and despite his foppish attire, he has nearly as nasty a right as Josh has, so I didn't like to interfere. But you see before you a very sad fellow. Lady Gwendolyn Darcy, on whom I had pinned my fondest hopes, has most unfortunately cast her handkerchief to a fellow from Perth, of all unlikely places, and means to set up housekeeping in Scotland. You don't happen to know of any other heiress who might suit me, do you?"

Certain he was teasing, she chuckled and said, "I know of only one, sir, a wealthy widow in Exeter to whom my uncle paid court for a time, but she must be at least in her mid-sixties."

"Why, that is of no account, ma'am. Only tell me what she is worth, and if it is more than two thousand pounds per annum, I shall bid you adieu at once and take the first coach to Exeter."

"Good gracious, sir, are you as hard up as that?"

"Worse," he said glumly. "My estates are so weighed down with debt that they'll soon slip right out of Nottingham and sink beneath the fens of Lincolnshire. Even my tailor has begun to press me to pay my bills, and one's tailor is very nearly the last one to dun a man, you know. I promised I would encourage all my friends to patronize him, but the damned fellow had the cheek to tell me he didn't want them, having no doubt they would be just as remiss in their payments as I am."

"Well, that was very unkind," Gillian said. "He cannot even know all your friends, and surely some of them would pay. There is a table over there, sir," she added with a nod.

"So there is," he said, moving to hold a chair for her. "I will leave you here and see what refreshments are offered, shall I?"

He was gone but a few moments, and in that time she tried to convince herself that she was not hopefully watching passing couples. When he returned and she still had not seen Thorne, she decided that the marquess must have chosen another supper room.

Crawley put a loaded plate down in front of her and seated himself, saying in a different sort of voice from the casual one he usually employed with her, "You won't see him, ma'am. He is under strict orders to give you a wide berth tonight."

Startled, she looked at him, feeling heat rise to her cheeks. "I . . . I wasn't. That is . . ."

His smile was warmer than she had ever seen it before. He said quietly, "He has been the very devil of late, ma'am, playing deep and drinking deeper. Thought you ought to know. That is, Mongrel thought so. Corbin warned him to keep his fingers out of the pie, but for once I agree with Mongrel. Josh has been a vastly different fellow since you entered his life, ma'am. All his friends were sorry when you cried off."

"Has he told you the truth about us?" she asked abruptly.

"Not much of it," he said, crooking an eyebrow. "He said only that he had met you once before he read of his betrothal to you and that he thought you had cause to be grateful to him."

"I did, indeed," she said with a reminiscent smile. "He was most fortunately at hand to rescue me when I was cut off by the tide. He did not tell me his true name, however."

"Baron Hopwood!"

"Yes. We were both very wet afterward, because there was a storm, and so when we returned to my home, he did not stay to meet my family. I told everyone about his kindness, and someone who did not believe the tale placed that announcement in the South Devon *Gazette*, never dreaming it would go any further. When it did, Thorne came to Devon, as you know, to straighten things out. His father . . . that is . . .'' She hesitated, uncertain whether she ought to say any more.

"You needn't explain," Crawley said gently. "I have known both Mongrel and Josh since we were lads together at Eton, and I know the duke's temper. Josh has been in his black books once or twice before, you see, and I daresay it was made quite plain to him this time that there was to be no scandal.''

She nodded. "I saw at once that a false betrothal would not answer, but Thorne refused to allow me to cry off, and now that I have done so, he is furious with me. Well, you know that, of course. I daresay he is unaccustomed to having his will crossed by anyone,'' she added forlornly, "let alone by a mere female.''

"Aye, he is that," Crawley said. His demeanor was thoughtful, and his attention seemed to have wandered.

Dorinda and Dawlish came up to their table then to ask if they wanted to stroll with them in the garden, putting an end to further confidences. When they returned to the house, Gillian's hand was claimed at once for a cotillion, and she forced herself from then on to keep her attention on her various partners. Not until Dawlish approached her again in the small hours of the morning did she feel able again to relax her guard.

"Mind if we sit this one out?" he asked. "My feet hurt and I'd give a fortune for a proper drink. Been gabbling for hours. My voice has well nigh dried up and disappeared.''

"I do not mind in the least, sir. In fact, I should welcome a glass of lemonade. I believe there are still refreshments in the little supper room off the gallery.''

"Oh, Lord, yes," he said. "One thing about my aunt is she don't starve her company. We'll find anything we might want.''

They met Thorne coming out of the little room, and to Gillian's amazement, her stepsister clung to his arm. Dorinda was laughing at something he had said, but she drew up in surprise and said, "Why, hello, Gillian, I wondered where you had got to. I declare, I've not laid eyes on you since we left you alone in the garden with Crawley.''

Thorne had been gazing into space, but at these innocent words his eyes focused sharply, and Gillian thought
for a moment that he would speak to her, and curtly at
that. She held her breath in anticipation, but he said only,
"You still here, Mongrel? Thought you'd have run along
home hours ago."

"Not such a cawker as that, dear boy," his cousin said
mildly, adding in an even more casual way, "Matter of
fact, we were just chatting about the masquerade to be
held at Ranelagh next week. Crawley and I are getting
up a party, you see, and Lady Gillian is going with us.
Care to join us?"

Dorinda said quickly, "It sounds like a delightful party,
and we shall be delighted to join you, I'm sure, but just
now you must excuse us, for Thorne has promised to
show me some new steps for a Scotch reel, and I hear
the music beginning. We must hurry, Thorne, or we'll
not find a single place left in the set."

Thorne bowed, his harsh gaze sweeping across Gillian
in such a way that she had all she could do not to tremble.
When they had gone, there was a moment's silence before Dawlish said, "He's three parts gone, you know. It
is to be hoped he don't trip over her whilst he's trying to
show her those dashed fool steps."

Gillian giggled, then clapped a hand to her mouth. "I
beg your pardon. I cannot think what came over me. One
would think that I, rather than his lordship, had been at
the wine."

"Daresay it ain't just wine, ma'am," he observed with
a sour grin. "More like to be brandy, and a good deal of
it. Got a head like a damn mule, Josh has, and he can
behave like one, too, when he's had a bit over the mark."

They went into the supper room. Discovering that they
had it to themselves and remembering what he had said
before, Gillian said, "You ought not to have said that
about the masquerade, sir. We had not talked of any such
thing, as you know very well."

"Oh, we hadn't talked of it yet," he said, grinning at
her. "I meant to speak to you, however. We—that is,
Corbin, Crawley and I—decided a few days ago that it
would be the very thing. That is to say, we thought it

would be fun to get up a party to go to the public festival at Ranelagh next week. Think of it—concert, fireworks, and a grand masquerade—and you may repose complete faith in us to protect you from any untoward experience. You will enjoy it hugely, ma'am. Do say you will go with us.''

Gillian had already reproached herself for letting Crawley see that she wore her heart on her sleeve. She would not make the same error with Dawlish. Knowing she owed it to herself and to her kind protectors not to mope herself to death, she agreed at once that she would be delighted to accompany them to Ranelagh, adding only, ''If my stepmother does not disapprove.''

''Oh, she won't do so,'' Dawlish said with another grin. ''We aim to invite her to go, and your uncle as well, ma'am. 'Tis to be a family party. Why, I mean to invite some of my relations, and Crawley means to invite his mama and Belinda.''

''Then I can scarcely say no, can I?'' Gillian said. Dawlish hadn't said as much, but his last, rather airy speech and the memory that he liked to be helpful led her to think he and his friends meant to encourage the marquess to attend the masquerade too. She tried to think of a grand costume to wear, one that would make him stare, but Dawlish, coming to Park Street to inform her that plans for his party were well in hand, shook his head and laughed when she asked for advice about a costume.

''No use in going to such a bother,'' he said. ''These public masques are always such crushes that it don't do to be going to a lot of trouble. Most ladies carry loo masks and wear dominoes over ordinary evening gowns. You have no notion what a nuisance a grand costume can be if it don't let you sit down comfortably. There is to be a concert as well as the dancing, you know, and one always likes to wander about the gardens. Take my advice and wear what will be most comfortable.''

Dorinda, coming into the drawing room in time to hear the comment, laughed and said, ''Oh, yes, I mean to wear only a silk domino over one of my white muslins. You ought to do the same, Gillian. The nights have turned warm, you know, and you will not want to be bothered carrying a shepherdess's crook or any such thing. Merely carrying one's indispensable is trouble enough.''

Gillian allowed herself to be overborn, particularly since her uncle also declared that costumes were a nuisance. "Take my word for it, girl," he said the next day in the morning room when she raised the subject, "the men who wear costumes won't be gents, and you won't want to make a figure of yourself if the other ladies in your party don't mean to wear them. Your stepmama won't wear one, surely, and nor will the duchess.''

"Oh, is the duchess going to be there?''

"Oh, aye, so Dawlish tells me, and his grace as well, I don't doubt," he added with a smile.

Gillian laughed. "Coming it too strong, sir. The duke does not look like a man who would enjoy a masquerade.''

"No, but since the news that the duchess would be there put that smile on your face, I thought I'd add the duke. He would enjoy the concert, for Ashley means to play a bassoon solo, and he is accounted to be the very best there is. And surely, no one will object if Langshire don't wear a domino.''

She left him chuckling at his own wit, and went to her father's library to see if the post had come yet. The earl had already left the house, but Dorinda was there, apparently reading a letter. She turned with a gasp, clutched the missive to her breast, then turned away again, her cheeks scarlet.

"Good heavens, Dorinda," Gillian said, "have you been indulging in a clandestine correspondence, that you must needs hide it from me?''

"Oh, no," Dorinda said quickly, "nothing of that sort. 'Tis only the invitation to—to . . . the Countess of Leicester's fete next week in honor of all her son's friends who were at Eton with him. You have already seen it, I'm sure.''

She was speaking too quickly, and Gillian knew she was not speaking the truth, for the countess's invitation had come the previous day and must surely be in the silver basket in Estrid's boudoir with others requiring acceptance or regret, but Gillian could see no good to be gained by pressing the matter, so she let it drop. There was little that Dorinda could do on the sly, after all, for Estrid kept a sharp eye on her.

Dorinda said abruptly, "Where is Clemmie? I have not seen her yet this morning."

Gillian shrugged. "No doubt she is with Miss Casey. They went to see the royal circus at St. George's Fields yesterday, you know. She has seen more sights of London than all the rest of us together, I believe."

"Well, yes, but I do not think she meant to go anywhere in particular today. I think I will just go and see if she is still abed. She will not want to miss her breakfast."

Gillian thought that Dorinda was more anxious to get out of the room with her letter than she was to see whether her younger sister was still abed, but she knew, too, that Dorinda had a soft place in her selfish heart for her little sister. They all did. Clementina was the one good thing, in Gillian's opinion, to have come out of her father's second marriage.

After conferring with Meggie, Gillian decided that if she was going to wear a domino, it must be a becoming one, so changing to a yellow muslin half dress made high in the neck with a collar trimmed with fawn-colored velvet, she ordered out a carriage to take her to the shops. In the entrance hall, she encountered Dorinda, just coming from the parlor anteroom.

"Oh, what a pretty hat," Dorinda said. Her manner was a trifle forced, but it was evident that she meant to be pleasant.

"Thank you," Gillian said, drawing on a pair of yellow kid gloves. "Did you find Clemmie?"

"Yes, she had already had her breakfast and was in the midst of a French lesson with Miss Casey. Are you going out?"

"I am going to Leicester Square to purchase silk for a domino," Gillian said. "Meggie assures me that there can be no reason to visit a modiste, since she can sew it for me, but I want to find just the right color."

"What an excellent idea," Dorinda said. "I shall go

with you if you can wait a minute or two for me to fetch my cloak and bonnet, and my indispensable.''

Though she wondered what had brought on this excess of affability, Gillian agreed, and the two young women spent a few pleasant hours visiting the linen drapers in Leicester Square. They examined numerous bolts of cloth and ended at last by purchasing enough for their dominoes. Dorinda selected a pale-blue silk to match her eyes, and Gillian chose a bright rose pink that she knew would make her eyes look stone gray.

''I like that color,'' Dorinda said, stroking the material with one slim, ungloved hand. ''I think I will take some of it and have a pelisse made to go with my pink Etruscan robe. A bit of fur 'round the hem will be just the thing, or perhaps a row or two of Naples lace. What do you think, Gillian?''

Privately, Gillian thought the color too bright for her stepsister, who looked much better in pastels than in more brilliant colors, but she could see that Dorinda had her heart set on the pink silk, so she agreed that it would look very dashing with the robe in question. She did point out, however, that Naples lace would create an effect rather more dashing than Dorinda might wish.

''Black with that shade of pink is much too bold,'' she said.

''Did you say Meggie has a pattern for your domino?'' Dorinda asked, evidently accepting the stricture. ''My maid is handy with a needle and thread, but I am not at all certain that she will know what is expected. May I send her to ask Meggie?''

''By all means,'' Gillian said, glad she had not offended Dorinda, as she so frequently seemed to do. She was beginning to think that when her stepsister exerted herself to be agreeable, she could be very pleasant company.

They met Lord Corbin on the point of being admitted to the house when they returned to Park Street. As always, he was dressed in the extreme of fashion, and his shirt points seemed to prevent his head from turning at all. Gillian hid a smile, reminding herself that he had an excellent seat on a horse and had proved to be a very good friend. Commanding her footman to remain with the carriage, she greeted his lordship warmly. "How very nice to see you, sir," she said. "I collect that you have been out of town. We missed you at the Langshire ball."

"Glad I was missed," he said, smiling at Dorinda, whose attention seemed suddenly to have been diverted by a carriage passing by in the street. "Been visiting friends in Kent, but I was in Bruton Street just now with a few feathers of my wing—friends, you know—and when they decided to stroll on to a coffeehouse, I decided I'd better use for my shillings and wandered along till I found myself in Park Street. I was sorry to have missed the ball," he added. "I trust it was a success."

His gaze was penetrating, and she knew he was not merely inquiring about the company in general, but Blalock opened the door just then, so she was able to smile at Corbin and say, "It was indeed, sir, a very pleasant affair. Do come in, won't you?"

"Thank you. Miss Ponderby, do allow me to take that parcel from you. Where the devil is your footman?"

"He has gone round to the stables with the carriage," Gillian said when Dorinda did not answer. "We had a good many parcels. He will bring them in the back way."

"But why did you not give him this one?" Corbin asked.

His question was clearly directed at Dorinda, and just as clearly Dorinda was determined to ignore him. Gillian watched them with interest, thinking that if her sister were as indifferent as she would have Corbin believe, she would not take nearly such pains to convince him of it. Gillian wondered suddenly if there was more to their relationship than she had thought—if, in fact, Dorinda's secret letter had come from Corbin. To break the silence, she said calmly, "Dorinda preferred to keep that one by her, sir. Blalock," she added, "take his lordship up to the third drawing room, if you please, and tell Lady Marrick that he is here."

"Yes, m'lady. Her ladyship is already in the drawing room, and lords Dawlish and Crawley are with her. Her ladyship has ordered tea. Will you take a glass of wine, sir?"

"I will," Corbin said. "And do take that parcel from Miss Ponderby, Blalock. It don't suit her to be carrying things."

"No, sir. Where shall I have it taken, miss?"

"Oh, to my bedchamber, I suppose," Dorinda said casually. "I cannot think why it makes any difference if I carry it or don't carry it. I shall be going up myself, after all, to tidy my hair and smooth my gown."

"In my opinion, you look perfectly splendid," Corbin said. "Lady Gillian don't mean to desert me, so why should you?"

Gillian chuckled. "I did intend to do the same, sir, but if you object, I see no good reason for us not to go up with you."

"Just what I thought," he murmured, looking at Dorinda.

She tossed her head. "I cannot think what you mean. You talk in riddles. You have neglected us shamefully for days, and did not see fit to attend the ball, so if we have found means of entertaining ourselves in your absence, you cannot be surprised."

"Oh, I should not be surprised at all," he said. "I don't doubt you've had a host of mooncalves swooning at your feet. Is that the way of it, Miss Ponderby?"

"They are not mooncalves," she said, lifting her chin. "I am sure I must have been solicited by at least three gentlemen for each dance at the ball and also at Lady Chard's rout last night."

"I did not know people danced at routs," he said, twinkling.

She glared at him. "They did last night!"

Gillian chuckled again. "They did indeed, sir. Several gentlemen rather the worse for wine got up an impromptu cotillion, but Lord Chard quickly put a stop to it."

They had reached the landing when Corbin said, "I am told that Mongrel expects me to make one of his party for the masked ball at Ranelagh. I hope you do not mind if I join you."

Before Gillian could reply, Dorinda said airily, "I am sure we have nothing to say about that, sir, though tickets cost ten shillings, sixpence, I believe, which may be beyond your means.''

"Do not heed her, sir," Gillian said quickly. "We shall be delighted to have you in our party."

Corbin nodded, smiling at her, but in the half hour that followed before the gentlemen took their leave, she became certain that he was trying to fix his interest with Dorinda and just as certain that Dorinda meant to ignore him. When Gillian demanded later to know why she was so determined to keep him at arm's length, Dorinda stared at her in surprise.

"Good gracious, Gillian, you cannot expect me to encourage Corbin! From all I can tell, he is the merest nobody. He's only a baron and certainly does not own a country house. Why, I'd not be surprised to learn that he's as poor as Crawley. Mama says it is as easy to fall in love with a rich man as a poor one—indeed, that it's much more sensible—so that is just what I mean to do."

In the days that passed before the masquerade, Gillian tried to determine exactly what her stepsister meant to do, but she had no luck whatever, although she was certain that Dorinda received at least one more secret letter. There were parties and dances, and an assembly at Almack's, but of their particular friends, only Corbin and Crawley attended the latter, and though Dorinda allowed each to claim her hand for a single dance, she did not allow any more. Gillian thought the entire evening was insipid.

She was looking forward—more than she would have admitted to anyone else—to the masked ball. She heard about Thorne frequently, because his friends seemed only too willing now to talk about him, but he had not seen fit to grace a single one of the parties she had attended, and she missed his company. She had realized now for some time that he was no mere masculine acquaintance but a friend whose company she truly enjoyed—at least, she told herself, she did when he did not scold her.

The day of the masquerade dawned at last but was gray and gloomy, and for a time everyone feared that a storm would put an end to the plan, but the rain held off, and Lady Marrick did not object when Clementina informed her that she and Miss Casey were venturing to the Tower of London to visit the armor collection there. Estrid said only that she thought Clementina was looking a little pale and perhaps needed to slow her pace a bit.

Clementina agreed at once. "When we return, I shall rest. Nurse told me little John is fretful this morning, so I promised to play with him later, so she can have her cup of tea with Mrs. Parish as she likes to do, without being in a fret about him."

"John is sick?" Lady Marrick looked concerned. "I thought that this new nurse was very good. I must look in on them this morning, though, for I did think he looked a bit pale yesterday."

She seemed truly worried, and that evening when everyone else was preparing to depart, she came downstairs and said with a frown, "I do not like to go away and leave him like this. He is feverish and I think he might really be sick."

"Oh, Mama," Dorinda cried, "you cannot mean that we are not to go, after all!"

"Oh, no, my pet, for what could I do that Nurse cannot? I have told her to send for the doctor if she is at all concerned, and so she will. I believe it must be something Clementina has brought home to him from her ramblings, for she is not feeling at all the thing this evening either. But there can be no reason to make you forgo your pleasure. None at all."

Gillian thought Dorinda's relief was excessive, but she did not give it much thought, believing that as usual her stepsister was thinking only of her own pleasure. She thought Dorinda was looking particularly fetching in her domino, and to her surprise, she discovered that her stepsister had used the rose silk she had purchased to line the pale blue. The contrast was arresting and most becoming to her golden beauty.

"What an excellent notion," Gillian said. "I wish I had thought of doing something like that, perhaps with a pearl gray or cream silk to line the rose."

Their dominoes were exactly alike otherwise, for Dorinda's maid had copied the pattern Meggie had given her. They wore their hair powdered, and the full-cut hooded silk cloaks covered them from head to toe. Loo masks fashioned from matching materials completed their costumes.

The gardens were alive with merrymakers, most of whom were dressed in a similar way. Festoons of lamps adorned with artificial flowers were hung from the trees and around the canal, and in the Rotunda the chandeliers were ornamented with natural flowers. The curtains that hung over the lower boxes had already been drawn to reveal supper tables, decorated with more candles and baskets of flowers.

Their party gathered by supper boxes previously reserved to their use by lords Dawlish and Crawley, and Gillian saw at once that Thorne was not there. Crawley, stepping forward with Corbin to greet them, said, "Thorne agreed to bring my mama and sister so that I could come on ahead. His parents mean to join us later too." He grinned. "His grace declined the honor of attending the masque, but he was willing to attend Mr. Ashley's concert."

Gillian returned his smile. The thought of Langshire carrying a loo mask was ridiculous. "It was kind of his lordship to offer his services to your mama," she said.

"It was." He grimaced. "My idiotic sister invited Dacres to accompany them and told him to come a half hour later than I'd instructed. However, perhaps something will come of that."

"I have seen her with him a number of times, sir," Gillian said. "They make a charming couple."

"I hope they may. He is worth forty thousand a year!"

Gillian chuckled. "You do not fool me, sir. You pretend you care only for money, but I doubt that you would encourage your sister to wed a man she did not like, just for his income."

"It is to be hoped she likes him, then. I had hoped for a time that Corbin might cast a glance her way, but he's been blind to every other chit since he first clapped eyes on the fair Dorinda. I only hope she does not disappoint him."

Gillian feared his hope was misplaced, but on the whole his words reassured her. If he had wanted his sister to marry his friend despite Corbin's lack of fortune, she had been right about him all along. A moment later, she saw the duchess strolling toward them, on the arm of her imperious husband.

Behind them, clad in biscuit-colored, tight-fitting knee breeches, Hessian boots, and a dark blue coat under a black domino, came their son with Crawley's mama and sister, and Lord Dacres. Thorne looked at her a bit searchingly, she thought, but turned away at once when Dorinda spoke his name. With a sigh Gillian moved forward to make her curtsy to the duke and duchess.

11

THORNE BENT HIS HEAD to hear what Dorinda was saying to him, but his attention was still fixed upon Gillian. She was looking particularly fetching, for she had put down her loo mask and in the golden glow of the myriad candles that lit the Rotunda, the deep rose color of the domino emphasized the color in her cheeks. He wanted to see her eyes, to see what color they were tonight, but she had scarcely paid any heed to his arrival. Clearly she was still at outs with him, despite the fact that she had finally condescended to reply to one of his notes of apology.

"My lord, you are not attending," Dorinda said, teasing him.

He straightened and smiled, collecting his wits. "Forgive me, Miss Ponderby. Something distracted me. It is an unacceptable excuse, I know. What was it you were saying?"

"Only that the night is already far more pleasant than the day has been, sir," she said demurely. " 'Twas a pity to have to come inside the Rotunda, though it is indeed a marvelous place, is it not? Oh, look! There are the queen and four of the princesses yonder in that box covered in scarlet fringed with gold.''

"Did you have an unpleasant day?'' he asked, looking dutifully in the direction she indicated and wishing at the same time that she weren't such a prattlebox. She was more beautiful than Gillian, but somehow Gillian had much more countenance.

Dorinda said, "I was referring only to the weather, my lord. It has been a prodigiously gloomy day, has it not?''

"It has,'' he agreed, glancing over to where Gillian was deep in conversation with Crawley and wondering what the devil Crawley could have said to her to make her eyes twinkle so. Whatever it was, her stepmother seemed not to have heard it. Lady Marrick was watching the crowd almost as if she searched for someone in particular, and Thorne wondered if Marrick had expressed the intent to abandon his gaming tables for the night to join them.

"I have never before been to Ranelagh,'' Dorinda said. "The lighted walks through the garden looked particularly inviting, do you not think so? And they say there will be a grand display of fireworks after supper, you know, before the dancing begins.''

Corbin's deep voice sounded from behind Thorne. "The walks are mighty fine indeed, Miss Ponderby. If you would care to stroll about, I should be pleased to act as your escort. We can join the throng going round and round the Rotunda promenade, or we can amble to the bottom of the garden and visit the Temple of Pan near the river, or have a look at the Mount Etna exhibit. They say that real lava flows from it into a pool of fire.''

Dorinda did not attempt to hide her annoyance at the interruption, but Thorne said, "She would enjoy it, Corbin. Do go with him, Miss Ponderby. He knows a deal more about the place than I do. My mother is motioning to me to join her, so I must beg you to excuse me.'' But although he turned toward the duchess, he did not go to her. He wanted to talk to Gillian.

She was still engrossed in her conversation with Crawley. They were standing near his mother and sister, who were chatting with Lady Marrick, the duchess, and the elegant Lord Dacres. Dacres, though he stood beside the duke, seemed enraptured by Belinda Crawley. Thorne told himself that he did not doubt his ability to detach Gillian from the others, but he suddenly feared to put it to the touch. It would be better to wait until later, he decided, when he could be private with her without causing a stir. Altering his course accordingly, he joined his father, who was looking particularly bored at the moment.

The orchestra played from a flower-decked platform beside a small stage that faced the queen's box, and when a company of children began to dance Spanish dances on the stage, Thorne and his companions retired to their supper boxes to be served with collared beef, collared veal, ham and tongue, sandwiches, Savoy cakes, pastries, and fruit, as well as tea, coffee, lemonade, ice creams, jellies, and biscuits. Thorne, looking over the vast spread, thought cynically that there was certainly no indication there that members of Parliament were spending every waking hour discussing the scarcity of food, and trying to discover practical methods of remedying the many grievances caused by that scarcity.

In no mood for lemonade, and knowing that the duke would likewise reject it, he caught the attention of a passing waiter and ordered several bottles of wine. Matters had been arranged so that Gillian had been seated in the next box, and since Thorne was certain he recognized the fine hand of his cousin Dawlish in the design for the evening, he determined to have a word with that young man before very much more time had passed. At the moment, however, Dawlish seemed interested only in the little dancers and was completely oblivious to his annoyance.

During the supper, Mr. Ashley played his bassoon, and a fat young woman sang several ballads. Glees and catches were sung by the children from recesses on each side of the stage, and out of respect for the duke, who actually wanted to hear the music, the others in his party lowered their voices, though others around them did not. The concert ended with a spirited rendition of "God Save the King," for which the entire company respectfully rose to their feet, and when it was done, the royal party turned toward the back of their box, for the curtains at the Rotunda's many tall windows had been swept back by the waiters so that everyone inside could watch in comfort the magnificent display of fireworks about to begin in the garden.

Part of the effect was lost due to the skies remaining overcast, but the display was brilliant nonetheless, for besides the usual star bursts and Catherine wheels, there were twenty illuminated sailboats on the canal from which skyrockets were discharged. The effect was dazzling, but at last it was done and the company turned back to the activities inside the Rotunda.

Many more people had arrived, most of whom were masked and wearing dominoes or costumes. The orchestra struck up again, playing a martial tune as a signal that the queen and the princesses with their retinue were ready to depart. A number of red-coated waiters cleared an aisle from the royal box to the exit, and a train of carriages, accompanied by a party of the Horse Guards, came up the long walk to collect them. Everyone else remained standing until they had been driven away.

"What a pity," Dorinda said, "that they cannot stay for the dancing. I am sure they would enjoy it."

Thorne smiled politely at her. "The royal family makes frequent appearances at public functions such as this one, Miss Ponderby, and I'm quite certain that there are at least two royal dukes present tonight who will remain for several hours, but it will be a long while before it is thought suitable for any royal princess to be present at a public masquerade."

Gillian, turning in time to see Thorne smile at Dorinda, stifled a sigh and turned away again. It was surely no business of hers if he chose to join the other gentlemen in making a cake of himself over her beautiful stepsister. Noting that many more people had joined the throng inside the Rotunda, she wondered why her uncle was not there. She had been expecting him ever since her own arrival, but had not caught so much as a glimpse of him.

The floor was cleared for dancing, and the orchestra struck up for a Grand March. Domino hoods were adjusted and loo masks lifted into place, and suddenly the Rotunda was alive with masqueraders. Gillian danced only with the men from her own party at first, telling herself it did not matter that everyone but Thorne asked her to dance. She saw him lead Dorinda out, then Belinda Crawley, and then the duchess, who accepted his invitation with a laugh and an engaging twinkle. The duke had disappeared toward the card room, evidently believing his wife would be well looked after without him for a time. Even Estrid was dancing. Gillian did not know her partner, but evidently Estrid had recognized the tall, slim gentleman in the black domino who had approached her and murmured an invitation to her to honor him, for she had blushed like a girl in her first Season and had gone with him without so much as a blink.

The numbers increased inside the Rotunda until it became clear that people without tickets had managed to slip past the gatekeepers. The numbers of people and the candles in the many chandeliers that lighted the room combined to make the temperature uncomfortably hot after a time, and so crowded did it become that Gillian wondered if she would find her way back to the box when her present dance was ended. She was with Crawley, and she had every confidence in his being able to see her safely back to her stepmother's side, but she had long since lost sight of Estrid—and of Thorne and most of the others, for that matter.

The pattern of the dance carried her away from Crawley for a moment, and when she turned back, she bumped into a tall, broad figure in a black domino who caught her hand and quickly pressed a folded note into it when she would have pulled away from him.

When she got near enough, Crawley bellowed into her ear, "Who the devil was that?"

"I don't know," she said, then repeated it louder when he indicated that he hadn't heard her. She showed him the note.

"Open it," he recommended when they paused for a moment.

She did so, and frowned. "It says I should come to the gravel walk behind the Mount Etna exhibition at midnight if I would find my heart's desire." She looked at him. "Who can have given me such a foolish note?"

He shook his head, letting his eyes roll up, as though he had not the least notion and thought the whole thing absurd, but Gillian had a sudden feeling that he knew all about it. Though the man who had given the note to her had been large enough to have been Thorne, she was nearly certain it had not been he, but Corbin was almost as tall, and she had felt from the beginning that the whole evening had been planned by Thorne's friends to bring the two of them together in some way or other. Smiling at Crawley, she tucked the note into her indispensable and let him skip her down the line.

Thorne had given up dancing and sat in his supper box with the duchess and Lady Crawley, watching the merrymakers. The Rotunda was so crowded now that it was nearly impossible to find anyone he recognized from their party, and the din was so great that conversation with his companions was impossible.

Lady Marrick suddenly appeared before them, blushing behind her black loo mask. She swept into the box and turned as though she meant to speak to someone behind her, then exclaimed, "Oh, how naughty of him! But that is always the way with masquerades, is it not, Duchess? One's partners never stay to make themselves known." She fanned herself rapidly with a program picked up from the table and looked around with a helpless air.

Thorne had risen to his feet when she entered the box, and he leaned down to his mother and said close to her ear, "Would it be dreadful of us, Mama, if we were to take a turn in the gardens? I am rapidly—"

But there was no need to finish, for the duchess leapt to her feet and said in a tone that carried to the other ladies despite the roar of noise around them, "We are going to take a turn in the garden before I swoon from this dreadful heat. Can we send a waiter to you with some lemonade, do you think?"

Both the other ladies accepted the offer with gratitude, and the duchess, placing her hand on Thorne's arm, fairly pulled him away from the box and around the flurry of dancers to the nearest exit. Once safely outside, she said, "Dearest, do see if you can capture one of those red-coated waiters and command him to take some lemonade to the box. There is one now. Catch him!"

Thorne did so, gave the necessary orders, then turned back to the duchess, who beamed at him and said, "That will hold them. We have been very clever, I think, dearest. Neither could offer to come with us, for they were bound to remain where Belinda and the other girls could find them, and for that I am thankful, for if anything is worse than enduring Amelia Crawley's chattering, it is attempting to remain gracious whilst Lady Marrick attempts to pretend she is unimpressed by my rank. The poor woman only makes me want to snatch her bald-headed!"

Chuckling, Thorne squeezed her hand on his arm and began to relax for the first time that evening. They were not the only ones to have sought the cooling river breezes. People wearing dominoes and carrying loo masks could be seen everywhere in the gardens. A band played from the temple-like structure near the canal, known as the Chinese House, and it was pleasant just to stroll. The garden's main walks were illuminated by the lamps hanging from the branches of the trees, but a few of the lesser walks had been left in discreet darkness.

A shepherdess carrying a crook ran past them, shrieking as she tried to elude a Harlequin in hot pursuit. Across the green lawn, a stately Cleopatra walked with a Roman-robed Anthony, and Queen Elizabeth strolled beside Sir Francis Drake. There were others in similar imaginative costumes, but many more wore dominoes. They looked, Thorne thought, like a host of colorful butterflies. And moths, he reflected, noting the vast number of black dominoes amongst the other, brighter colors.

There were also gawkers, those members of the public who for a small sum had purchased tickets of admission that, while they did not allow entrance to the Rotunda, did allow them to watch the glittering activity in the gardens, to enjoy the music and the beauty of the lights reflected in the river Thames, and to stroll beneath the elms and oaks that lined the gravel walks.

Thorne caught a flash of rose pink and turned to see a young woman who he was certain must be Gillian, her hand on the arm of a man in a black domino, strolling away from them some distance ahead. She lowered her mask carelessly and turned her profile, and he saw that it was indeed Gillian. When she laughed, twinkling up at her partner, Thorne realized he was gritting his teeth and promptly returned his attention to the duchess. The band music grew louder near the bottom of the garden.

Thorne's patience was wearing thin. He found himself wondering about Gillian's chilly attitude, and for the first time it occurred to him that she might not have sent the note he had received. Surely, he thought, if she had, she would have cast at least one speaking look his way during the evening. He had been led by that note to believe she would greet him with some warmth, at least. Instead she seemed to avoid looking at him at all, and he had not managed to get a word with her. It was almost as if his friends, having conspired to throw them together, were now in a conspiracy to keep them apart until the appointed hour.

If, indeed, she had not sent the message herself, he realized that it would behoove him to tread carefully. His first message to her, apologizing for having lost his temper, had got short shrift. His second had been politely received, however, and she had agreed to meet him. At least that was what he had assumed when her note had come, apparently in reply to his.

What if that was not the case? What if she remained cold toward him and came to the rendezvous, as perhaps he did himself, believing what was not true. What if the timing of the note he received had been only a coincidence? He could scarcely ask the others outright what they had done, in case he was wrong about the whole and they had done nothing. He wanted to find Gillian, to have things out with her and discover the truth, but he could scarcely walk away and leave the duchess in the garden.

* * *

Gillian had found her uncle. In truth, he had found her when she had been on the point of leaving the floor with Crawley. He had come upon them, unmasked, indeed wearing nothing over his normal evening attire but the sort of plain black domino that so many gentlemen wore. Gillian had greeted him with delight, dismissing Crawley and agreeing at once to take a turn in the garden with Mr. Vellacott, but she had scolded him as soon as they were outside, where she could make herself heard.

"Where have you been, sir? I have been on the watch for you ever since we arrived. You missed a very fine supper."

"Oh, I had my supper," he said airily. "Why the devil were you dancing with Crawley? Man's a fortune hunter. Needs an heiress more than I do myself. Well, stands to reason he does, since I don't need one. Wasn't born without a shirt, even if m' father did see fit to leave the bulk of his wealth to your mama. Never bothered me a whit. My Millicent came to me with a fine dowry, and so, for all her faults, did Grace. I'm well fixed now, damme if I'm not, so I needn't ever again fall into a parson's mousetrap. I can just enjoy myself. Crawley, now—"

"Don't concern yourself, sir," Gillian said, twinkling at him. "I do not believe for a minute that Crawley seeks to capture me or my fortune. Indeed, I think he acts more out of friendship than from any other motive."

"Oh, does he now? And what makes you think that, m' dear?"

"Well . . ." She wrinkled her nose, wondering if she ought to take him into her confidence. When he twinkled back at her, looking like a child awaiting a treat, she decided that in such a crowd as this one she would be extremely foolish to wander about at midnight without an escort. Laughing, she said, "Oh, very well, but I tell you only because I will need an escort and I do not want to spoil fun by demanding that one of the others go with me. I am very nearly certain that Crawley, Dawlish, and Corbin are all in a string to mend matters between Thorne and me."

Vellacott gave her a straight look. "Do you want things mended between you, m' dear?"

Giving back look for look, she said, "I do, sir. I have been most unhappy since our quarrel."

"Then go to the lad and tell him so," Vellacott recommended.

Gillian bit her lip. "How can I? The last time I saw him privately he shouted at me, and the only time I have seen him since, he had Dorinda on his arm and didn't so much as bid me good evening. But if the others are doing what I think they are, it must be because they believe he wants to mend matters just as much as I do, so will you come for me at midnight, sir? The assignation is to be in the walk behind the Mount Etna exhibit."

"Very well, m' dear, but now let us stroll back toward the Rotunda. There is a particular beauty who deserves just a few more minutes of my time before I must abandon her for you."

Gillian laughed and let him take her back inside. They were intercepted by Lord Dawlish before they reached the box, and when he asked her to dance, she accepted readily, hoping he might say something to reassure her that he had things well in hand. He didn't say a word that she could pretend had any double meaning, but neither did he say anything to dash her hopes.

Thorne had lost sight of Gillian and her cavalier, and in order to hurry the clock, he guided his mother to a deserted table in a pavilion near the water, where they could watch the lights and the boats sailing on the canal. Waving to a strolling wine seller, he purchased a bottle of Madeira and poured a glass for each of them. Less than a half hour later, they were joined by lords Corbin and Crawley.

Taking a seat and stretching his legs, Corbin said, "Found Crawler by the canal but dashed if we haven't lost Mongrel and the others. The beauteous Dorinda gave me the slip a half hour ago, and I'd not seen the rest for some time before that."

Crawley said, "My sister's with Dacres, strolling down the long walk, and I thought I saw Lady Gillian across the canal, walking near the Mount Etna exhibition with her uncle Vellacott. It's nigh onto midnight, so they will soon be serving a late supper. People are already coming out of the Rotunda in droves, so I daresay the dancing is done for a time and the others will be ready for something to eat or drink. What say you look about for the others, Corbin, while Josh and I go see who is still sitting in the supper boxes? Don't wander about for long, though. Most likely, their last partners will deliver them safe and sound to Lady Marrick's box. Just hope she's still there," he added. "Seen her dancing more than once tonight, always with the same skinny fellow in a black domino. Wears a full mask, so I can't say who he is, but it's my belief Marrick ought to spend less time at the tables and more time dancing attendance on his wife— begging your pardon, I'm sure, your grace."

The duchess smiled at him. "Never mind about my pardon, sir. Just go and find the others. I shall be perfectly content to remain here with Corbin until you and Josiah do so. We can have our late supper here, in fact. It is growing a trifle chilly, but I refuse to set foot back inside that hotbox."

Crawley turned toward Thorne, who said, "You'll have to hold me excused, I'm afraid. I've got an assignation at the pavilion near the card room." Giving the others a mocking grin, he turned away. Then, looking back rather quickly, he caught the look of consternation that passed between his two friends and laughed to himself, sure that they knew he had caught on to their plan and were wondering if he was pleased or irritated by it. Let them wonder, he mused. It would do them no harm.

Gillian, having met Mr. Vellacott a little earlier than planned, strolled with him across the canal bridge to the Mount Etna exhibit and went inside to take a look at the marvelous display, which depicted the volcano above the cavern of Vulcan, where the Cyclops forged the armor of Mars to music by Handel and Haydn. Smoke thickened, the crater vomited forth flames, and lava rolled down the side of the mountain into a flaming pool.

There were halos around the garden lights when they came out again, and around the lighted sailboats on the canal, and Gillian realized that a fog was collecting. They would have to leave soon, before the road near the river became too dangerous to travel. But first . . .

She drew a breath and said, "Do you know the time, sir?"

He drew his watch from his pocket and opened it. "Just on twelve now," he said. "Do I go with you all the way?"

"No, but do stay where you can see me," she said. "I am very nearly certain that I know what they are about, but just in case the matter is completely otherwise . . . well, sir, I do not want to find myself alone in the dark with some lunatic."

He grinned at her and they moved toward the walk that led behind the exhibit. Just as Gillian was about to take leave of Mr. Vellacott, she heard her name called and turned to see Crawley striding rapidly toward her.

He did not mince words. "Mongrel must have muffed it," he said. "Josh is going to the pavilion near the Rotunda card room to meet you, and here you are expecting to meet him—at least, I think you must have known it was going to be him—along here."

"So it *was* your plan," she exclaimed, "just as I thought!"

"Well, don't go congratulating yourself yet," he said. "If you don't get along to the right place, Josh will probably call for his carriage and go along home, and that wouldn't suit us at all. Man's been like a bear with a sore head for a week, and just when we think we have managed the thing to a fare-thee-well, Mongrel scrawls the wrong damned things on his notes."

"Lord Dawlish wrote a note to Thorne like the one I got! But would he not recognize his cousin's hand?"

"To be sure he would, but Mongrel didn't actually write it, you know. Needed a woman's hand. But look here, m'lady, we mustn't tarry. Unless of course, you are as miffed by our intrusion into your affairs as Thorne is likely to be if he finds out. What he will tolerate if it goes smoothly is one thing. If it don't, I don't even want to think about what he might do."

"Do you want to come with me?" she asked.

But he refused, saying he owed it to Corbin to get back

to help him collect the others. The fog was gathering in earnest, and he was sure that everyone would be wanting to get along home within the hour. "Thorne will see to you, though, ma'am, or your uncle will if things don't go as well as we hope."

His last words were not encouraging, but Gillian, shrugging off the shiver of fear that came when she heard them, took her uncle's arm and fairly dragged him back across the bridge.

Thorne forced himself to stroll casually along the gravel walk behind the Rotunda and came at last to the path leading past the boxlike card room toward the canal. The walk beside the Rotunda was well lighted, but once he turned into the side walk the light was much dimmer. He knew that anyone watching for his arrival would see him outlined by the lights behind him, but the walk also had hedges bordering it, and he wondered suddenly if Gillian had been foolish enough to come alone to meet him. He would have something to say to her about that if she had.

He walked past the side entrance to the card room just as the door opened and someone came out. Light from inside spilled onto the gravel walk and radiated a little distance, showing him a marble bench ahead and a flash of rose pink silk.

She was sitting on the bench alone, still hooded and turned shyly away from him. The sight of her so foolishly alone, so vulnerable, made him want to shake her, but he held his temper, speaking her name in a normal tone so as not to startle her.

When she did not turn, he was certain that he was right, that she had come because she thought he had asked her to do so, but was still out of charity with him. Still, she was here. The card room door opened in another brief flash of light, then shut.

"Gillian," he said again, moving to sit beside her and touching her shoulder. "Turn and talk to me, sweetheart."

He saw her stiffen at the endearment, but still she did not turn. Indeed, she seemed to huddle down, seeking some sort of comfort from the thick folds of her domino.

"Gillian," he said more loudly, "come now, don't be foolish. We must talk to each other just as you once said we should."

There was a step on the gravel behind him, and as he turned a familiar voice said, "Josiah, is that your voice? Whatever are you doing out here like this?"

He turned, saw the unmistakable figure of the duke beside another, much plumper and shorter masculine figure, and got quickly to his feet. "It's all right, sir," he said with a chuckle. "I'm not creating a scandal this time but merely trying to make all right and tight with the woman I want to marry."

"Perhaps you would like to introduce the lady to Mr. Fox," the duke said lightly.

"Certainly, sir, though I am certain that he has already met her at our ball. Come here, sweetheart, this is no time to be shy." The figure in the rose domino stood up, and before he had taken in the fact that Gillian appeared to have grown rather taller, Dorinda swept back her hood and made a deep curtsy.

"Ah, yes," Mr. Fox said, making a leg, "Miss Ponderby, is it not? Well met, madam. I shall dance at your wedding."

Rising quickly from her curtsy, Dorinda flung her arms around Thorne and said, "Oh, sir, I hadn't the least knowledge that you wished to marry me, but I am ever so happy to accept your offer! Only I'm afraid you didn't really mean it, and you will say you didn't, and I shan't get to marry you, after all!"

The duke said grimly, "He will not do that, Miss Ponderby. For that you have my word."

Thorne, trying to release himself from Dorinda's clutches, met his father's stern gaze and knew at once that it would do him no good at this point to protest. It wasn't Dorinda's fault that he had mistaken her for Gillian, though the wretched girl ought to have made herself known to him long before she had. Then, to his horror, before he could collect his scattered thoughts, he saw Gillian standing behind the duke and Mr. Fox, with her uncle Vellacott. Her eyes were as wide as saucers. She stared at the tableau their little group formed for only a moment before she gathered up her skirts, turned on her heel, and fled.

12

GILLIAN RAN AND RAN, the tears streaming down her face, blinding her, her silk domino billowing behind her and her muslin skirts making it impossible for her to run freely. Gravel got into her sandals, hurting her feet, but still she ran, wanting only to put as much distance as she could between herself and the dreadful scene she had witnessed. She was barely conscious of the people she passed, figures who stopped and stared at her, others who jumped aside to let her run past them, still others who did not, who cried out when she brushed past them. Suddenly she was caught in a pair of strong arms, caught, swung around and held. For a brief, joyful instant she thought it was Thorne who had caught her, but to her sorrow, her captor was Crawley.

"Whoa, there," he cried. "You cannot run full tilt through these gardens, ma'am. It simply ain't done." Then, drawing her off the path into a temporarily deserted side path, he said in a different tone, "What went amiss? Here now, don't cry, for God's sake. I haven't even got a clean handkerchief."

"And I've lost my indispensable," she said, realizing that in one of her near collisions the strings must have broken. "Meggie will say it just goes to show that a proper pocket, tied around one's waist in the old style, is much more practical." She sniffled. "Oh, I must be a mess, Crawley. Whatever possessed the lot of you to think you could mend matters?"

"Well, that is what I was coming to tell you," he said. "I found Mongrel, and he swears he never told Dorinda to write the bit about the card room, that the meeting was supposed to have been behind the Mount Etna exhibit.''

''Evidently one thing my sister failed to mention to any of you,'' Gillian said bitterly, ''is her determination to marry well. She has decided that a marquess will suit her, and Thorne is evidently happy to accommodate her. I saw him with his arm around her, and it was not the first time. He just declared to his father and to Mr. Charles James Fox, who will no doubt tell everyone else in London, that she is just the bride for him. He is welcome to her, I'm sure.'' But she sobbed on the words.

''Well, I don't believe for a moment that Thorne wants to marry that wench,'' Crawley said. ''For one thing, he knows perfectly well that Corbin is infatuated with her, and for another it ain't for the love of the fair Dorinda that our Josh has been acting like a bear with a sore head this past week.''

''But I have seen how he smiles at her,'' Gillian said, ''and in any case it will not matter now that he has declared himself as he has, for Dorinda will never agree to cry off, and the duke will not allow Thorne to do so. You know he won't.''

''No,'' Crawley said, ''that's true enough. Good God, what a coil! That girl wants thrashing, and I'll be bound she'll be sorry she ever entrapped Josh if he does marry her. He'll make her the very devil of a husband.''

Gillian was able to take small comfort from that, though she told herself quite firmly that she was wrong to hope Thorne would beat Dorinda weekly. She sighed. ''It just goes to show that I was right all along,'' she said. ''If only people would say outright what they mean instead of always wrapping things up in clean linen, the world would be a much easier place to live. If you had not tried to trick us into meeting—''

''Now, hold on,'' Crawley said. ''We only wanted to help. If you had been frank with Thorne at the outset, and had told him that you cared for him—''

''But I could not,'' she protested. ''I do believe in candor whenever it is possible, but only think of how I would have been perceived, sir, if I had done any such thing! A proper young woman does not march up to a man and tell him she thinks he's the perfect husband for her.'' Feeling heat in her cheeks, she added hastily, ''Why, just to say that much to you makes me want to sink right into the ground. Only a truly hubble-bubble person behaves in such a way. What would he have thought of me?''

''There is that,'' he agreed. ''Plain speaking ain't as simple a matter as it sounds. You may be thinking that Mongrel, Corbin, and I ought to have gone bang up to him and said, 'Look here, Josh, you're making an ass of yourself by behaving as you are. Just go and apologize or do whatever you must to make things right again. A fine scene that would have been. Most likely you would have had to attend our funeral services shortly afterward. He would not have appreciated being told what to do, I can tell you that. And no more would you have liked it, my lady, so don't try any more of your faradiddles with me.''

Gillian sighed again, wiping her damp cheeks with the tail of her domino, since she had nothing else to use. ''You are right, of course, and so was Thorne when he said much the same things to me. It is a lowering thought that although one always thinks one's own notions are best, no one ever likes to take advice. But all the same,'' she added, ''it is not wise to try to manipulate one's friends like so many puppets either.''

He grimaced ruefully. ''No, you are right about that. I daresay Josh will have a few things to say to us that I for one don't want to hear. I think the best thing will be to play least in sight for a few days, at least. If we thought he was out of sorts before, it will be as nothing to what he will be like now.''

Gillian wanted to believe him, but she still feared that Thorne would not find it so difficult to accommodate himself to the notion of marrying Dorinda as Crawley seemed to think he would. There was no time to debate the matter, however, for Crawley had seen Corbin and the duchess, followed by Lady Marrick and his own mother and sister. He called out to them, and they turned down the little path to meet them.

"Here you are, my dears," the duchess said.

Gillian thought she perceived a thoughtful look in her grace's eyes, but it disappeared swiftly as greetings were exchanged and questions were asked about the whereabouts of those members of their party who were still missing.

The duchess said, "Corbin was very kindly escorting me to find Langshire. Have you seen him, Crawley?"

Gillian waited only until Crawley said he had not before she said, "His grace was with your son and my stepsister in the little path by the card room a few minutes ago, ma'am. Mr. Fox was there as well, and my uncle Vellacott."

"Goodness, what a party! Oh, but here is my nephew and Lord Dacres. Perry, darling, you may give me your arm to find your uncle, and I daresay Lady Marrick will want to accompany us, since I am told that her daughter is with him in some pathway near the card room. So indiscreet of his grace, do you not agree? And Lord Dacres, here are Lady Crawley and Belinda, who have been wondering where you had got to. I believe her ladyship is ready to depart, and I am sure you will want to escort her. Ah, but Crawley," she added when Dacres had instantly agreed with her suggestion, "dear Gillian looks as if she would like to go home. Perhaps you will be kind enough to escort her if her stepmother does not object. Take one of our carriages if you must. There are enough for the rest of us, I believe."

A little stunned by the duchess's sudden chatty decisiveness, Gillian looked at Crawley and saw that he was nodding. "But I cannot," she said. "It would be quite improper of me to let you take me home in a closed carriage, sir."

"Fustian," said the duchess. "Crawley will not molest you."

"Certainly not," Crawley said, grinning.

Gently her grace added, "He would have to deal with me if he did so and, I think, not only with me."

Realizing that the duchess had no idea what had transpired only moments before, Gillian was at a stand. The last thing she wanted to do was to announce Thorne's engagement to this entire group, for Dacres and his two charges had not gone yet, and even if they had, she did not think she could do it. She was spared the ordeal by the arrival on the scene of Mr. Vellacott.

"Ah, here you are, m' dear. Been searching for you. Bad form to have run off like that, you know. Makes a poor impression on the masses to see a young girl running through the gardens." Seeming to take notice for the first time of the others, who were listening to his words with open curiosity, he smiled and said. "Quite a to-do, there was. Just like a play—or a farce. Can't say I've been so entertained in weeks. Not since the king fainted dead away at Drury Lane and had to be revived by no less than thirty persons, all gathered about him arguing over what was best to be done. Poor fellow came to himself before they'd made up their minds. What was I saying?"

The duchess, eyeing him in that same sharp manner that Gillian had detected earlier, said, "You mentioned a to-do, sir. What can you have meant, I wonder?"

"Well, your grace, I ain't generally a talebearer, but it does appear that that young rascal of yours has gone and got himself betrothed again."

"What?" Stunned, the duchess looked at Gillian.

Gillian looked at her feet.

"Oh, yes," Vellacott said, clearly enjoying himself. "Devil of a thing, for he is now betrothed to the lovely Miss Ponderby."

Estrid shrieked, "What! Dorinda?"

"The very same," Vellacott said. "A nice catch, don't you agree, ma'am? And the duke saying in no uncertain terms that there will be no crying off from this one."

"No, indeed," Estrid said. "Oh, I must go to my darling girl at once. To think, she will be a marchioness! Oh, was anything ever so wonderful? You may go with Crawley if you choose, Gillian, though I think you would do better to wait and come with Dorinda and me. Surely, you will wish to offer her your best wishes for her happiness."

Gillian remained silent.

Vellacott said, "What's this? Go home with Crawley?

Oh, I don't think that is wise, do you, my dear? Much better if I go with you, to lend a touch of propriety to the occasion.''

The thought of Mr. Vellacott putting himself in the role of chaperon gave Gillian a sudden urge to laugh, but she was afraid to do so, for she had a very strong feeling that if she were to allow herself so much as a chuckle, she would succumb to hysterics on the spot, and no doubt would then be carried away to Bedlam, where she would cease to be a trouble to anyone at all.

Crawley's hand on her arm steadied her, and when the others walked away, she watched as if she were in a daze. The fog had drifted down and around, making halos everywhere there was light, and little wisps of it floated through the trees and around the hedges lining the paths. She saw all this in a silent world, for it was as if the noise and merrymaking around her had faded into the distance. Only Crawley's hand on her arm was real, and she let him guide her farther and farther away, until they had come to the gates and passed through them, and the carriage had been called for. Not until Crawley lifted her into the carriage and she had felt it tip first with his weight and then with her uncle's did the world right itself again. But even then she had no wish for conversation, and the journey to Park Street seemed to take a very long time.

She could see both men in the golden glow from the carriage lamps, but it occurred to her that the dense fog outside made it look as though they traveled in some space removed from reality, and she was barely conscious of the fact that a conversation had begun. She took no notice of their words until her uncle said, ''That Dorinda lass wants a sharp lesson. Such foolishness!''

''Foolishness, sir?'' she muttered. ''I know you think that Dorinda did something dreadful tonight, but I am not by any means certain it was entirely her fault, for his lordship has never shown any displeasure in her company and has, in fact, smiled and laughed with her as he does with no one else.''

''Poppycock,'' Vellacott said. ''He don't seek the chit out, never has. 'Tis you he likes, my girl, and you ought to know it. And if he don't like you, it can be only because you have done your best of late to put him off. If he don't want to marry Dorinda, he'll soon find a way out, you mark my words.''

''But he cannot. Even when he found himself betrothed to me, he did not try to get out of it. He was angry because I cried off, not because he wanted to marry me but because he feared I would injure my reputation, and he was at pains to see that I did not. He will not want Dorinda ruined either. Nor will the duke. He made himself quite clear, sir. You heard him.''

''Oh, aye, and vastly entertaining it was too. To think of Fox being there! Was there ever such a thing? But that lad is no milk-toothed boy, m' dear. He's a man with a mind of his own, and you can be certain he will find a way out if he wants it.''

Crawley had been silent, but now he said quietly, ''He might be able to manage, Mr. Vellacott, but he would have to estrange himself from his father to do so, and I am by no means certain that he is willing to do that. He generally wants nothing more than to please his father. Josh has long wanted to take a hand in the family affairs, but whenever he has offered a suggestion, the duke has said he ought to leave it to those who know their business best. Josh has never gone against him before, you see, and I doubt he will now. We may have to put our heads together, to think if there is any way we can help him out of this mess.''

''No,'' Gillian said sharply. When Crawley looked at her in surprise, she said, ''You must not help anymore, sir. You will only make matters worse. Pray, heed my wishes.''

He spoke soothingly, but he did not actually promise that he would leave the marquess to manage his own affairs. A few moments later their carriage came to a halt. They could not so much as see the flagway or the houses beyond it. Their carriage was entirely cut off from the world by the fog. Crawley leaned out and spoke to the driver.

''What is this delay?''

''Accident ahead, sir. Nothing very serious, just a tangle. Daresay they didn't see each other for the fog.

It's thick as cotton wool out here. I didn't ought to have come this way, sir, but I thought we'd avoid some of the traffic from the theaters and Piccadilly if we cut along lower down. Forgot it would only get thicker by the river. Sorry, sir.''

"That's all right. We are not in any great hurry. If you need to call up a link boy to light the way for you, do so.''

"Aye, sir,'' the coachman said.

They were on their way again not long after that, and if the journey was not as quick as Gillian might have wished, she did not really mind. She liked Crawley and felt safe in his company, and her uncle provided a buffer so that she might talk only when she wished to. Her thoughts were in a jumble. She knew now that she loved Thorne, and she knew, too, despite what the others thought, that there would be nothing anyone could do to make matters better. Dorinda would marry the marquess, because Dorinda was determined to do so and because Estrid and the duke would see that no one interfered with this betrothal.

They reached Park Street to discover the others there ahead of them, and to Gillian's surprise the house was in an uproar. The disturbance appeared to have nothing to do with Dorinda's betrothal, however, for Blalock greeted them at the door with the information that Miss Clementina had been took real bad with the influenza and they'd had to have the doctor for the baby as well.

"Influenza!'' Gillian exclaimed, looking at him in horror. "But people die of influenza!''

"Oh, aye, they do,'' Blalock said, "but if I may be so bold, m'lady, the case is not so dire as that. To be sure, there was some concern earlier, what with Miss Prynne and Miss Casey both insisting the doctor should be sent for at once, but a saline draught produced excellent results in both patients and the doctor assures us that they both will survive the ordeal. Not but what her ladyship was put into a rare passion when she learned that the little one was ill. Turned pale as death herself, she did. And his lordship was in a pucker as well.''

"His lordship? Is my father at home, then?''

"Yes, m'lady. Everyone is in the third drawing room. But it isn't so much having sickness in the house, if I might say so, m'lady, as . . . well, it is not my position to say . . ."

"Blalock, for the love of heaven, what is it?"

"Well, my lady, if I might put the matter delicately, his lordship were a trifle put out before ever he learned there was sickness in the house. His last words before he ordered Lady Marrick to come to him the moment she assured herself of her children's well-being were that it needed only this! I am sure I had no notion of what he meant, however."

Glancing at her companions, Gillian began to thank them for their escort, but Vellacott cut her off at once.

"If you think we are going to miss any of this, you just think again, my girl. You might find yourself in need of a champion or two, in any case. If Marrick is put out, he won't like the fact that you didn't come home with the others."

"He probably will not have noticed, sir," she said.

They entered the drawing room in the midst of what was only too clearly a confrontation between Marrick and his lady. Dorinda stood to one side, apparently trying to make herself invisible, and Marrick was bellowing at the top of his lungs. Gillian had expected to find Dawlish, Corbin, and even Thorne there, but none of them were present.

Marrick shouted, "A fine thing, madam, for your husband to learn in a club card room of your doings, from not one helpful friend but three! You will cease to pretend you know nothing of this business and tell me a round tale, or by God—"

"Or by God, what, sir?" Estrid demanded, arms akimbo. "Here I arrive home to find my children at death's door—your heir, I might remind you—and do you care for their safety? No, sir, you make wild accusations about your wife. And in front of your daughter at that—your daughter, I might remind you, who has just this night become betrothed to the Marquess of Thorne."

Marrick waved this news off with a rude gesture. "The devil take the marquess. If Dorinda thinks to wed him, she is all about in her head. From what I've seen, that young man likes nothing better than to see a young woman make a cake of herself over him and then send her packing. I want to know about you, madam, and that damned fellow you were dancing with all night at Ranelagh. And I'll have a round tale, or by God, you'll rue the day!''

Gillian had stopped with the others upon the threshold, and at these words she felt Vellacott start beside her. She looked at him, but he was watching Marrick. Crawley was silent. Gillian saw Dorinda gazing at her with a look of triumph in her eyes, and was conscious of an urge to stride across the room and strangle her. She repressed it and turned her attention firmly to Estrid, who was fairly sputtering in her fury.

''You dare to threaten me, sir! You dare! Well, I would have preferred to make a private conversation of this, for I am not one to wash my linen in public, but you have asked for a round tale, and so you shall have one. You, sir, married me only because I would not go to your bed without you first put a ring on my finger, and once we were wed, I kept my part of the bargain by providing you with the heir you had wanted for so long. And what was my reward for that? Neglect, sir, that is what! You scarcely even stop to pass the time of day, let alone to talk to me. You ignore your son, and you ignore your estates, leaving everything to your daughter to run. And you deceived me, sir, letting me believe you were wealthier than what you are, never telling me that full half of what I thought was yours was your daughter's, so that I made a complete fool of myself.''

''Look here, Estrid, we are not talking about me,'' the earl said, red to his ears as he became aware of his increased audience. ''I questioned your maid, and what did I discover but that you've been sneaking out of the house at night to make some sort of damned assignation with the fellow. I won't have it. By God, I won't! Who the devil is your lover?''

''I wouldn't tell you if I knew,'' she cried. ''He is not my lover, for all that, but merely a kind and charming gentleman who tells me I am beautiful and thoughtful, and a wonderful person. He tells me things I need to hear from someone, sir, and since I never hear them from you, why I shall continue to—"

"But in a graveyard, Estrid? For the love of God, can you not find a better place to meet than that?"

"Indeed, sir, I met him tonight, as your friends have so kindly informed you, and it was delightful to be held in a man's arms and have him whisper lovely things in my ear."

" 'Tis for your husband to whisper such things!" the earl bellowed. "Now, listen to me, Estrid—"

"When was the last time you whispered such things, my lord? When? I want a man who will take care of me, who won't expect me to look after everything myself. And if I have to find him outside my own home, at least I have found some pleasure—"

"By God, I'll kill the villain. He's no business to be making love to my wife, and so I'll tell him, and as for you—"

"Marrick, wait," Vellacott said quietly.

Gillian, standing in mute shock and having been wishing for the past few minutes that she were anywhere else, turned sharply to look at her uncle. From the moment Estrid had mentioned a graveyard, she had suspended her thoughts, not daring to allow the one tickling the back of her mind to take form. But now, looking at her uncle, she knew what he would say.

"I am the devil you seek," he told the earl.

Estrid gasped.

"By God, sir," Marrick said furiously, "if I had my sword—"

"I'd hope you would keep it sheathed," Vellacott said, smiling at him, in no way abashed by his anger. "I am in the habit, as you know, of visiting my first wife's grave whenever I come to London. I did so the night I arrived, and I came upon a beautiful woman who was there to visit her first husband. She did not know me. The graveyard was very dark. I spoke quietly when I first made known my presence, and I did not introduce myself. I did not know her until I heard her speak later in this house, when I confess, I was ripe for mischief. She has never known my identity. She was lonely and I provided a bit of romance, but there was nothing out of the way. If you wish to mend matters, you have only to escort her yourself henceforth.''

Marrick was perfectly still for a moment when Vellacott finished speaking, and no one else said a word. Then, turning to his wife, the earl said, ''Forgive me, Estrid. Since I shouted my mistaken beliefs at you in front of all these people, I will do you the courtesy to say here and now that it was not only that I wanted you in my bed. I fell in love with you, madam, with your frank, open ways, and with your incredible beauty.'' He cast a quick glance at Gillian, then added, ''I loved my first wife very much, but her father was not a man I could like. Vellacott made it plain from the outset that he had no faith in his daughter's choice of a husband. He was willing to indulge her but not to trust me with his lands or his money. So he tied everything up in her and her children and sent his own man to keep watch over everything. I soon fell out of the habit of attempting to call any of the tunes for myself, even where my own was concerned. I grew instead into the habit of letting her have her own way, of letting Hollingston do as he pleased, and later of allowing Gillian to take over where her mother had left off. Then, when you wanted to run things in the house, it just seemed as if it was all too much for me. I didn't know how to call the tunes anymore by then, so I felt trapped between the two of you.''

''Well, my lord,'' Estrid said in an acid tone, ''it's not been so easy for me, either, if you must know. After all, I had lived with a man who ordered everything, whose servants treated me as if I were a duchess, and who never let me want for anything until he had the misfortune to die and all his fortune was found to be entailed, with only a widow's jointure to keep me and my girls. When you tumbled onto my doorstep, it was as if Providence had dropped you there. I'll tell you to your face, it wouldn't have mattered then if you had been a Gypsy. I'd have taken you once I learned you were wealthy, but as it chances, I . . . well, I found I loved you, too, and that's the word with no bark on it.''

Marrick looked at the others. "If you will have the goodness to excuse us, I believe my wife and I have private matters to discuss. As for you, Vellacott, your mischief here is done. My wife will not require your kindness anymore."

To Gillian's surprise her uncle chuckled. "Do you mean to bar me from the house, Marrick?"

"No, no," the earl said. "I believe you've done me a service, so you will always be welcome, but you'll have to visit your Millie's grave alone. Come, my dear," he added to Estrid, "we will continue this discussion in your boudoir, I think."

When they had gone, Gillian said quietly, "The word with no bark on it, that's what Estrid said, and that is what should be the case with all of us. Dorinda, I want to talk to you!"

"Well, I do not want to talk to you," Dorinda said. She had stood staring at her mother and stepfather with wide eyes, but now, with Gillian advancing angrily upon her, she gathered her forces to meet the attack, saying hastily, "It is no good looking at me like that. You had every chance with him. You like plain speaking, so I shall tell you to your head that you were a fool to let him go. He may not be as handsome as Corbin or as pretty behaved, but he is a marquess, and he has money. You didn't want him, so you need not think you can keep me from taking him."

"You tricked him! It is as clear as can be that somehow you played a may game with those notes that were sent to us, and you certainly turned your domino inside out, for I saw that with my own eyes. It will not do, Dorinda."

"Do you think he does not like me, Gillian?" Dorinda demanded, and when Gillian could not answer her, she added, "There, you see, you know he does. And furthermore, I will have you know that he escorted us home, he and Lord Dawlish. That ridiculous Corbin went off in a huff. And Thorne was as kind as could be. He said he would come round to discuss matters tomorrow, so you see he will want to be talking of settlements, and I shall certainly not deny him the pleasure." And before Gillian could say another word, she turned and left the room.

"So much for that," Crawley murmured.

Gillian turned ruefully to the two men. "What an arch-wife I must appear to be. I do apologize. And though I confess that I do not know whether I am on my head or on my heels, does not this little scene we have just witnessed prove that plain speaking is truly the best way? Had they not said all they did to each other, my father and Estrid would still be traveling on different roads." She sighed. "I declare, if I had any sense whatever, after all this, I would marry the first man willing to swear an oath always to tell me precisely what was in his mind!"

Crawley promptly fell to his knees and put his hand over his heart. "Permit me to tell you that I am that man, *dear* lady. I tell you flat out that I want to marry you only for the sake of your vast fortune and all it can do for my humble self."

"Don't be so absurd, sir," she begged.

"Aha," he said, getting to his feet, "so you have learned nothing whatever from all this and still offer a man Spanish coin. You ought to be ashamed of yourself."

Stung more than she cared to admit by his careless words, she said, "The notion tempts me, sir. Indeed it does, for I swear I mean it when I say I prefer candor to equivocation."

"Precisely my point," Crawley said. " 'Tis why I repeat the obvious fact that your fortune would make it possible for me to live in the style I like best. You cannot marry Thorne, after all, for no amount of plain speaking will change what has come to pass this night. The duke will not allow him to create another scandal, and for him to jilt your sister would certainly cause one. I do not ask for your answer at once, but I do ask you to consider it." His tone gentled considerably when he added, "You will be happier in a household of your own than if you must continue to live with your stepmother after Dorinda has married Thorne. Just one more moment, Vellacott, and I will come with you, but I want to say first, my lady, that I will return first thing tomorrow morning to see if you are a woman of your word.''

Certain now that he was serious, Gillian took care not to offend him, saying only that she would think carefully on the matter. The two men took their leave then, but Vellacott turned back long enough to say, "Don't dismiss him out of hand, m' dear. Only think what your life will be like if you refuse him."

She did and her thoughts were not pleasant. She went upstairs to look in on Clementina, and found Meggie sitting beside her bed.

"Go away, Miss Gillian. It wouldn't do for you to catch it from her. She'll do. She's sleeping like a lamb now, and the little one will get better as well. Go to sleep yourself."

Instead Gillian went to try to have it out again with Dorinda, but it was no use. Dorinda not only refused to let her in, but shrieked at her through the door that she meant to be a marchioness and live in a fine country house, and that was that.

Alone in her own bed, Gillian stared at the ceiling for a long time, thinking about what a mull she had made of her life through not having had the courage of her convictions, just as Thorne had said. She had been a fool, she thought, to insist upon crying off before finding out what his true feelings were—at least, she had if his friends were right—just as he had been a fool in so many more ways. Counting them, she sank deeper and deeper into depression until at last she cried herself to sleep, and when she awoke the following morning, she discovered that somehow, overnight, she had decided to accept Crawley's offer.

13

THORNE HAD SPENT the night at his house in Brook Street. His first inclination, to dash after Gillian, had been impossible at the time. His second, to drown his sorrows in a few more bottles, he had rejected out of hand. Realizing that he would do better to think things out carefully before taking any action at all, he had held his emotions in check long enough to see Lady Marrick and Dorinda to their doorstep, but he had refused their invitation to step inside with as much politeness as he could muster and had taken himself directly home afterward.

Having spent a practically sleepless night trying to think of a way out of his predicament that would neither ruin Miss Ponderby nor alienate his father, in the blazing light of mid-morning he awoke from his uneasy slumbers to the realization that Gillian had been right about one thing at least. He had got into the fix he was in by not speaking out at once.

He had taken snuff from the first moment of learning that Gillian dared to interest herself in the running of what he had thought were her father's lands. The subsequent discovery that she had every right to interest herself, and indeed, had more authority to effect change than he did himself, had been a bitter pill to swallow. He had behaved badly, and he knew it. Moreover, he was rapidly coming to understand what she had meant when she accused him of making judgments before he had all his facts and to believe that he was as responsible as the duke was—if not more so—for their present uncomfortable situation.

But here he was, sitting over his late breakfast, thinking of Gillian instead of putting his mind to the problem at hand, which was how to extricate himself from the tangle that had been woven about him. He was fairly certain now that Dorinda, for reasons of her own, had been the manipulator behind the scenes the previous night. He had blamed his cousin Dawlish, but Dawlish had certainly never intended him to wed Miss Ponderby.

He was still picking at his food when his footman brought in a tray with the morning post, and he waved it aside. "Just leave it. I'll look through it later," he said.

"Begging your pardon, m'lord, but Lord Dawlish is below. I told him you wasn't at home, but he insists on speaking to you."

Thorne sighed. "Very well, send him up. And you might as well bring him coffee, Ferry, and anything else you think he might like." When Dawlish entered a moment later, Thorne looked at him from beneath his brows and said, "Mighty formal this morning, Peregrine. You needn't stand there looking as though you expect to be flogged. Sit down. Ferry will bring coffee."

"I don't want anything, Josh. I came to apologize, and if you're going to be kind about it, it will make it much worse. I wasn't certain you'd even agree to see me."

"Much you would have cared for that. Sit down, man. I cannot abide your fidgeting."

"Oh, very well," Dawlish said, flinging himself into a chair, "but I never meant it, you know. I asked that idiotic chit to write a note, telling her what was planned, but I never thought she'd play all-hide with the meeting place and then use our plan to trap you into marrying her."

Thorne, realizing in a flash that he had been right about the real plan, had to fight to keep his temper, and he could see by Dawlish's widening eyes that he was only partially successful. "So this farrago can be laid at your door," he said, his words measured, his tone carefully calm.

Dawlish squirmed in his chair and reached out toward the silver tray full of letters near his arm, fingering them nervously. "I said I was sorry, Josh. We only wanted to help."

"I see," Thorne said grimly. "Well, I'll tell you what

I think of your help." And he proceeded to give his cousin the trimming of his young life in a calm but deadly voice. If it did nothing else, it relieved Thorne's pent-up feelings, and he felt a good deal better by the time he ran out of things to say.

Dawlish sat silently through it all, making no attempt to vindicate himself or to stem the tide of words, but they seemed to flow around and over him, leaving little impression. He continued to fiddle with the letters on the tray, pushing them this way and that, looking more at them than at his cousin, though he did glance at Thorne whenever he was commanded to look at him. Then, suddenly, he looked sharply at one of the letters uncovered by his manipulations, snatched it up, and said, "Why the devil would Crawley be writing to you, for goodness' sake? We are to meet him in a couple of hours, are we not?"

"I shall not have time for that today, I fear. Are you listening to what I am saying to you, Peregrine?"

"Oh yes, of course, Josh. Sorry. Only I couldn't think why he would write to you, you know, when we see him all the time. It might be important, don't you think?"

"I don't care if it is. Crawley's problems have nothing to do with me. I have matters of my own to attend to. I am not going to marry that girl, Perry, but I must get out of it as gracefully as I can for the benefit of everyone concerned."

"Oh, yes, of course. If there is anything I can do—"

"Don't suggest it! In fact, if you have nothing better to do than to sit goggling at me, I wish you would leave. I am going to Langshire House. Can I drop you anywhere?"

"No, no. I'm just going 'round the corner to call on a friend. I won't keep you any longer. And, Josh, truly—"

"I know," Thorne said gruffly. "You just wanted to help." He watched him go, then got to his feet, intending to order his chaise at once, but his gaze fell upon the letter Dawlish had drawn apart from the others. It was Crawley's bold handwriting, certainly. He picked it up. No doubt the man needed a loan and didn't like to ask again in person, though that was not really his way of going about such things. Breaking the seal, Thorne read swiftly, his fury growing with ever word.

"Josh," the note said, "I've asked Lady Gillian to marry me. My affairs are in such a tangle that only money will set them right. I can't wait to see if Dacres comes up to scratch, nor can I afford to purchase a special license here in London. Cheaper ones may be had at Fledborough in Nottinghamshire—in fact, the cheapest in all England, I am told—so we will go there today. She agrees it will be best, in view of what transpired between you and Miss Ponderby, and she don't want a fancy wedding anyway. Sorry, old fellow, but I promise I'll look after her, and it will solve all our problems. Yours, Crawler."

Gritting his teeth, Thorne crumpled the letter into a ball and threw it onto the table. His first inclination was to find Crawley and throttle him. His second was to find Gillian and strangle her. He glanced at the clock on the breakfast room mantel and saw that it was nearly eleven o'clock. No doubt they were long gone. They would take the Great North Road, which he knew well, but there was no point in chasing after them until he had his own affairs in hand.

Shouting for Ferry, he snatched up the note again, deciding it would be far more pleasant to stuff it down Crawley's throat when he had the chance than merely to leave it. He had no worries that his servants would read it. They knew better. When Ferry entered, Thorne said, "I shall want my phaeton and the chestnuts ready for me in two hours' time. If I am not back by then, tell them to keep them moving but not to unharness them. I shall want them ready to leave at a moment's notice. And have my curricle brought 'round at once. I am going to Langshire House."

He wasted no time, leaving the curricle in the drive at Langshire House with Tim Cooley to walk his horses. He found his father in the library.

"Sir," he said, walking swiftly toward the duke, "I must talk with you."

"Come in, Josiah, and sit down. I have been expecting you. I've no doubt you will wish to discuss your marriage settlements and other such things. You will want your allowance increased—''

"No, sir," Thorne said, drawing up a chair, "I do not. I ought to have spoken up long before this, but I have really only just come to realize that I have never made my feelings about certain matters plain to you. I wish to do so now. Afterward, if you still insist upon it, we can discuss whatever you like."

The duke, instead of taking him to task for his boldness, as he had half expected him to do, merely gestured for him to continue. Taking the bull by the horns, he did so, and forty minutes later left the house with a spring in his step, but with the knowledge that a much more difficult task lay ahead of him.

When he drew up in Park Street, he saw that someone was at the door before him and fairly gnashed his teeth at the thought that he might have to wait a time before he could be private with Miss Ponderby, Lady Marrick, and the earl. But then he saw, just as the door opened, that the other visitor was only Corbin.

Leaping down from the curricle the moment Cooley had run to the leaders' heads, Thorne hurried up the steps. The butler and Corbin had seen him and they waited. Corbin regarded him with a rather wary expression.

Thorne didn't mince words. "If you would repay me for the tangle you and Mongrel managed to create for me, you will take yourself off and let me deal with this alone."

Corbin smoothed his elegant neckcloth and removed a bit of lint from his dark sleeve. "Well now, Josh, that's just what I can't do," he said. "I believe I've as much a stake as you do in the outcome of this business. Moreover, if you were hoping to speak with Marrick or his lady, you are balked at the outset. They are not here."

Dismayed, Thorne turned to the butler, but Blalock was nodding his head. "He is quite right, m'lord. Lord Marrick and his lady have gone for a drive in Richmond Park and do not expect to return to the house until sometime late this evening."

Thorne was at a standstill, but Corbin said calmly, "We will see Miss Ponderby, if you please, Blalock. At once."

The butler hesitated. "I do not think that would be allowed, sir, if I might be so bold as to say so, there being no proper chaperon on the premises, so to speak."

"Dash it all, man, we don't want a chaperon. Be damnably in the way, I can tell you. Miss Ponderby is here, is she not?"

"Oh, yes, sir, but—"

"Then you just take us up to see her. No need to announce us, either, for we are not going to give that young woman a single chance to play least in sight. I daresay she'll be in the morning room at this hour, will she not?"

The butler, faced with two gentlemen who clearly meant to have their way, proprieties notwithstanding, said weakly, "I ought to call the footmen to put you out, m'lord."

"If you think they can," Corbin said, "by all means call them. Haven't had a good set-to in days. Daresay the exercise will do us good." His tone of voice was no longer the lazy drawl he affected but a crisp, challenging one, and Thorne hid a smile, knowing Corbin was no ordinary Bond Street lounger.

Blalock capitulated. "The young ladies are in the morning room, sir. I might remind you that Miss Clementina has been very ill and is by no means recovered." He paused, but when his words appeared to have no effect, said, "I will take you up."

Thorne had not the least notion what he was going to do, but he no longer objected to Corbin's presence. He certainly could not demand a private interview with Miss Ponderby when neither of her parents was in the house. He and Corbin were stretching the bounds of propriety to breaking point, as it was, by seeking her out with only her little sister to protect her reputation.

They did not speak as they followed the butler upstairs, and the gallery was carpeted, so their steps were silent ones. The morning room door stood ajar, and quite clearly they heard Clementina say, "Oh, Dorrie, you are always so wonderfully kind to me! To think you have been reading aloud for an hour without so much as a complaint, all because I was upset to learn that Gillian had gone. You are truly the best of sisters.''

Thorne grimaced, but to his shock the next thing they heard was Clementina crying out, "Oh, Dorrie, what is wrong? Why do you cry like that? You said it was your fault that Gillian had gone away, but that cannot be so. Oh, pray do not cry!''

Corbin jumped forward to stop Blalock before he could be seen from inside the room. Catching the butler's arm, he signaled to him to remain silent, but grimaced at Thorne, making plain his distaste for any eavesdropping, and his intention nevertheless to engage in a bit of it.

Thorne had much the same mixed feelings, but he had heard Dorinda mutter something and Clementina respond, and he realized that he wanted desperately to hear what Miss Ponderby was saying.

They moved a step nearer and heard her say, "Oh, Clemmie, I am such a wretch, but indeed, I did not know he loved her.''

"Lord Crawley? But why should that make you cry? I did not know he loved her either. In fact, I should be very surprised—''

"No, not Crawley, Thorne! But how could I know? I am not the perfect sister you believe me to be. I am utterly wicked. I cannot stand to have you think ill of me, but when you discover what I have done, you will hate me just as they all do.''

Clementina said gently, "Don't be a goose, Dorrie. I do not care a rap for what you have done. I shall always think you the very best of sisters.''

"But I am selfish and greedy. You know I am, and I cannot change, Clemmie. I do not want to spend my life making and scraping and hoping that the man I marry won't leave me with children to support as Papa did Mama. It terrifies me to think how easily that can come to pass if one is not careful. But I have done such dreadful things! And I never meant to harm her.''

"Gillian?" Clementina said. "But what have you done?''

"I tricked Thorne into a betrothal last night, with me.''

"Oh, Dorrie, no!''

"Yes, but I did not know he loved her until it was too late. I know that you said he cared for her, but when they didn't seem even to want to speak to each other, I thought you must be mistaken, but when he came to me last night—thinking I was her, you know, for I had turned my domino inside out—he called me *sweetheart* and *my love*. But by then it was too late. I had seen my chance the minute Dawlish told me what they had planned, wanting to bring his lordship and Gillian together again, you see, and I took advantage of it—just as I took advantage of seeing the newspaper office directly across the street when Mama and I went to Honiton to buy ribbons that day."

"Dorrie, you didn't! You were the one who put that notice in the papers? Oh, Dorrie, you had very much better hope that Thorne never finds out. He would be so angry with you!"

Thorne had not meant to listen so long, but had stood transfixed when he heard Dorinda say he loved Gillian. He did love her, but to hear the words spoken by someone else had been enough of a shock to stop him in his tracks for that extra, important moment. Now, exchanging a grim look with Corbin, he stepped past him into the open doorway and said, "I am afraid the hope is a forlorn one, Miss Clementina. I heard every word."

Both young ladies shrieked when they saw him, and Dorinda leapt to her feet, looking about her in panic, as though she wanted to run from the room. Before Thorne could continue, Corbin said from behind him, "You have gone your limit now, Miss Ponderby. By God, what you deserve is a good—"

"Never mind that now," Thorne said sharply. "Miss Ponderby, has Marrick sent an announcement to the papers yet?"

Dorinda, keeping a more watchful eye on Corbin than on Thorne, said, "I do not think so, sir. He and my mama left very early this morning for Richmond Park, and they did not seem to be in the least interested in any affairs but their own. But so many people heard what transpired last night—Oh, sir, can you ever forgive me? It was a dreadful thing, I know, but I—"

She had glanced at Thorne when she blurted the apology, but her gaze went swiftly back to Corbin. She was looking at him as though she had never seen him before, and indeed, Thorne thought, glancing at his friend, she had surely never seen this side of him. Corbin was standing beside him, his countenance stern and unyielding, his anger a nearly palpable thing. Thorne looked again at Dorinda, and decided he could safely take his leave. He paused only to say, "I want to be clear about this. There is no engagement between us. I am going to marry Gillian."

Dorinda turned toward him then, dismayed. "Oh, but sir, she drove out with Lord Crawley some time ago. He wrote to me saying he means to marry her, and I think from things he said before and what Gillian wrote to Clementina, that perhaps they mean to elope . . . that perhaps they are doing so even now," she added.

"Yes, I believe they are," he replied calmly. "I had a letter from Crawley this morning, informing me of the fact. It was kind of him to want to help, but I believe their marriage must be stopped, do not you, Corbin?"

Corbin glanced at him. "Oh, certainly, my dear chap. They will be bound for Gretna, I daresay."

"No, only to Nottinghamshire. Who do you suppose was kind enough to inform him that a special license might be had there more cheaply than in London?"

Corbin did not look at him. His gaze appeared still to be fixed upon Miss Ponderby.

Thorne didn't wait. He turned to Clementina. "I stand in your debt, Miss Clementina. When you are well again, I shall take you sailing on my yacht. You will enjoy that, I daresay."

"Oh, yes, sir," she exclaimed. "I should like it above all things. But please, Lord Thorne, do not be too angry with Dorinda. She is not a wicked person, truly she is not!"

He smiled. "I am not in the least angry with her now, child, but you may have to protect her from Corbin. He looks fit to throttle her. I leave them in your most capable hands, however, for I must catch a pair of elopers."

Clementina smiled back at him. "And you will not

forget, sir, that you are to take me on your yacht one day. Promise!''

"Oh, I will not forget, my dear. I always pay my debts, as Crawley is about to learn to his cost.''

He left them then, hurried down the stairs and out to the street, only to be hailed by Mr. Vellacott, who was strolling toward him on the flagway.

"Where are you off to in such a dither?'' Vellacott demanded, raising his quizzing glass to peer at him.

"To catch your niece and keep her from marrying Crawley.''

"Marrying Crawley? But I doubt she has any such intention. Are you quite sure?''

Thorne shot him a mocking smile. "I am very sure that she will be a widow before nightfall if she does so.''

"Dear me,'' said Mr. Vellacott, slipping his glass back into his fob pocket, "how very fierce you are, sir.''

"I am learning the art of plain speaking, Vellacott. Pray congratulate me, and excuse me. I am off. Tim, release them!''

Gillian's intent to accept Crawley's offer of marriage lasted only until he arrived in Park Street that morning. Her father and stepmother had left the house before she came down to breakfast, and she found herself the sole occupant of the morning room. Still, she found it nearly impossible to think straight about what she ought to do.

Living with her father and Estrid, despite the present truce, did not appear to be an acceptable answer to her dilemma. Even if she and Estrid could work out an agreement between them, she was not certain she could continue to live in amity with her father if he had decided, as it appeared he had done, to resume control of his wife, his family, and his estates. Either he and his daughter would be constantly at outs with each other, or Gillian would find herself bowing more and more to parental rule. That, of all things, she would dislike the most, after so many years of making decisions and having the freedom to do as she pleased where the estate was concerned. Just the thought of trying to explain to him what she had done with regard to the new seed would be both difficult and frustrating. The earl thought of Mr. Coke of Norfolk only as an excellent host for the annual sheep shearing at Holkham Hall, or the amusing shooting parties at Longford. If he knew of Coke's vast reputation for agricultural innovation, Gillian was not aware of it. And if she mentioned Lord Percival Worth's experiments to him, he would merely say that the son of the Duke of Morency ought to have better things to do with his time.

Thinking of Lord Percival reminded her that Thorne had been visiting at Braunton Burrows the day they had met, but her musings were interrupted just then by Blalock, who informed her in disapproving accents that Lord Crawley had called and was insisting that his visit was expected. "I told him that her ladyship was not at home, m'lady, but he insists that it is you he has called to see. Shall I send him away?"

Gillian sighed, knowing she could not marry Crawley. "No, Blalock, show him up. I will send him away myself."

When Crawley entered the room and moved forward to greet her, she held up a hand. "Stop where you are, sir. Blalock is already distressed that I have agreed to see you at all, and I should not like him carrying tales of me to my father just at present. I ought to have called my abigail to come in, but I did not, to spare your feelings."

He grimaced. "That sounds very much like a refusal, my dear. I hope it is not."

"It is, sir. I have thought and thought. One moment your proposition seems like an answer to my every problem, but the next I see only a lifetime of misery for the both of us."

"I would make you a much more pleasant husband than Thorne, my dear," Crawley said, smiling ruefully at her.

She smiled back. "I do not doubt that, sir. One does not think of his lordship as the sort to be a *pleasant* husband. I am sure he would be demanding, and arrogant, and ungrateful, and that he would shout at me when I was only trying to tell him something he ought to know, and . . . and, oh dear, Crawley, I fear that I have left my handkerchief abovestairs. Oh, pray—"

Breaking off, she turned away so that he would not see her tears, but when a large white handkerchief was pressed into her hand, she took it gratefully and blew her nose.

"You love him very much," Crawley said.

"Oh, yes," she said, sniffing. Dabbing her eyes, she turned back, forcing herself to overcome her tears. "Forgive my foolishness. I am not usually such a watering pot. They came on so quickly, I didn't realize. . . . But you must see that I cannot marry you, sir. It would not be fair. I like you very much, but I could never love you like that . . . and . . ."

Making a sound very much like a growl, Crawley turned away from her, muttering, "Your stepsister ought to be soundly thrashed, and I hope that when—But never mind that," he added briskly. "I'll tell you what you need, ma'am, and that is an outing. I've my phaeton below with a fresh team hitched to it, and I should like nothing better than to take you for a nice, refreshing drive. The day is a splendid one, so do not tell me you won't come. 'Tis bad enough that you have capsized all my hopes of becoming a wealthy landowner. Don't tell me you won't even come for a drive with me. You needn't worry about the proprieties, for I've my tiger with me today."

He looked at her in much the same way as a puppy hopeful of a scrap from the table, and she could not help but give a watery laugh. "Almost you persuade me, sir, but I should not."

"I see how it is," he said. "You prefer to wait to have it out with your stepsister, or perhaps to offer her your congratulations on her excellent generalship. You may tell her for me that I think she should go at once and offer her services to that rascal Bonaparte. He might appreciate her methods."

Gillian had not thought about attempting to confront Dorinda again, and she was not by any means sure she wanted even to talk to her now. There was nothing to be done. The betrothal was a fact, and the duke would not allow Thorne to back down. Dorinda would merely flaunt her new status. It was not a picture Gillian could contemplate at the moment. Impulsively she said, "I will go for a drive with you, sir. Indeed, I welcome the opportunity to escape from the house for a time. Only let me leave word for Clementina. She has been ill, you know, and I don't want her to fret if I do not go to her." Dorinda would sit with Clementina, and Gillian did not think it would be good for the little girl if Gillian were there with them as well. Not if all she wanted to do was to scratch Dorinda's eyes out.

"An excellent notion. If you do not mind, I will also leave her a message to wish her better health, and another to Miss Ponderby, to wish her . . . well, I shan't say what I wish her," he added with a comical grimace.

When the notes were written and Gillian had collected her things, she let Crawley assist her to the seat of his curricle. He climbed up beside her, called to his tiger to set them loose, and they were off. Gillian settled back against her seat to enjoy the warmth of the sun on her face. Crawley was fully occupied for some time with traffic, and so she had no need to maintain a flow of conversation, and by the time she realized that he was not merely driving her around the block or into Hyde Park, they had reached the Edgware Bar and he had drawn up to pay their toll at the gate.

Gillian waited until they were clear of it, and then, fully conscious of the tiger perched behind them, she said in a casual manner, "Are you perchance abducting me, sir?"

Crawley grinned at her. "I had thought about it," he said, "but they've developed a nasty habit of hanging men who abduct heiresses, and I do not think your papa can be depended upon to look kindly upon my suit. Were that not the case, I'd have snapped at the chance to carry you off, for I've decided I shall be happy only as a wealthy man. I must tell you, however, that I hope you will tell Thorne, when the opportunity arises for you to do so, that you have agreed to make me a very happy one."

Her heart seemed suddenly to be pounding in her chest. "I do not think I understand you, sir. Even if there should be cause for me to tell him such a thing, I could not do so."

Crawley's gaze rolled upward. "Then may I tell you it has been a pleasure knowing you, ma'am, and that if there is indeed an afterlife, I look forward to renewing our acquaintance."

Watching him carefully, Gillian said, "Do you anticipate an early demise, sir? You look very healthy to me."

"Thorne will most likely hasten my departure from this earth, ma'am, when he catches us, if you say I carried you off."

A sigh of relief escaped her. "You expect him to follow us, then. But my dear sir, why should he?"

"Well, he'd better, considering that I was kind enough to send him a letter informing him of my intention to make you my bride—an intent, I feel bound to warn you, that I said was a mutual one. Mongrel promised faithfully to see that Thorne read the damned thing before he left the house today, so I dashed well hope he follows us, or else, my dear ma'am, we may very shortly find ourselves deep in the suds."

Gillian burst into a peal of delighted laughter.

14

CRAWLEY TURNED INTO the New Road toward Islington, and his attention was instantly claimed by his team, for suddenly there were shouts ahead and a large herd of cattle thronged the street. The air was foul with them, but drovers quickly cleared the way, and the traffic began to move again.

"Bound for Smithfield Market, I don't wonder," Crawley said a moment later. "Daresay that lot's bound for slaughter."

"What a pleasant outing we are having, to be sure,"

Gillian said, grimacing at him. "Pray, where are *we* bound?"

He grinned back at her. "Well, ma'am, in the letter I left for Josh, I said we were bound for Fledborough in my own county of Nottinghamshire, because special licenses may be had cheaply there. That means the Great North Road, of course, and we are taking the shortest route I know to meet it, through Barnet."

"I do not believe I have had the pleasure of visiting Barnet," Gillian said. "Is it far?"

"Oh, a matter of some ten or eleven miles," he said, grinning at her. " 'Tis a fine place and historical too. A famous battle was fought there during the Wars of the Roses, and the folks have put up an obelisk in honor of it. Town sits on a hilltop, so there are some splendid views to be had."

"My dear sir, I am not particularly interested in fine views or in historical obelisks. I am persuaded that we ought to turn back at once, before this plan goes the way of your previous schemes. Goodness knows what my family will be thinking when I fail to return, but you may count upon Dorinda, at least, to see to it that your plan does not succeed."

"Corbin has promised to look after the fair Dorinda," Crawley said. "We need worry only about Josh, and I doubt we need to worry about him too soon. We left your house at ten, and Mongrel gave it as his considered opinion that Josh wouldn't stir out before noon, so that gives us a couple of hours on him. You may be easy, believe me. I don't want him catching us too soon."

With some asperity Gillian said, "Be easy, sir? That is just what I cannot be! You must know better than anyone what his lordship's temper is like."

"None better," Crawley said cheerfully. "He will be ripe to murder me if we have read him correctly."

"And me," Gillian said. "You did say you had done your best to make it look as if I had agreed to this mad plan of yours."

"I did, but I took the lion's share of the credit, just in case he didn't believe me."

"Good God, sir, but you must know that if he does care as you seem to think he does, he really will murder you!"

"My dependence is entirely upon you, ma'am. You must distract him long enough for me to take to my heels."

He was laughing at her, and she knew it, but she could not be easy. They were coming into Islington, and though she knew he must be right and it was far too soon to expect the marquess to be on their trail, she could not help looking back over her shoulder as they passed the Peacock. There was no sign of him.

Crawley said in a different, more serious tone, "Look here, you must not be on the fret, you know. I think you know Josh cares for you. The problem with him is that—"

"That he likes to have his own way about things," Gillian said grimly, "and I cannot see that this idiotic plan of yours will change that."

"Did you hear how he introduced your stepsister to his father last night?" Crawley asked.

"He said she was the woman he meant to marry," Gillian said in a small voice.

"I would wager every opportunity for wealth to come my way for a year—well, a month, anyway—that he was speaking of you when he said that. You turned and ran the minute you saw Dorinda, so you might not have seen the look on Josh's face, but if he knew it was *her* face he was going to see when he said those words, you may call me anything you like."

"But what can that matter," Gillian said, "if his father will not allow him to go back on his word?"

"Josh can handle his father," Crawley said. "He just sometimes needs a little prodding before he will take his courage in hand and do it. You mightn't think it when you hear the old blighter speak, but he's mighty fond of Josh, for all he gives him a wigging nearly every time they meet."

"Yes, I have noticed the affection between them," Gillian said. She thought for a moment about what he had said, then said, "Do you mean to say, sir, that you have abducted me—for without mincing words, that is what this is—merely to stir his lordship to rebel against his father?"

Crawley's amusement was clear. "I don't know that I

would put it that way myself, ma'am, but I suppose that's it. At best, Josh would think the matter out from every angle and consider all the things that might happen, and chances are, he would murder the fair Dorinda before anything else was accomplished. And if we hadn't acted quickly, your father would have put a notice in the papers today. Once I saw what took place with your stepmama last night, I thought we might have a respite, since Marrick had his own affairs to consider and mightn't send the thing out first thing. But even if he did, you know, I doubt, after last time, that the paper will put it in before clearing it with Josh or his father. I have it on excellent authority that his grace came the duke over the poor fellow who printed the last one. So if Josh moves quickly, I think the betrothal can be scotched.''

"He will not like having his hand forced, I think."

"We will concern ourselves with that when the time comes," Crawley said grandly. "I hope he comes up with us by Welwyn. This team is good for two stages at an easy pace, but I shouldn't like to try taking them as far as Stevenage. If I wind them, Corbin will have my liver. Moreover, we'd never get back before midnight, and I fear that your reputation—"

"Oh, are we concerned now about my reputation?" Gillian said with a sigh. "I'd never have thought it, sir."

"Are you vexed? I'm sorry if you are. You needn't be, you know. I promise you, we'll make it all right and tight again."

She sat back to try to enjoy the scenery, hoping very much that Thorne would come after her. She could think of no better end to the crazy journey than for him to take her in his arms and tell her he loved her. On the other hand, she could not convince herself that anything had really changed between them. He still would resent the fact that he could control neither her money nor the vast estates that would one day be his. The very thought that he must wait for the duke's death in order to come into his own, she knew, did not sit comfortably with him. It was a pity, she thought, that the two men could not simply divide up the wealth now and each have a part. Or that she could not give half of her fortune to him. But such solutions would not work. Neither Langshire nor Thorne would want half a loaf, and she knew her grandfather would not have approved of any plan that would allow her to give her fortune away to someone not of Vellacott blood.

The battleground Crawley had mentioned was actually to be found at Hadley Green, half a mile north of Barnet, where he proceeded at once to put her in possession of the details of a battle that had taken place there well over three hundred years before. Gillian paid little heed. She was not interested in the houses of York or Lancaster, only in the House of Langshire.

Though Crawley kept his team to a pace that not only spared them but that compared more to a snail's crawl than the speed expected of such a team, they had passed through Hatfield and come within three miles of Welwyn before Gillian, looking back for what must have been the hundredth time, saw a cloud of dust in the distance and felt a leap of hope in her heart.

Before she could speak, the tiger riding behind them said, "Be a carriage coming up fast, m'lord. Best hug the shoulder."

"Could it be the royal mail?" Crawley asked, grinning.

"No, m'lord. Not near enough dust nor enough speed. Looks to be a sportin' carriage, and a right fast one at that."

Gillian looked at Crawley and saw his grin. "Is it he?"

"No way of knowing till he's upon us," Crawley said. "I'd have thought it would be another half hour to an hour, but if he's been driving like the devil—which I'll be bound he has—it's Josh, all right. Shall we try to outrun him? I daresay we might beat him to Welwyn. These horses have got to be a good sight fresher than his. He's probably driving job horses by now, for if he hasn't changed at every stage, I don't know him, though come to think of it, I daresay the duke keeps his own teams on this road. It is also the way to Langshire, after all."

Gillian was paying him no heed. She had turned around on her seat and was watching the carriage behind them. And it was as well for them that there was no turnpike ahead just then, for the tiger was likewise looking to the rear. But Crawley did not increase his speed, so it was not long before the other team caught up with them.

Crawley pulled to the side as if to let the faster team pass him, but the other carriage swept past and swerved, forcing him to bring his horses plunging to a standstill. "By God," he muttered, "if that were anyone but Josh, I'd have a few sharp things to say to the fellow."

But it was Thorne. Tossing his lines to Tim Cooley, he jumped down and strode back to their carriage with murder in his eyes. "Come down from there, my lad," he said to Crawley. "I'd like a word or two with you in private. Behind that hedge yonder looks to be a good place for a quiet chat."

"Does it?" Crawley said, his tone even, all sign of his previous humor gone.

Gillian held her breath. She was not at all certain what she ought to do. She could not allow Thorne to have any sort of "chat" with Crawley, for she knew perfectly well what he meant to do to him. But she was not by any means certain that she wanted to talk to him herself in the mood he was in. It was a pity, she thought, that they had not reached the safety of Welwyn High Street, for even Thorne must have thought twice about starting a brawl there. But here on the highroad she was afraid he might.

Thorne said, "Do you come down, or do I come fetch you?"

"We're fairly evenly matched," Crawley said. "I fancy I can hold my own, my buck, so long as you don't resort to weaponry. Dashed if I'll face you with pistols, though, so don't think you'll force anything of that nature on me."

"I have no intention of giving you the satisfaction," Thorne said. "I mean only to teach you not to meddle in my affairs."

Gillian had had enough. "Stop it, the both of you," she snapped. "I have allowed myself to be made a figure of curiosity to all the ragtag and bobtail along the highroad by being driven along it in an open carriage, but I will not become an onlooker to a bout of childish fisticuffs."

"But he did say we should go behind the hedge, my dear," Crawley murmured irrepressibly.

"And leave me here to be gawked at by every passerby," she retorted. "And don't bother to point out that there are none," she added, seeing him make a great thing about looking up and down the deserted road, "for the fact of the matter is that this is the Great North Road and one cannot depend upon its remaining deserted for long. In fact, there is a wagon coming now from the north. My lord," she said, looking at Thorne, "please believe me when I say that this is not what it looks like."

"No?" He turned that stern look of his on her. "But perhaps you do not know what it looks like to me."

"Well, of course I do. It must look as if Lord Crawley and I have . . . that is, as if he has . . ."

"Precisely, my love. Will you call it an elopement or an abduction? I warn you that either term may well overset the strong hold I am keeping on my temper, so choose carefully."

Something in his tone made her look at him more shrewdly. He looked angry, but clearly Crawley was not the least bit afraid of him. Indeed, the idiotic man looked as if he were having all he could do to keep from bursting into laughter when by rights he ought to have been shaking in his shoes. And Thorne looked . . . She wasn't sure how he looked, but she decided that if he were even half as angry as his expression suggested, she ought to be trembling, and she was not. She was beginning to get angry, and his casual endearment had only augmented that anger.

"I suppose you mean to say that you know perfectly well that this whole idiotic business was merely a ruse on Crawley's part to bring you chasing after us," she said grimly. "Well, I must tell you then, my lord, that I had no part in it, nor did I agree with his rather muddled thinking on the subject."

"Traitor," Crawley murmured. "My tombstone will read, 'Thanks be to the lady who sent me to an early grave, 'twas less than I deserved.' "

Gillian bit her lip.

"Just so," Thorne said, looking right at her. "He does

have a tendency to be a trifle melodramatic. I have noted the fault in him before. I shall postpone my chat with him, however, if you will agree to drive back to London with me.''

Uncertain whether the sudden clenching sensation in her midsection was due to elation or terror, Gillian looked doubtfully from one man to the other.

Crawley said, ''I am not altogether certain that I should advise her to take you up on that offer.''

''In that event, you would be wise to keep silent,'' Thorne said. ''She is coming with me. In fact, I think we will take your rig. I've a fancy to drive Corbin's chestnuts again. You may take my phaeton back to town.''

''The devil I will! Those nags look blown, and I doubt I've got enough on me to pay for a new team. In fact, dashed if I don't think I ought to continue to Welwyn—to Fledborough, for that matter. Marriage to an heiress is the only thing that will save my groats, so I'm dashed if I can see why I ought to give Lady Gillian into your tender keeping if she don't choose to go.''

''I'll give you a roll of soft,'' Thorne said, ''and you can drive into Welwyn to make the change. Moreover, if you will tote up the reckoning, I will pay all your current bills for you, so you can start the quarter with a clean slate.''

''Good Lord, Josh, you needn't do that!''

Thorne glanced at Gillian. ''I don't want anyone thinking I deprived you of a fortune, Crawler. You may repay me at your leisure. Now get down from that damn carriage, and take your tiger with you.''

''Oh, to be sure,'' Crawley said as he leaned over to wrap the traces around his brake handle. ''You will want your own man.''

''No, I don't. You may take him with you as well.''

''But good Lord, Josh, you can't drive along the highroad with Lady Gillian perched up beside you. It ain't done!''

''As we see,'' Thorne said, casting him a look of mockery.

''Well, but I did have my tiger, and—''

"Crawler, do get down while you can still move without assistance."

"Oh, very well, you needn't look at me as though you still mean to murder me. We meant only to—"

"To help? I thank you, but I beg you will keep your beneficent urges to yourselves in the future."

Crawley paused on the step, glancing from Gillian to Thorne. "I say, Josh, you did take care of everything in London, didn't you? It won't do at all for you to be careering along the highroad with her if you are still betrothed to Miss Ponderby."

"I am happy to tell you that I am not. I left her explaining herself to Corbin. I am sure it was a vastly entertaining conversation, but I did not stay to hear it. Nor do I wish to converse any longer with you." He pulled a thick roll of bills from his pocket and handed them to Crawley. "Change horses as often as you like. And if you should chance to pass us on the road, do not feel obliged to stop to pass the time of day."

Crawley took the money, then thrust his hand out. "Good luck to you, Josh. I hope you mean to tell me the particulars later, for I don't mind telling you, I'm as curious as a cat."

"But think what happened to the cat," Thorne murmured.

"Oh, very well, I'm gone." Calling to his tiger to hurry, he turned and waved at Gillian. "I shall do myself the pleasure of calling in Park Street tomorrow, ma'am, to see how you go on."

Gillian returned his wave, but she was watching Thorne. The serious look had returned, and she was not certain what to say to him. He swung himself up and gathered the reins into his hands, waited only until the farm wagon had passed them, and then deftly turned the carriage in the roadway. He didn't say a word.

After some moments of this treatment, Gillian looked directly at him and said, "Did I hear you say that you left Dorinda explaining matters to Lord Corbin, sir?"

He nodded.

"But why to Lord Corbin? I could understand it if she

had had to explain to Papa or to Estrid, but surely you should not have left her alone with Corbin."

"Well, I did," he said. "I chanced to meet him on the doorstep, and when we discovered that your father and Lady Marrick had gone to Richmond Park for the day—"

"Richmond! Papa? But why on earth—"

"It seems they had matters of their own they wished to discuss. Doubtless, you know more about the matter than I do, since you live there and I do not. I cannot conceive of why they would do such a thing. Nor do I care. I want to—"

"It must be on account of what happened last night when Papa discovered that Estrid had been meeting Uncle Marmaduke in the cemetery, and had danced with him at Ranelagh."

"Your uncle and Lady Marrick? Come, what nonsense is this?"

"Oh, it is not nonsense, sir, but merely what comes of plain speaking," Gillian said, shooting him a mischievous look. "Papa was in a taking because one of his cronies told him Estrid was making a cake of herself over some fellow in a black domino, and when he taxed her with it, the whole tale came out. Before she and Uncle Marmaduke had ever met properly, he chanced to meet her in the churchyard one night. Apparently she has been in the habit since coming to London of paying her respects to her late husband, just as Uncle Marmaduke frequently visits his first wife's grave and has little chats with her. Well, the short tale is that he flirted with Estrid and she didn't see him clearly enough to recognize him later. But he recognized her when he met her in Park Street, and he has such a wicked sense of mischief that he went right on being her mysterious cicisbeo, even to the point of making an assignation to meet her at Ranelagh. And of course, Papa has not paid any heed to her, not seeing any reason to do so, but now I daresay he has seen the error of his ways. Their marriage is not perfect by any means, but I do think that in their own ways they are fond of each other."

"It is not *their* marriage I wish to discuss, however."

The breath caught in Gillian's throat, but she rallied

quickly. "But if they have gone to Richmond, that is all the more reason you ought not to have left Dorinda alone with Corbin."

"Nonsense. If he is wise he will give her the trimming of her life, and then they can go on as they have begun. She will make him the devil of a wife, but he wants her, so I suppose in the end he will have her."

"He may want her," Gillian said, "but I very much fear she will not have him, sir. It is a pity, too, because Dorinda has a soft spot in her heart for him and I think they would suit each other, but she is determined to marry a country house, and Corbin is a mere baron, besides having to be so careful with his money."

Thorne gave a shout of laughter. "My poor innocent! Corbin may be a baron, but he is anything but 'mere.' Good God, do women know nothing of men's affairs? My sweet, do you have any idea what it costs a man to be a member of Brooks's, or to join the Four Horse Club, or even to dress himself? Why, what Corbin spends on clothes in a month would clothe the British army for nearly the same amount of time! He's rolling in money."

"I did know that Crawley had once hoped Corbin would marry Belinda, but I thought that was only because they were such good friends. Is Crawley rich, too, then? Is that all a hum?"

"No, he is not rich, but he could be well enough to pass if he would settle down and tend his estates. It looks very much as if Dacres will come up to scratch, and he will make a generous settlement if he does. But enough rattle, my love, I do not wish to speak of—"

"Don't call me that," Gillian said. "It is the second time today you have done so, and I do not like it. You have developed this feeling that you must look after me, sir—that's all. You think that since I managed to come within your orbit, you somehow have reason to order my life for me. But you don't love me, and you *hate* that I control my own fortune."

The carriage had been moving along at a steady speed, but suddenly Thorne slowed the team and turned them into a narrow dirt roadway that led off at an angle from the highroad. The byway was hedged on both sides and when it curved, the highroad was lost to sight altogether Thorne drew up and wrapped the traces around the brake handle.

"What are you doing?" Gillian demanded. "Take us back to the road at once."

"There's no going back, my love," he said quietly turning to face her. "Even I am not skilled enough to turn this rig in this narrow lane. We shall have to drive on, and unless I miss my guess, this is a private road, so we will find ourselves turning around in someone's farm yard. Before that happens, I have a number of things to say to you, and I cannot make you stop prating of unimportant matters if I must keep half my mind on the team. You never had any intention of marrying Crawley I hope."

"No, of course not. He said he was taking me for an airing."

"Then you never agreed to any of this? By God, I will teach him a lesson!"

"Well, actually . . ."

"What? Come now, you are such an advocate of candor. Do not fail me now."

"I did think for a very short time that I might marry him," she confessed. "He spoke of candor, too, but he clinched his argument—with my uncle's assistance—by pointing out how dismal my life will be with Papa now that Estrid has made all her feelings clear and Papa has confessed that he truly loves her and never meant to hurt her. He has always resented the fact that he never has had complete control at Carnaby Park since he married my mother and my grandfather sent Hollingston to look after the place. But Papa means for things to be different now and while I do not think he will do anything dreadful, I cannot think that I shall have the same freedom there that I had before."

"Good," Thorne said.

"I beg your pardon?"

"I am merely following your command, my love, and saying what I think."

"Oh. Well, after last night I am beginning to agree with you that it is not always such an excellent idea."

"No, no, you were perfectly right. One cannot always be fretting about how others will react. Everyone does that to some extent, I know, and it is not always wrong, but I came to see that a number of my own problems stemmed from the fact that I had never openly discussed my position with my father. I had tried to insinuate my feelings into his awareness, I suppose, rather than simply telling him what they were. But now—"

"You spoke to him, then? Oh, what did he say?"

Thorne put an arm around her shoulders. "Before I allow you to direct me onto yet another byway, love, we will finish what we began, I think. I do love you. I do not hate that you control your fortune. I behaved childishly when I learned of the fact because I was furious that you had not told me, particularly in view of your so often spouted views about plain speaking. Since I resented the fact that I had so little control of what would one day be mine, learning that you controlled yours was more than I could stomach at the time. How would you like to spend half of each year in Ireland, by the way?"

She stared at him. "Ireland?"

"We have an estate there that has proved to be something of a nuisance. My father has frequently threatened to send me there if I did not mend my ways, but it never occurred to me before that I might find the solution to my problems in that threat. We talked at some length earlier today, and when I explained to him that I have been spending a good deal of my time this past year learning about estate management from quite unexceptionable sources, he agreed to deed the place over to me to use as a sort of experimental farm, after the manner of Holkham Hall. You will note that I don't attempt to explain to you what I mean by that."

She smiled. "You once said you did not believe I knew anything about crops, sir. What can I know of Holkham?"

He chuckled. "It occurred to me that you mentioned quite a number of things showing a knowledge one does not expect to find in females. Still, you did not view my friendship with Coke, or the fact that when we first met

I was coming from Braunton Burrows as evidence of anything but simple friendships.''

"No, that is quite true. Were those men your teachers?"

"They were. I had alienated my father's steward by throwing suggestions at him without taking the trouble first to learn how things worked, and I fear I did not have enough humility to present myself to him as a student. It was easier with men like Worth and Coke. When I did speak to my father, however, I could talk like a sensible man, and he listened with much more understanding than I had expected. Much of what I gained today, my love, I owe to you. I rescued you once," he added softly, "but I believe you have returned the favor now."

She touched his face and gazed into his eyes, finding nothing of the chilly mockery that she had so often seen there, but only warmth and love. When she stroked his cheek, he caught her hand and kissed it, his lips warm against her soft skin. She said quietly, "I must remember to thank Dorinda."

"Ah, yes," he said, "I think we must both thank her."

"You know, then?"

He nodded. "She confessed that it was she who created our first betrothal, but I think we must attend to the second one without any help, don't you? Or perhaps we could simply drive on to Fledborough and procure one of those licenses Crawley spoke of for ourselves. In any case," he added, drawing her slowly toward him and watching her with a wicked twinkle in his eyes as he did so, "I suggest that we discuss the matter at great length before we decide just which course to follow. What do you think?"

She was arched against him, her breasts crushed against his chest, her eyes closed, and her face tilted up expectantly. When he kissed her lightly on the tip of her nose and drew back, she opened her eyes wide and looked at him reproachfully. "Surely you can do better than that," she said.

"Certainly I can," he said, grinning, "but you must tell me precisely what you want me to do."

Snuggling happily into his embrace, Gillian said, "It is just as I said, my love. Plain speaking is certainly best.'